W9-CJR-242

Tales of the American West
The Best of Spur Award–Winning Authors

This outstanding collection represents the entire spectrum of the Western experience—such as Richard Matheson's tense, gritty tale of a man forced to face the gun of a young thug, to Glendon Swarthout's masterpiece detailing an encounter between U.S. soldiers and the Apache. From the frontier's natural beauty to the devastating horrors of war, these amazing award-winning stories depict the West in all its stunning glory.

Includes the 2001 Spur Award–winning short story "All or Nothing" by Gary Svee

and
Spur Finalists

"I Never Saw a Buffalo"
by Frank Roderus
and
"The Anniversary" by Win Blevins

Tales of the American West

The Best of Spur Award–Winning Authors

EDITED BY

Richard S. Wheeler

A SIGNET BOOK

SIGNET
Published by New American Library, a division of
Penguin Putnam Inc., 375 Hudson Street,
New York, New York 10014, U.S.A.
Penguin Books Ltd, 27 Wrights Lane,
London W8 5TZ, England
Penguin Books Australia Ltd,
Ringwood, Victoria, Australia
Penguin Books Canada Ltd, 10 Alcorn Avenue,
Toronto, Ontario, Canada M4V 3B2
Penguin Books (N.Z.) Ltd, 182–190 Wairau Road,
Auckland 10, New Zealand

Penguin Books Ltd, Registered Offices:
Harmondsworth, Middlesex, England

Published by Signet, an imprint of New American Library,
a division of Penguin Putnam Inc. Previously published in a New
American Library edition.

First Signet Printing, June 2001
10 9 8 7 6 5 4 3 2 1
Copyright © Western Writers of America, 2000

All rights reserved

 REGISTERED TRADEMARK—MARCA REGISTRADA

Printed in the United States of America

Without limiting the rights under copyright reserved above, no part of
this publication may be reproduced, stored in or introduced into a
retrieval system, or transmitted, in any form, or by any means (electronic,
mechanical, photocopying, recording, or otherwise), without the prior
written permission of both the copyright owner and the above publisher
of this book.

PUBLISHER'S NOTE
These are works of fiction. Names, characters, places, and incidents either
are the product of the author's imagination or are used fictitiously, and
any resemblance to actual persons, living or dead, business establish-
ments, events, or locales is entirely coincidental.

BOOKS ARE AVAILABLE AT QUANTITY DISCOUNTS WHEN USED TO PROMOTE
PRODUCTS OR SERVICES. FOR INFORMATION PLEASE WRITE TO PREMIUM MARKETING
DIVISION, PENGUIN PUTNAM INC., 375 HUDSON STREET, NEW YORK, NEW YORK 10014.

If you purchased this book without a cover you should be aware that this
book is stolen property. It was reported as "unsold and destroyed" to the
publisher and neither the author nor the publisher has received any
payment for this "stripped book."

(The following page constitutes an extension of this copyright page.)

The editor gratefully acknowledges permission to reprint the following copyrighted materials:

"The Cat King of Cochise County," originally published in *Louis L'Amour Magazine*, copyright © Loren D. Estleman, 1995.

"Too Proud to Lose," originally published in *Fifteen Western Tales*, and later published by Berkley Books in *By the Gun*, copyright © Richard Matheson, 1955, 1994.

"The Attack on the Mountain," originally published in the *Saturday Evening Post*, copyright © Glendon Swarthout, 1959.

"The Face," originally published by Swallow Press in *The Best Western Short Stories of Ed Gorman*, copyright © Ed Gorman, 1991.

"Sue Ellen Learns to Dance," originally published by Browder Springs Publishing in *Texas Short Stories*, copyright © Judy Alter, 1997.

"The Indian Summer of Nancy Redwing," originally published by Doubleday in *The New Frontier: The Best of Today's Western Fiction*, copyright © Harry W. Paige, 1989.

"The Big Two-Shoot Rifle," originally published in *American Rendezvous*, copyright © R. C. House, 1982.

"Just as I Am," originally privately published by the author, copyright © Joyce Gibson Roach, 1990.

"Charity," originally published in *Louis L'Amour Magazine*, copyright © Sandra Whiting, 1995.

"Continuity," originally published in *Louis L'Amour Magazine,* copyright © Elmer Kelton, 1995.

The following stories appear here for the first time:

"Comes the Hunter" copyright © Jory Sherman, 2000.

"The Anniversary" copyright © Win Blevins, 2000.

"I Never Saw a Buffalo" copyright © Frank Roderus, 2000.

"All or Nothing" copyright © Gary Svee, 2000.

"The School at the Bucket of Blood" copyright © Jeanne Williams, 2000.

CONTENTS

Introduction

The Spur Awards, given out annually by the Western Writers of America, have been the hallmark of excellence in the field of western literature for almost half a century. The first Spur Awards were presented back in 1954 in five categories: best western novel, best historical novel, best work of juvenile fiction, best review, and best short story. Over the last forty-five years, they have expanded to include several nonfiction categories as well as best original paperback novel and best screenplay. But when one looks back on the evolution of the western in modern literature, it is the short story that really helped to define the genre as a whole, from its roots in serial publications and pulp paperbacks up to present-day collections and anthologies.

From the 1930s to the 1950s, the western short stories published by pulp magazines and in occasional slicks such as the *Saturday Evening Post* were largely confrontational, and the stories were resolved by the spilling of blood. At the same time, the stories enshrined a certain body of virtues, chief among them being bravery, loyalty, courage, and enterprise. There had always been in western short stories a tender regard for the downtrodden, or the "little guy," such as the small hardscrabble rancher, and many of them posited the overly ambitious empire-building rancher or politician or mining mogul as the black-hat. So powerful and pervasive were these stories that they were incorporated into the national psyche, and especially in the ideals of American manhood. But by the 1960s, exhaustion had set in, and the writers of western short fiction began roaming farther afield. Today, very few western short stories are confrontational in the old blood-and-thunder sense. Modern western fiction has also broken free of the old frontier time frame, and can occur in any era including the present.

This anthology, composed of both Spur-winning short stories as well as short stories by Spur-winning or Spur-finalist writers, is a veritable showcase of modern western fiction. These are the stories and authors that have been judged by their peers to be the best of the best in the genre. Some of the novelists featured in this collection have won multiple Spur Awards, among them Elmer Kelton, Jeanne Williams, Loren Estleman, and Glendon Swarthout. In addition to Spur-winning short stories by Judy Alter, Joyce Gibson Roach, and Sandy Whiting, this collection also features several never-before-anthologized short stories by such renowned authors as Jory Sherman, Win Blevins, and R. C. House.

These stories are marvelously diverse, reflecting the broad spectrum of the American frontier experience from its roots in the 1800s up until today. But all have the Spur Award in common, that mark of excellence that lifts this collection into a dazzling realm never before seen between two covers.

Two of the stories date back to the 1950s, when the traditional western action story was in its heyday. Richard Matheson's "Too Proud to Lose" transcends the usual shoot-out tales of that period by delving deeply into the soul of a man who must face the gun of a young hard case with something to prove. And Glendon Swarthout's tragicomic masterpiece about soldiers facing the Apaches bears little resemblance to the usual frontier army yarns of that era.

A few of the more recent contributions would scarcely be recognized as westerns by readers of the old pulp fiction magazines, pointing to the expansion of themes and issues in western literature over the past few decades—much to the benefit of the genre. Women and children are far more evident in recent literature than in traditional western tales, becoming central characters rather than peripheral ones. Some writers in this collection probe such things as a righteous couple coping with the rumor that a grandmother was a dance hall girl in the bad old days, or a hunter making a grave and wise decision about sparing a mother bear and her cubs, or the consequences of riding in a 1940s Wild West show in the middle of New York City.

Western stories are no longer brief action dramas, but explore the human condition in swift, sure strokes. Harry Paige's Spur-winning story, "The Indian Summer of Nancy Redwing," is a memorable exploration of a young Sioux woman's desperate wish to have a happy birthday. Gary Svee's heartrending story of the lengths to which Norwegian immigrants would go for food, shelter, and medicine during the Great Depression is a powerful study of the hardship visited upon settlers by a perfidious land. Others take off on amazing tangents. One of these is Loren Estleman's "The Cat King of Cochise County," a comic delight reminiscent of the best work of Mark Twain or Bret Harte, and every bit as good.

And what brings them all together is the Spur Award, that coveted plaque featuring glimmering rowels, intended by the founders of Western Writers of America to spur excellence in the literature of the American West. I am pleased to offer an extraordinary collection of stories by a star-studded collection of award-winning writers.

—*Richard S. Wheeler*

The Cat King of Cochise County

Loren D. Estleman

This comic masterpiece is Estleman at his best. It is a tale about the entrepreneurial genius of one Chickenwire, and the woe that befalls him and his cargo en route to Tombstone. This sort of tale was a frontier staple, and puts a reader in mind of Mark Twain, Bret Harte, and Dan De Quille. It was first published in Louis L'Amour Western Magazine *in 1995, and this is the first time it has been anthologized. Loren D. Estleman is the winner of four Spur Awards, two for novels and two for short stories, and is widely considered to be one of the finest novelists writing in our time. He is also a well-known mystery novelist, specializing in the Detroit area near his home. He has devoted virtually his entire life to writing fiction, but has written many pieces of stirring nonfiction as well.*

People in Salt Lake City called Chickenwire Chickenwire on account of the device he'd come up with to keep chickens from being eaten by Elder Evilsizer's Boar, Deuteronomy.

The business had started when Sister Gertrude, the elder's primary wife, had fed the carcass of a hen to the hogs because she wasn't sufficiently certain of what had killed it to cook it and didn't feel like digging a hole. The hogs, particularly old Deuteronomy, discovered a taste for chicken, and after that whenever a bird strayed near, the last image its pea brain carried to Pullet Paradise was of the boar's hairy snout and gnashing teeth. Feathers, bones, beaks, and claws were all grist for Deuteronomy's mill; often only a furious pattern in the dust of the barnyard and a pepper of blood remained to tie up the mystery of the diminishing local chicken population.

It wasn't long before the aging swine's dietary preference led it to neighboring farms, which was the reason a committee of whisker-faced, sad-eyed Mormons showed up at Chickenwire's mercantile store to ask him for some miracle that would protect their best layers from the predatory pig. Shooting the offender was out of the question. So, too, was demanding that Elder Evilsizer take measures to keep his boar at home where it belonged. The violence of the elder's disposition, compounded by his reputation as one of the last of the Destroying Angels involved in the Mountain Meadows Massacre, was legend, preventing any word or action on the part of his gentler neighbors that might call down his wrath.

Chickenwire's response was to fashion a net from spools of wire he had rescued from a wagon abandoned by Western Union in the Shoshone country north of the Great Salt Lake. He reasoned that by stretching the screen around stakes encircling the birds' scratching ground to keep Deuteronomy out, and above their heads to keep the chickens in, the farmers might put an end to the bloodshed without inviting retaliation.

The theory proved sound. The wire was bought, the pens built, and the pig, after a number of unsuccessful attempts to breach Ilium, was forced to settle for the turnips in its trough, together with such game as it could find out on the great alkali plain.

Moreover, the idea turned out to be an invention that outlasted its original necessity. Months after Deuteronomy got hold of a bad prairie hen and finished his existence on the Evilsizers' dinner table, orders for the remarkable wire continued to stream in. There were still wolves and stray dogs to contend with, and the participating Mormons' many wives had reported a secondary benefit in being able to cross their yards without dragging their hems through fresh droppings. Chickenwire, whose vision was not always equal to his entrepreneurial spirit, had reason when he parted with his last thirty feet to regret not commandeering the entire wagonload when he'd had the chance.

When he came to think about it, however, he thought perhaps it was just as well he ran out when he did. The wire was devilish to work with, having slashed up a dozen pairs of leather gloves he'd hoped to sell at a profit, and he was confident that as word got around that his store was no longer a source of the stuff, the farmers would stop calling him Chickenwire. Born Michael Aloysius McDonough, he had been known as Iron Mike in the California gold camps, where he'd made his grubstake knocking down miners for wagers. He much preferred that address; although the thirty years since he'd given up prospecting and come to make his way as a Gentile among the Latter-Day Saints had packed forty extra pounds around his impressive musculature, he still introduced himself as Iron Mike.

He'd liked the raw life of the camps. Successful man of commerce that he was, he missed the rough company and unpredictable nature of a place that could double its population almost overnight once a major lode was uncovered, or lose a citizen in a heartbeat when the same card turned up twice in a poker game in one of the tents. Most of all he missed the candor. The Mormons were much like everyone else as to percentages of good and bad, but altogether too civilized for a man who liked to know right off what sort of person he was dealing with. In the camps you knew where you stood. If a man didn't like you he came at you with something, fists or a shotgun or some kind of club. In Salt Lake City he mouthed pleasantries to your face while spreading stories behind your back that the flour you sold contained rat poison.

It was fitting, then, that Chickenwire McDonough's vague dissatisfaction with his current circumstances should be turned into action by a man from the camps.

From the moment the fellow entered the store, some two or three weeks after the last ten yards of wire had been sold, it was obvious he was no Mormon. His beard was too scraggly, for one thing—more the result of late unfamiliarity with a razor than deliberate cultivation—and his filthy slouch hat, sun-blanched flannel shirt, and torn overalls were as far from the sober black that the faithful wore to town as one could come. He read aloud from a list scribbled in thick pencil on a greasy scrap of paper he held close to his sunken, red-ringed eyes. They were the items that a man traveling a long distance would request: axle grease, flour, cartridges, iodine for cuts and fistulas, beans, brogans, coal oil, and flour sacks of Arbuckle's.

"Homesteading?" Chickenwire totaled the order in his ledger.

"Prospecting." The stranger's vocal cords grated against each other like hacksaw blades. "Bound for Montana and silver."

"I hear silver's growing scarce up that way."

"I don't care. It's too cold there for rats and that's good enough for me."

"Rats?"

"They're big as rabbits in Arizona. Had me a nice little claim a day's ride out of Tombstone, but the rats run me out. I can put up with lice and Apaches and highwaymen, but I sure don't warm to waking up with a large gray rat chewing on my big toe."

"Can't you trap them?"

"Not the ones in Cochise County. They're too smart for traps. Some of 'em's smarter than either one of my partners. I sold out to them finally and hauled my freight north. My partners, not the rats; though they're big enough to do their share of the digging, and that's a fact."

"The cats down there must be lazy."

"Not lazy. Scarce. Cats go with barns. Ain't no barns down there, no farmers to build 'em. Just miners and Mexicans. Mexicans don't keep cats."

Chickenwire ran broken-knuckled fingers through his whiskers. "How's the dirt?"

"Rich as Vanderbilt. The Can-Can Restaurant sells ham in champagne sauce. Two bucks a throw, and they ran out every Saturday. Them nuggets don't get time to knock the dirt off on their way to some fancy man's pocket in town."

The prospector paid for his supplies in silver and carried them out. Chickenwire never saw him again, and in time forgot his features. But what he'd said changed the merchant's life.

When young Lemuel Dent reported to the mercantile the next morning for his part-time delivery duties, he found the proprietor gummy-eyed from lack of sleep but sparkling with energy from some unknown source.

"How many friends you got, boy?"

Lemuel considered. His employer was perched on his stool behind the counter with a brand-new ledger flayed open before him. The pages were black with figures and the countertop was a litter of short chewed yellow pencils. It was obvious he'd been doing sums all night. At inventory time, Chickenwire's temper was shorter than his pencils, and a thing to tread carefully around. "I don't know," answered the boy; and because that didn't seem specific enough he added, "Some."

"Round them up. There's a quarter in it for you if you can have them here by noon."

Youthful avarice flared in Lemuel's eyes, slightly crossed since an encounter he regretted with a mule's left hind foot on his tenth birthday. "What do I say?"

"Tell them there's money to be made."

In the boy's absence, more than one potential customer found Chickenwire's door locked and the

CLOSED sign in the window. Had they been able to peer around the shade, they'd have seen the store-keeper removing slats from his inventory of wooden crates and replacing them with scraps of wire formerly deemed too short to mess with. By the time Lemuel rapped at the door, accompanied by eight of his closest friends and one or two boys he didn't like at all, Chickenwire had finished nine of a projected twenty cagelike contraptions, complete with doors hung on leather hinges and secured with tenpenny nails on the sliding-bolt principle.

Mopping his great bony brow with a smeared bandanna, the proprietor surveyed this bounty of boys barefoot and brogan-shod, overalled and knicker-bockered, dirty-faced and scrubbed pink. At length he grunted his approval and ostentatiously surrendered a disk of shining silver to the young man responsible, who pocketed it without ceremony. This transaction was observed closely by his companions, who then looked to Chickenwire for their share in the bonanza.

"A fifth part of that," he announced. "Five cents, if you don't know your fractions. A nickel I will pay for every stray cat you lads bring to me between now and sundown. A dollar extra to the young fellow who delivers the most. *Healthy* cats, mind. I'll not pay for mange or palsy. Fly, now!"

The command provoked a thunder of feet and a brief scuffle on the threshold as a number of lithe bodies attempted to pass through a single doorway at the same time.

What occurred in the streets between midday and dusk on that date has achieved regional immortality as the Great Cat Hunt of Salt Lake City, and requires no extrapolation here. Suffice it to say the next day's *Deseret News* reported two discharges of rock salt by homeowners at undersize prowlers vaulting over back fences with wailing felines clamped beneath their arms, and one close call involving a dray wagon when a skinny youth in corduroys dived in front of the horses to snatch a flying Siamese. By the time these and similar incidents were connected with the increased demand at apothecary shops for iodine to treat cat scratches, and the whole traced to their source, Chickenwire McDonough had crossed the territorial line, unaware of the animus against him.

In his defense it must be stated that when the day was done and the merchant found himself, among the noisy multitude, in possession of two cats wearing collars and bells, he instructed the boys who had brought them to return them to their owners: "*Stray* cats, I said! " The rest he paid for. The promised bonus went to Fatty Ambrose, whose corpulence did not prevent him from depositing no fewer than seventeen cats in the mercantile's back room.

The tally, once the boys had been ushered out with pockets jingling, came to forty-six, including thirteen tabbies, ten calicos, seven black witch's familiars, six tigers, one blue Angora, and nine hollow-flanked alley veterans of indeterminate color and pattern. Reluctantly—for he calculated their collective worth to be sixty dollars—Chickenwire released six cats by way of the back door; two per cage was crowding things well enough, and he needed to eliminate as many casualties due to disease and fights as possible during the long journey ahead.

Every inch of which, he reasoned, would prove well worth the inconvenience.

For if the miners around Tombstone were content to part with two extremely hard-earned dollars for a dish of plain ham swimming in fizzy wine, how much would they pay on a one-time-only basis to be rid of the rats that plagued their digging and made their lives miserable in the tents when they slept? Ten dollars hardly seemed unwieldy. Thus, upon an initial investment of three dollars and twenty-five cents for inventory, plus an approximate fifty dollars to outfit himself for the trip, which would be covered six times over when he sold the store and its stock, Michael Aloysius McDonough stood to gross four hundred dollars at the end of the trail—far more than the amount required for a place to live and a healthy interest in a claim that showed promise. The adventurer in him embraced both the odyssey and the camp camaraderie for which he pined; the speculator in him warmed itself at the fire of the riches that would be his.

Elder Evilsizer, six feet four inches of fierce, white-bearded piety with a back as straight as a Winchester barrel, heard out Chickenwire's proposition the next morning from the bentwood rocker on his front porch an hour's ride from town, where he was accustomed to keeping an eye on his hired man to ensure he plowed a straight furrow and avoided his secondary wife's rose bushes.

"Two hundred dollars," he said.

Chickenwire shook his head. "Three hundred is the price, and a bargain at that. I have nearly a thousand tied up in the building and stock."

"Two hundred dollars."

The conversation continued in that vein for some minutes, at the end of which Chickenwire, no longer a storekeeper, drove away from the farm with twenty ten-dollar bank notes in his inside breast pocket. The sum was a disappointment, but the elder was the only member of the community who could put his hand on more than a few dollars at a time. Most of the others traded in chickens and homemade quilts.

Although he considered his own delivery wagon, a medium-size Studebaker designed for use as an ambulance by the federal army during the late war, more than adequate for his excursion, Chickenwire gave the blacksmith down the street from the store thirty dollars to replace a doubtful spring and reinforce the tires, axles, and hounds with iron. While that was being done he fed the cats, changed the shelf paper he had placed in the cages to collect waste, and organized the necessaries he had excluded from his transaction with the elder to carry him a thousand miles. Among these the item that consumed the most space was sardines—nearly a hundred tins packed in oil to sustain both him and his cargo. Casks of water, a bearskin for protection against the arctic blasts that sometimes occurred even in the desert, repair tools, and medical stores completed the kit. This last precaution came to mind while he was scratching a bothersome new itch, turning his thoughts toward witch hazel and the like.

The wagon was ready the following day. He loaded his supplies carefully, distributing the burden equally so that the construction would not pull against itself while lurching over uneven ground. He hitched it to a fine chestnut and bay he had taken in trade for an overdue bill owed by a farmer who had gone bust on the worthless ground west of the lake, and stacked the cages atop one another in the bed, lashing them securely. The cats, cranky from captivity and sensing more unpleasantness ahead, screeched and hissed and tried to claw him through the wire. And then he was on the seat and away, without once turning to look back at the enterprise that had supported him for close on three decades.

Allowing time for delays, he calculated the trip would take a month to complete. In the jockey box were railroad survey maps of the Utah and Arizona territories. Behind the seat, within easy reach, he had placed a Springfield carbine for shooting antelopes and jackrabbits when he tired of sardines, and a Walker Colt for shooting Indians and the highway-men when they tired of local prey. The very thought of hazard set his blood to singing. He marveled that he'd stuck out city life as long as he had.

Three cats died the first week.

He blamed himself for the first, a moth-eaten tabby whose bones showed, but whose ravenous appetite and nasty disposition had convinced him the animal was heartier than it appeared and worth bringing along. After three days it stopped eating. On the fourth morning it was as cold and stiff as jerky. Then a pair of cage mates, a black and a calico, got into a savage fight, and although Chickenwire separated them by moving the calico in with the dead tabby's cage mate, the torn and bleeding combatants took infection and perished within twenty-four hours of each other. He cast out the carcasses, cleaned both cages, and used them to relieve the crowded conditions elsewhere. Thirty dollars shot to hell.

The itching he'd noticed back in Salt Lake City had by this time turned into an angry rash on his neck and between the fingers of both hands. Despite the application so far of half a bottle of witch hazel, it kept him awake nights in his bedroll and stung like bees when he sweated in the heat of the day. His eyes had become puffy, too, and uncontrollable fits of sneezing plagued him for an hour after he fed the cats or changed the paper in their cages. Although he knew nothing of allergies, he was no fool, and immediately connected this sudden breakdown in the aggressive health of a lifetime to his furry charges. But he had stood worse for much smaller rewards. Come Tombstone he would be shut of the business.

He found the Fremont River three times wider than on his last crossing. Unseasonal rains in the Wasatch Mountains had made a mockery of its banks and accelerated its current, uprooting small trees and dismantling century-old beaver huts as if they were built of playing cards. Circumventing it would take him three days out of his way. While he felt he could put up with the itching and sneezing for the extended period, he was not as confident of the cats, two more of which were off their feed. Chickenwire tied one end of a hundred-foot length of hemp to a rock on the bank, unhitched the horses, swam the chestnut over with the other end of the rope in hand, and made it fast to a fir tree on the opposite bank. He then worked his way back, hand over hand along the rope, swam the bay across, and worked his way back again.

After two hours' rest he spent the remainder of the day caulking the wagon.

When that job was finished he wanted desperately to make camp, but he feared the river would continue to swell throughout the night and become uncrossable by morning, leaving him stranded with his horses on the wrong side. He double-fastened everything, taking special pains with the cages, and, standing in the wagon bed up front, grasped the rope with one hand and pushed off with a shovel. The current snatched greedily at this fresh flotsam, trying to turn it downstream, but using the shovel as a paddle and gripping the rope until his fingers cramped, Chickenwire guided the wagon toward the opposite bank by force of his own might.

Halfway across, he felt the shovel slip and nearly fell overboard as he lunged to retrieve it. The river tore the handle free and took it away, the spade end ducking and bobbing until it was out of sight. Lest he follow, he grasped the rope in both hands, inadvertently creating a pivot. The rear of the wagon swung around, a corner dipped beneath the surface, the cargo shifted, and one of the leather harness straps that held the cages in place burst with an earsplitting report. The top cage toppled off. Chickenwire, struggling to maintain his grip on the rope, watched helplessly as the cage containing two cats splashed into the water. The doomed animals squalled piteously; and then they, too, like the shovel, were beyond seeing.

The sudden absence caused a change in balance that brought the swamped corner up out of the water. Now the captain of the craft allowed the current to push it the rest of the way around and, sliding his hand along the waterlogged hemp, worked his way to the stern, which had now become the bow. He took with him the Springfield carbine. Leaning over the tailgate, he lowered the wooden stock into the water to act as paddle and rudder. Five minutes more and the submerged wheels came to rest against the original bank. He laid aside the carbine, leapt out, and with the river eddying around his hips, exhausted his remaining strength hauling the wagon up the slope and out of the Fremont's clutches.

In blue twilight he lay in the sparse grass on the south bank, soaked to the skin, caked with mud, his chest heaving and his heart hammering in his ears. He was sure it would stop. When it did, when his breathing slowed and he found he could move his limbs more than an inch at a time, he dragged himself to his feet and proceeded to assess the damage.

The wagon and its surviving contents had come through remarkably well. In addition to the cage, he had lost a water cask and a case of rifle cartridges, and two sacks of flour had become saturated. Some of the pegs holding the wagon together had loosened, but he was sure he could tap them tight with the blunt edge of his ax once they'd dried. The lost cats were the tragedy. One was the blue Angora, a beautiful, sweet-tempered female he'd hoped to palm off on some sporting lady with a soft heart and deep pockets for twenty dollars and recoup some of his losses.

However, he was a practical businessman who knew that every venture carried risks. If just half his cargo came through, he stood to realize a seven thousand percent return on his original investment—more than enough to satisfy any plunger, let alone one interested mainly in arranging a comfortable stake for mining. And so when the cats and horses were seen to and his bed prepared, dreams of avarice claimed him until the sun hit him in the face like a skillet.

In his charge was a particularly obstreperous tiger, a slat-sided alley fighter with one eye, a broken tail, and an ear that drooped from a lacerated muscle, who, unlike most of the others, had refused to adjust to the confined quarters. From dawn to dusk it spat and sprayed, and at feeding time swiped a set of claws nearly an inch long at the hand that opened its cage. Chickenwire bled copiously until he fell into the habit of pulling on a pair of the leather gloves he had used to work with the wire. More than once he had considered releasing the disagreeable creature to starve in the desert, but there were many miles to go and the value of each item in his inventory was climbing. Instead, rearranging the cages to restore balance, he placed the tiger's in the corner left vacant by the incident in the river. Should history repeat itself, the sacrifice would not leave him inconsolable.

Arizona offered no obstacles until the Colorado River, an unfordable torrent that made the Fremont seem a sleepy creek by comparison. There a weather-checked little ferryman loaded with big-handled pistols under a sombrero wider than his shoulders walked around the wagon, evaluating its features and cargo, and offered to take him across for twenty dollars.

"I never paid more than a dollar to cross water in my life!

Quick as thought, the little man drew both pistols

and thumbed back the hammers. The weight of the barrels bent his wrists. "Then I reckon you best do your business this side."

Chickenwire chewed his whiskers, then paid over the requested amount. Halfway across the charging river, propelled by an ingenious lock-lever device attached to the guide rope, the little man stopped the ferry and demanded the rest of his passenger's poke.

"You're holding me up?"

"I got expenses," said the ferryman. "What good's your stake if you can't get across?"

"What good is it if I don't have it at all?"

Out came the pistols. "I done my talking, mister."

"I don't have it on me. It's in a false bottom in this cage. I'll get it." Chickenwire undid the latch on the top cage.

"Back off! How do I know you ain't got a hogleg hid out there?"

"That's foolish." He started to open the door.

"I'll blow you into Mexico if you don't back off!"

Chickenwire stepped back, raising both hands. Belting one of the pistols, the ferryman covered him with the other and swung open the door. The tiger cat pounced. Cursing, the ferryman snatched his hand back, bloody. Chickenwire stepped in, knocked aside the pistol, and threw a left hook from as far as the gold camps of California. He felt the ferryman's jaw give way and caught the pistols as he fell. He slammed and latched the cage door and pointed the pistol at the man groaning on the deck. "Can you swim?"

"What? No!" The ferryman was supporting himself on one hand and trying to hold his jaw together with the other.

"Pity." Chickenwire laid the pistol inside the wagon bed, lifted the man beneath the arms, and pitched him over the rail. The big sombrero could still be seen riding the whitecaps long after its owner had gone under. Watching it, Chickenwire wished he'd thought to take back his twenty dollars.

He lost the best part of a week detouring around the Grand Canyon, whose size he had greatly underestimated, whipped the horses brutally over the San Francisco Mountains to make up the time, and sweated off twelve pounds crossing the desert west of San Carlos. Three calicos, a black, and an alley mongrel perished in the heat. The buzzards that perched in the mesquite bushes near his camp had grown too bold to frighten off, even when he fired at one with the Springfield and sent it dashing to the ground. He wasted no more ammunition on this project, there being more birds than he had shells.

The rash had spread over most of his body. When a sneezing fit came upon him he was forced to alight from the wagon and lead the horses, putting as much distance as possible between himself and the cats. Nothing else would bring relief.

It was during one of these intervals that he encountered his first Apache.

The suddenness of it took his breath away. He had been directing his eyes to the ground to avoid the glare of the sun, and when he raised them the Indian was there, straddling a rattle-boned paint not fifty yards in front of him. The man was naked but for a breech-clout and high-topped moccasins, and carried a long-barreled rifle slung behind his back from a strip of braided rawhide. His eyes were fissures in a face the color and apparent texture of the pottery bowls that the merchant used to accept in trade from the tame Shoshone who had come to his store for supplies. This, however, was no tame Indian.

Instinctively, Chickenwire dropped the reins he was holding and lunged toward the wagon and the Springfield behind the seat. The seat exploded. He lost his balance and sat down hard in the sand. The Apache, having unslung and fired his rifle in less than a heartbeat, was already seating another charge, ramming it home with a thin wooden rod as long as the barrel of the ancient flintlock. It was ready to fire again before Chickenwire could regain his footing. He stood with his hands clear of his sides as the Indian heeled his paint up to the wagon.

Up close, the newcomer appeared to be younger than the white man had thought at first. His eyes, graphite colored, glittered between narrowed lids as they took in every detail of the wagon and its owner. At length he stepped down and, making it clear that he would raise and discharge his weapon at the first sign of resistance, inspected the horses in their traces, examining their teeth and haunches and squatting to feel their fetlocks.

Rising, the Indian pointed to the chestnut, then his own horse, repeating the gesture several times. Chickenwire stared doubtfully at the paint, which looked even bonier close up and motheaten besides, but nodded, observing that even an outmoded firearm was of enormous advantage in horse-trading. He unhitched the chestnut and accepted the horsehair attached to the paint's bridle.

The Indian showed no inclination to leave. Waving the white man away from the wagon and the rifle inside the bed, he walked to the rear and peered inside. For a moment he contemplated the strange cargo in silence. Then he reached inside, fumbled with the latch on one of the cages, opened the door, and pulled out a yowling black by the scruff of its neck. Now he grinned for the first time. Guessing his intent, Chickenwire took a step in his direction. Immediately the flintlock came up. The grin vanished.

Chickenwire stopped, raised his hands high. He watched as the man swung aboard the chestnut, expertly checking its attempts at rebellion with his knees as he slung the weapon over his shoulder and forced the cat into a reclining position, head down across the horse's withers. Then he wheeled, uttered a high-pitched cry, and was gone, galloping toward the horizon with his long hair flying unfettered behind him.

The puzzle of the cat's value to the Apache occupied the merchant's thoughts for a long time afterward. Companionship? An ingredient in some tribal ritual? Food for the family tepee? At which point he sought a better subject.

The paint proved a bad trade. It had never been broken to any kind of wagon, and when its new owner attempted to maneuver it between the traces, it fought the bridle and tried to rear. When he dug in his heels, the horse arched its back, causing a sudden slackening in the reins, then rocked back on its hind legs and clawed the air. Ducking to avoid a slashing hoof, Chickenwire lost his grip on the reins. The paint spun and clattered away in the direction its late master had gone. In another minute only a cloud of dust remained to mark its passage.

This was not a good turn. Chickenwire was stranded in desert country with a wagonload of cats and a tired bay unequal to the burden.

He jettisoned everything that wasn't absolutely necessary. Axes were superfluous in that arid landscape, where buffalo chips served for firewood. Coffee, bacon, and flour were luxuries when sardines sufficed, weary though he had grown of them. Toiletries, tobacco, a fine old walnut rocker his grandfather had made and which had accompanied him all the way from his Ohio birthplace—out everything went. Doubling up the more compatible cats allowed him to discard a number of cages.

The load was still too much for the bay. When the animal stopped and hung its head after barely a dozen yards, Chickenwire raged, stamped about, and tugged at his beard until the roots popped. Then, as in a trance, he hoisted five cages to the ground and unlatched the doors. Nine cats bolted in nine directions. Despite his distaste for the noisy, irritating creatures, he hoped they would find enough roadrunners and pack rats to sustain them.

When the tenth cat did not emerge from its cage, he looked inside. One of the muddy-colored beasts of mysterious lineage lay licking a moist, pink, mouse-sized squirm with a squinched face. Two more were huddled inside the curve of the cat's body, sucking energetically at teats.

Chickenwire's face felt funny. He realized he was smiling—beaming, for the first time in recent memory. Enormous as were the odds against three kittens surviving the journey, he looked upon the miracle as a sign of hope. He secured the door and gently lifted the cage back into the wagon. Now he altered his plan to toss out a full case of sardines after releasing the cats and saved out a dozen tins. Mothers required more food.

New life does not greatly improve a grim situation. Not counting the kittens, he was down to half his inventory, with a wagon that was still too heavy unless he climbed down and walked beside it at regular intervals, and better than a hundred miles to go before Tombstone and the promised land. And he had a fresh scratch on his hand courtesy of the scrappy tiger, registering its disapproval at the prospect of a roommate after all this time. Already Chickenwire regretted his softhearted decision not to abandon the tiger to the desert with the others as a reward for helping out with the larcenous ferryman.

The monsoons caught him shortly after crossing into what he determined to be Cochise County, home of Tombstone and an area larger than some European countries. The rains transformed the earth to ropy mud that sucked the wagon down to its hubs, slowing him to a crawl and obliging him often to step into the vacant harness next to the bay and pull with all his might when it stuck. At night he lay shivering in his bedroll, coughing up specks of blood, still sneezing and itching but too weak to scratch.

A kitten died. Two grown cats succumbed to pneumonia. He shared that malady and was certain that before long he would share their fate. Still he pressed on.

When a second kitten died he shed tears, but he wasn't sure whether they had more to do with his genuine sorrow or his runny eyes.

Huddled in his soaked covers beneath the wagon, he dreamt Death came to him. Deep in the folds of Death's black hood shone the yellow-green eyes of a cat.

Late into the next day he remained supine and swaddled. The sun was low when the plaintive meowing of his famished charges aroused him. His skin felt cool. The fever had broken.

After two days he felt strong enough to continue. In the meantime a calico had succumbed. He disposed of the carcass, moved its cage mate in with another, and threw out the empty cage. Resigned now to tragedy, he looked in on the mother and remaining kitten, and was surprised to find that both were doing well. The young one seemed even to have grown. Rather than encouraging him, however, the news found him numb. He was past all emotion.

The rains stopped. Almost immediately he longed for their return. He could actually see the puddles turning to steam, the earth drying and cracking like old plaster. He had not been out of his clothes in weeks; his own caked sweat grated beneath his arms and behind his knees. When he treated himself to a swallow of water from his suddenly dwindling supply, the liquid stung his weather-checked lips like acid. Despite reasonable rationing among the cats, two more calicos and a tabby dried up and died. He wondered what the next generation would make of the derelict cages along his trail.

Three days from Tombstone, he came to an arroyo that stretched to the horizon in each direction. It was steep and strewn with boulders, but he calculated that going around it would cost a week, with nary enough water left in his casks to sustain a man for half that time, much less a man and thirteen and a half cats. Gripping the brake lever to control the descent, he gave the reins a flip.

The bay picked its way over rocks of unequal size and loose shale, making gasping snorts as the wagon lurched behind, threatening to throw it off balance. A third of the way down, the animal lost its nerve and stopped. Chickenwire, who could feel rubble shifting beneath the wheels, cursed and smacked his whip at the horse's rump. It whinnied, shook its mane, and took another step.

A piece of shale the size and shape of a bishop's hat turned under its hoof. A knee buckled. The wagon lunged.

Chickenwire released the brake and lashed the whip, shouting at the top of his lungs. The bay bolted.

When the wagon's left front wheel struck a boulder, the merchant heard wood splinter. He was standing at the time and threw himself clear as the wagon heeled over and skidded on its side into the lead, pulling the screaming bay down the slope all the way to the base. Cages flew. The yowling of the terrified cats echoed in the arroyo for a full minute after the dust had settled.

Dazed, Chickenwire lay listening as the horse's cries grew feeble and finally stopped. When at length he tried to push himself up, his wrist bent suddenly, shooting white heat to his shoulder. He didn't know he'd passed out until he opened his eyes and saw a pair of caked boots inches in front of his face.

"You dead, hoss?"

They were the first words he'd heard since the encounter with the ferryman. He made a reply, but his throat was parched and it came out a dry rattle. Boots squatted. Pain lashed Chickenwire again as his arm was lifted and probed from elbow to hand. The man smelled of sweat, earth, woodsmoke, and bacon. "That's as broke a wrist as ever I seen, hoss." He raised his voice. "Syke, fetch me that busted shovel and a canteen."

He was turned onto his back. A hand supported his head as he swallowed a blessed draught of mossy-tasting water. While Boots fashioned a splint from a splintered wooden handle and a length of hemp, Chickenwire observed that the arroyo was alive with men in filthy Levi's and flop-brimmed hats—miners, if he remembered his camp days at all—calling information to one another from their positions next to the ruined wagon and scattered cats. He learned the bay was dead of a shattered spine and that most of the cages were empty, having broken open on impact and freed their captives. Three contained dead cats.

"What about the rest?" he asked.

The man called Syke, shorter and stouter than the horse-faced Boots, returned from the wagon, mopping the back of his neck with a red bandanna. "Six in the wagon and one don't look too good. And a kitten, though I wouldn't count on it lasting. The mother's dead."

"Dutch Bill's got him a goat," Boots said. "He might could get it to suck goat's milk from a neckerchief. Don't know what your plans was, hoss, but we sure can use cats in these here parts. We got more rats than prospectors."

Chickenwire made a decision.

"Take them."

Boots's eyes rolled white in a face stained with silver clay. "This here's a problem. It ain't nothing to josh about."

"I'm not joshing. You saved my life. I'll need a horse, too, and water and provisions to get me to town. Divide them up how you want. If I never see another cat it will be too soon."

The miners moved swiftly, as if afraid he'd change his mind. Within the hour a gentle dun mare was produced, complete with a worn saddle and pouches filled with tins of beef and tomatoes. Boots helped Chickenwire straddle the mare and hung a canteen on the horn. One of the other miners, an honest lot, had found the merchant's poke and brought it to him.

From his high seat Chickenwire surveyed the wreckage of the wagon and its contents. "Help yourself to whatever you can salvage. I've had my life's portion of sardines, as well."

"Good luck to you, hoss," Boots said. "My chewed fingers and toes sure do thank you."

That night, thawing the evening chill from his bones before a fire and trying not to think about his throbbing wrist in its makeshift sling, Chickenwire pondered his future. The remainder of the money the elder had paid him for his store in Salt Lake City, while not enough to buy into a good claim, might net him a partnership in a store in Tombstone. In a year or two he might set a sufficient amount aside to invest in pay dirt. The enterprise would be a success after all, and it would not depend on cats. After all those weeks in their company he could still hear them meowing.

Meowing.

He caught himself looking for the source of the fancied sound and smiled. The tinkling of the pianos in the all-night saloons would drown out the echoes soon enough. He would find the cure for his rash in the arms of a sporting lady. Chickenwire was picturing the enameled women in their bright dresses when a specter came into the firelight and slunk toward him, meowing.

He sneezed, and the fresh pain in his arm made him curse. The cat—for it was the one-eyed, vile-tempered tiger he had despised for a thousand miles—shrank from the oath, hissing and flattening its single undamaged ear; then started forward again.

Obviously, the beast had been among those that had escaped when the wagon overturned. How or why it had trailed him to this spot didn't concern him. The species filled him with rage. With his good hand he reached for the Walker Colt under the saddle he was using for a backrest, cocked it, and rested the barrel atop his raised knee, sighting in on the tiger's chest.

"Cat, you just went and spent the last of your nine lives."

Ignoring the weapon, the animal came forward the rest of the way. At his knee it paused and ducked its head, rubbing its body against his leg. As it did so, a velvety rumble issued from deep inside its throat. The sound caught a little from a lifetime of disuse.

Chickenwire said, "Well, I'm damned," and let down the Colt's hammer gently.

Early Tombstone cherished its characters nearly as much as it did its heroes and villains. Well into a new century, when old-timers wearied of recounting the exploits of the Earps and Clantons and Johnny Ringo, they would wet their whistles and launch into the story of how Itchy McDonough, part proprietor of the Golden Gate Mercantile on Fremont Street, came to town with nothing to his name but an old mare and his one-man cat, Elder Evilsizer.

Too Proud to Lose

——

Richard Matheson

This is much more than a classic confrontation story about an aging sheriff and a youth who wants to kill him. It is a story that brilliantly plumbs the dread, disgust, and morbid thoughts of a man who thinks he might soon die. It is also a fine study of intimidation and challenge. It is the work of legendary Spur Award–winning novelist and screenwriter Richard Matheson. The author has written in many genres, including horror and fantasy, and wrote teleplays for Rod Serling's famous 1950s TV series, The Twilight Zone, *as well as the screenplay for Steven Spielberg's* Duel. *His first western novel,* Journal of the Gun Years, *won a Spur Award in 1991, and he has subsequently published several other western novels. This remarkable, taut story first appeared in* Fifteen Western Tales, *published in 1955.*

Lew Torrin woke slowly that morning. His eyelids kept falling shut again and again before they finally stayed open.

Today. It was the first word that crawled across his sleep-thickened mind. Today he had to meet Frank Hamet, and one of them was going to die.

He turned his head on the pillow and looked out the window, mouth tightened. It was a bleak morning, gray and sunless. Even under the blankets he could almost feel the November frost that would make his blood run slow, deaden his reflexes. Lack of sunlight would hurt his vision . . today, when his eyes would have to work perfectly or he'd die.

Die. He pushed away the thought and sat up quickly. A groan rumbled in his chest. A full night's sleep and still he was tired. He dropped his legs over the edge of the bed and sat staring at his veined hands, their backs almost bronze from the Arizona sun. He flexed the long fingers and tried to work limberness into them, but he couldn't. They were stiff; something was gone from them.

I'm forty, he thought, I can't expect to be the same.

His chest rose and sank heavily. That didn't change anything. He still had to meet Frank Hamet.

He reached out and picked up his watch from the bedside table. My God, he'd slept ten hours! Why hadn't Mary woken him?

The question was pointless; he already knew the answer. She'd let him sleep because she knew his exhaustion.

She didn't know about Hamet though—and she wouldn't know.

Lew Torrin still sat there, heavy-muscled shoulders limp, hands hanging slackly over his thighs. He wished he could lie down and sleep another ten hours. All the energy was gone from him. It was the way a man lived in this time: full grown at sixteen, burned-out at forty.

His gaze moved to the leather of his belt and holster hanging on the bedpost and settled on the worn handle of the Colt .44. Today that piece of apparatus would save his life or he would die.

It was unbelievable.

He stood up and lost himself in the activity of dressing, staring around the room to keep his mind from thinking. His eyes moved from the bowl and pitcher to the rumpled bed; to the carved chest at the foot of the bed; to the hook rug Mary had made years ago; to their wedding picture on the wall; to the pictures of Lucy and Sarah taken in front of the tree last Christmas.

He kept looking at all of them while he pulled on his Levi's, buttoned up the flannel shirt, and sat on the bed to pull on stockings and boots.

Is that me? He couldn't help the question as he stared into the mirror at his dark blond hair graying at the temples, his tanned face creased from squinting and worrying. He ran his finger over the thin white scar on his temple still there from the fight.

He shook his head slowly as he drew the watch out of his shirt pocket after putting it in. Eleven. In two hours he had to meet Frank in the field behind the graveyard. His head kept shaking. It seemed impossible.

His mouth tensed. Well, it's *not*, he told himself angrily. That was the worst thing with being his age. It wasn't failing reflexes, or muscles that couldn't get enough rest, or even fear. It was this endless thinking that made things so hard.

He pinned on his badge before the mirror, looking at its dull burnished glitter. Sheriff of Dannerville for twenty years and nothing to show for it but this lit-

tle piece of metal on his chest. Why did a man do it?
Why did he devote himself to keeping the law in a
town, following the steps of his father and his father's
father?

For the life of him, he didn't know.

Torrin grabbed his gun belt and dragged it up over
the bedpost. He walked quickly across the shadowed
room, his boots clumping on the floorboards. Don't
start thinking, he told himself. It's better not to think.
Go into it blindly, thoughtlessly. It was simple, really.
Twenty years of keeping law, that didn't matter. Eighteen years of marriage, that counted for nothing. There
were only two things—living and dying.

He came slowly down the stairs, the smell of hot-
cakes and bacon and strong coffee floating up to him.
As he descended, he felt the heaviness of his body
bearing down on one leg, then the other. He felt the
weight of the pistol belt dragging on his arm. He
heard the measured ticking of the clock as he moved
past it and saw, from the corners of his eyes, the sluggish arcing of its pendulum. He heard his boot heels
thumping on the stairs and saw the dull glow of the
polished banister. The heavy panels of the front door,
the clothes tree with his hat and leather jacket on it.
Everything—all the things of his house, of his life,
that might, in two hours, be suddenly ended in a wash
of agonized blackness.

Don't think! The words exploded in his mind. But
then he heard the sound of Mary's feet moving with
quick precision in the kitchen and everything welled
over him again—all the inconceivable details massing
against the black backdrop of dying.

She looked up from the stove. "Good morning, dear," she said.

He tried to smile but couldn't manage more than a stiff twitching at the corners of his mouth.

Her face grew sympathetic. "Still tired?" she asked.

"No, I feel better," he said.

"Good. Sit down now. I'll get your breakfast."

He moved to the chair and slung the gun belt over one of the back posts. No, I won't tell her, he thought, feeling a sudden churning in his stomach as he realized he wanted desperately to tell her about it.

He sank down in the chair and clenched tight fists under the table where she couldn't see.

"You shouldn't have let me sleep so long," he said.

"You needed it," she told him. "Jake can handle the office for one morning."

Lew stared at the clean dishes before him, the coffee mug, the silverware. This will be the last food I eat, the thought came, and he tightened angrily at the cruelty of his own mind.

"The girls gone?" he asked quickly, hoping to drown away thought with words.

"Been in school since nine," she said easily, coming over to get his plate.

He caught her hand impassively and she looked down at him, a spark of surprise in her eyes.

He forced a smile. "Thanks for . . . letting me sleep," he said.

"I wish you could sleep all day," she said.

Then she went to the stove and his hand dropped back. So do I, he thought, so do I wish I could sleep all day.

Suddenly his hands clenched into bloodless fists

on his lap and he wanted to cry out, No! No, it isn't fair! Why should I throw my life away for some hellion who never did a decent thing in his life?

"Are you cold, Lew?" she asked as she brought the food to him.

He swallowed hard. "A little," he said. "Looks like it's getting ready to snow."

"Pretty soon now," she said and put down his plate.

"Looks fine," he said and smiled up at her.

"I'll get your coffee," she said, and his fingers twitched impotently in his lap as he fought off the impulse to grab her hand again. He drew in a shaking breath and braced himself That's enough, he ordered himself. That's enough.

While he ate slowly, he tried not to think, but he kept thinking about Frank Hamet.

Lew had known Frank's father. He'd seen old Joshua Hamet killed by a runaway horse, been a pallbearer at the funeral, taken up the collection that helped the Widow Hamet start the small dry goods shop that provided her income.

And he'd seen Frank grow from a pampered baby to a brat flinging stones at passing horses, playing hooky from school. He'd seen Frank grow into a lean adolescent who started drinking and gambling too soon and took up with the wrong kind of friends.

And now this same Frank Hamet had challenged him and would be waiting in a field to kill him.

"Aren't you hungry, Lew?"

Mary's question made him look up with a startled expression on his face.

"Aren't you feeling well?" she asked.

"No, I'm just . . . oh, I don't know." He managed a

grin. "Guess I'm not used to so much sleep. I'm still groggy."

"Why don't you stay home today and let Jake handle things?"

"No, I—"

"There's nothing important to do is there?"

"No. But—"

She smiled gently. "All right, dear. But please take it easy."

He lowered his head so she wouldn't see him swallow. "I will," he said.

He finished the coffee and stood up, hands trembling a little as he buckled on the gun belt that seemed to weigh a hundred pounds. Then he drew out his watch. Eleven-thirty. He leaned over and kissed Mary's cheek. "I'm going," he said, feeling something cold in his stomach.

She put her hands on his arms. "Don't work too hard now," she said. "*Please.* And come home early for dinner."

He looked at her another moment, trying to print her face in his mind: the curl hanging loosely across her right temple, the soft brown eyes, the glowing cheeks, the warm full lips, which he kissed now, feeling her body against his.

"See you at dinner," she said softly.

"Good-bye," he answered.

He could hardly feel his legs as he walked across the kitchen. I'm leaving her, he thought. I'm leaving my wife and I'll never see her again. He kept his lips pressed together to hold back the sound he felt pushing up in his throat, and his body felt like a block of stone.

Then he was in the hall, putting on his jacket and hat, hardly conscious of his body, he was so numb with dread. Not for his life, but that he would never see Mary or the girls again. He actually took a step back toward the kitchen, meaning to go in and tell her and plan out what she should do if he didn't come back.

But he checked himself and stood there buttoning up his jacket, face a mask of resolution. He wasn't going to tell her. He didn't want her to go through what he was going through.

Before he went out, he looked around the hall and knew, in that moment, how very much he loved this house because in it had been all the happiness of his life. The bringing home of his bride, the years of domestic pleasures, the births of Lucy and Sarah; all the thousand little things that added up to the total of a man's existence.

At one o'clock they might all be ended.

He went out quickly into the cold, frost-edged air and walked down the path, shutting the gate behind him, then plunging his hands into his jacket pockets again. Every jolting bootfall was like a blow against his heart, and he didn't dare look back.

"Hello, Sheriff!"

He heard a thin voice call out and, turning his head, saw five-year-old Mickey Porter playing in his front yard. He smiled with effort and waved to Mickey. A son, the thought came without warning, that's the worst part.

He realized then that he'd avoided that thought most of all. He felt that it was arrogance on his part to feel so strongly about the continuation of his line.

It's something I was taught, he reasoned with himself. My grandfather told my father and my father told me. Torrin means law in Dannerville. That was it, a slogan, a saying that you learned by rote as if it were a law of the universe. Torrin means justice, means law.

Torrin meant Torrin—that was all it meant. Lew felt it strongly. The line would end and nothing would be lost by it. The world would go on, children being born and old men dying, and Torrin would become a forgotten name; the dust-heavy title of an ancient strain who tried to keep the law in a little Arizona town and finally passed from being.

He was so lost in thought he almost rammed into the Widow Hamet.

"Sheriff Torrin," she said, looking up at him as he towered over her.

Automatically, he caught the brim of his hat between two fingers and drew it off, his gray-tinged blond hair ruffling in the wind.

"Please, put your hat on," the Widow Hamet said in her thin voice. "It's much too cold."

He smiled politely and put his hat back on. "You . . . want to see me?" he asked.

"Yes," she answered. "Deputy Catwell told me you were still at home."

He nodded, feeling himself tighten. This was only stalling, he knew, only words that would lead to other words, words he didn't want to hear.

"Sheriff, I know I have no right to come to you like this," she said.

"Of course you do," he said, not wanting to say it. "You're an old friend."

She tried to smile but couldn't. "I mean, I know it's Frank's fault. I—can't defend him, Sheriff, I know it's his fault. But—"

He didn't say anything. He looked down at her, feeling empty.

She drew in a quick breath. "Isn't there any way?" she asked.

He felt himself stiffen with anger that Frank had told his mother and driven one more knife into her already wounded heart.

"I'm sorry you know about it," he said, knowing it wasn't the answer she wanted.

"Sheriff Torrin, I *tried*," she said, her eyes pleading with him. "I begged him not to do the terrible things he's done. I begged him not to fight with you. I know there are no arguments for him but . . ." Her voice broke. "He's my boy," she said. "Don't hurt him, Sheriff. Don't hurt my boy!"

He stood there numbly, staring down at her as though from a great height. Then he heard a voice speaking and knew it was his own but didn't know where the words came from.

"I'm sorry, Missus Hamet," he said. "I can't stop the fight now. I would if I could, but I'm helpless. It's gone too far. Unless Frank backs out, I can't do anything. I'm sheriff, and I have to go through with it."

He wondered what had happened to the Widow Hamet, and it wasn't until he'd walked thirty feet that he realized he'd stepped past her quickly and walked away without another word.

He strode past Martin's gunsmith shop, past the saddlery, the feed store. He walked past people and knew what they were thinking. He said good morning to no one. His face was expressionless as he walked steadily toward the jail. Far off, he heard the church bell toll noon. In an hour, he thought. An hour.

He tried to regain the strength-giving rage he'd felt a few moments before by thinking of all the things Frank Hamet had done.

The day had come when shooting roared in the Lazy Wheel Saloon, and he had run there to find Frank in a drunken rage, firing his pistol while friends watched approvingly.

He'd taken away Frank's pistol, dragged him from the saloon, and tossed him into jail. And Frank, shamed in the eyes of his friends, had screamed at him, face mottled with fury, the cords in his neck standing out.

"I'll kill you for this, Torrin! I swear to God, I'll kill you!"

He hadn't believed Frank. He'd turned away from the abusive cursing and left him there for twenty-four hours. And when he'd released him, Frank had said nothing.

The jail was locked. Lew let himself in and walked across the room, listening to the faint crackling of flames inside the woodstove. Sinking down wearily before his desk, he leaned back and looked up at the clock pendulum moving from side to side in rhythm with the ticking. It's my life, he thought, ticking away while I sit here.

It had begun soon after the jailing incident. Wherever Lew rode or walked he would, seemingly by accident, come across Frank. Frank would never look at him. He'd be sitting in front of his mother's shop, or in front of the hotel or the saloon, or standing by a hitching rack, or sitting in back of the saloon—examining his pistol.

That went on for weeks.

Then came the drawing and the firing. Whenever Lew rode outside of town he'd come across Frank practicing. Frank would draw and fire at something, very quick and sure; more so with each passing week.

And that was all. Never an overt move, never anything that could possibly be interpreted as a challenge. Only this carefully planned and executed intimidation. Months passing and Lew's nerves getting tighter and tighter because he knew just what Frank was doing and had no power to stop it.

It got to the point where he actually found himself taking extra rides outside of town in order to practice drawing and firing.

Then a reaction set in and he stopped, feeling like a fool for doing it in the first place. And, trying to pretend he felt nothing, he'd gone on about his business, every day watching Frank get faster and knowing that, one day, Frank would know himself fast enough.

The day had come. But still there was nothing overt.

Frank started grinning at him.

That was all—just grinning. At first Lew thought it would be easy to ignore, but when the whole town started watching, it began to tell on his nerves. Frank seemed to devote his time to plaguing Lew with grins and then, little by little, with carefully measured insults spoken behind his back which, sooner or later, reached Lew's ears.

Until finally, one day—a day of frustrating irritations—Frank had snickered as Lew passed in the street and Lew, goaded to sudden fury, had whirled on him and knocked him into the street. There had been the fight—a clawing, kicking, frothing Frank against him. And when the fight had ended, a beaten Frank had flung his challenge and everything was crystallized into a simple alternative: life or death.

Lew Torrin's eyes refocused on the pistol in his lap and, suddenly, he jerked his finger out of the trigger guard and thumped the pistol down on the desk.

He sat there wondering if he should write a letter to Mary. His will had been made years before; it rested safe in the bank vault. But shouldn't he write a letter now to let her know how he felt?

He picked up a pen and ran its dry, ink-black tip across the back of his hand. Dear Mary—words ran through his mind—I'm writing to you because, in forty minutes, I'll be dead . . .

The door opened and Jake Catwell came in. "Mornin', Lew," he said.

Lew nodded, then felt himself tighten as Jake glanced up at the wall clock. For a moment he became afraid that the fight was so widely known Mary might hear of it.

"Everything all right?" he asked Jake.

"Sure," Jake said. "Fine."

Lew nodded again and took some papers from the top drawer so he'd have something to look at besides his hands and the pistol on the desk. Jake slung off his mackinaw and tossed it on the bench.

"Cold as hell out," he said. "Probably snow today."

Lew didn't answer. He was suddenly conscious of

the fact that he was still wearing his leather jacket in the warmth of the room.

"Let Melter out," he said abruptly.

"Thought we was keepin' him two days."

"No, let him out. Tell him to go home and stop drinking."

Jake snickered as he headed for the cells. "That'll be the day," he said.

Lew sat there and heard the muffled voices of Jake and Sam Melter in the back. He thought of how simple this whole situation would have been for his father, because his father had lived in a time when a man never got a chance to slow down and worry. There were more than drunks to put in jail then, civic picnics to police, petty merchants' squabbles to settle, fights to referee or end. In those days there were murders and robberies and endless gunplays to keep a man at a keen edge of readiness.

Not now.

Jake came back in. "Go see if the stage is in," Lew told him. "Expecting some posters."

"Ain't due in for half hour yet, Lew."

"It might be early."

"Never is."

"Will you do what I say!"

Jake looked at him a moment, then shrugged once. "Okay, Lew," he said, putting on his mackinaw again. He walked to the door, then turned. "Good luck, Lew," he said.

Lew kept his head down, and when the door shut, he felt the rush of cold wind across his hands and face.

*　　*　　*

He looked up at the clock again. Almost twelve-thirty. In fifteen minutes he'd walk over to the stable. He could start now and walk to the graveyard, but he didn't want to do that; he'd get too tired. No, the thought came, I'll ride to the graveyard.

He almost ran right into Mary as he went out.

She threw herself against him, her face twisted with terrible fright, her hands clutching at his arms.

"Lew!" she gasped. "Why didn't you tell me?"

His stomach muscles jerked in as he looked at her flushed face. She had only a thin shawl over her dress. "Mary," he said confusedly, "what are you—"

"How could you go without telling me?" she asked.

He swallowed. "Who told you?" he asked.

"Frank's mother," she said quickly. "Lew, you're not really—"

"Come in, Mary, come in; you'll catch your death of cold standing out here."

"But—"

"Come *in*." He led her into the warmth of the jail and sat her down at his desk.

"There," he said. "Wait for me here. I have to go."

"Lew, you're not going to—"

"Mary, please," he begged. "This is my job. I have to do it, can't you see that?"

She sat wordlessly, staring up at him as he took out his watch and looked at it. A quarter to one. "I have to go," he said again.

"Lew, please," she started. "You—" She stopped and lowered her head with a sob. "You should have told me," she said brokenly. "Why didn't you tell me?"

His hands closed into fists, and he stood there staring down at her helplessly, thinking, I've got to get out of here. I've got to get out of here.

"It's all right," he said huskily. "I'll . . . come back."

She was up and in his arms then, shaking terribly. He kept patting her back with numb fingers and staring at the wall clock. One o'clock, I have to be there at one o'clock, he thought.

He kissed her cold cheek then and turned quickly. "Good-bye," he said, and he felt her watching him as he walked out of the jail into the cold November afternoon.

He walked quickly to the stable, not sure of what he felt at that moment. It wasn't fear, he knew, but it wasn't strength either. It was more a sense of complete inevitability.

No, he wouldn't think about it. He hunched his shoulders forward and rode slowly down the street, head lowered to keep the wind from his face. He could feel it buffeting coldly against him as he watched thin wisps of his horse's steaming breath.

Then, suddenly, without knowing why, he lifted his head and squared his shoulders. He looked straight ahead into the wind, noticing from the corners of his eyes how people watched him as he rode by. Remember me like this, he thought, proud and unafraid.

At two minutes to one, he reined up at the edge of the graveyard and tied his horse to the picket fence. For a moment, he stood there patting his horse's crest. Then, abruptly, he unbuttoned his jacket and slung it over the pommel, pulled out his pistol and checked it, then replaced it, satisfied.

He was ready.

He pushed through the gate and started across the deserted graveyard. Far out in the field, he saw a cluster of waiting men. He walked faster, anxious to be there and get it over with. He heard his boots crunching down the stiff grass as he threaded a path among the tombstones, eyes directed at the slender figure standing in the middle of the field, waiting, right hand on pistol butt, right arm cocked out languidly.

His mouth tightened. Be cute, he thought, be as cute as you like, little boy—I'll end your cuteness if it kills me. At his sides, his hands grew rigid. He hardly felt the cold.

He reached the edge of the field and entered, and all the men stopped talking abruptly and looked at him with the withdrawn curiosity of watchers at a killing. Feeling nothing, Lew Torrin looked around from man to man, avoiding until last the tight face of Frank Hamet, thirty yards away.

As their eyes met, Frank's hand left his pistol butt and fell to his side. Lew felt his arm muscles tighten in readiness.

Then, abruptly, he let his gaze drop. Slowly, almost lethargically, he took out his watch, pushed in the catch, and saw the front cover spring open.

Still twenty seconds to go. He stood there, head down, watching the second hand. Let him wait, he thought, amazed at his own calm, let him wait for me. He said one o'clock. One o'clock it would be.

Fifteen seconds, fourteen, thirteen. Lew Torrin stood erectly, not even glancing up at Frank Hamet. Eleven, ten, nine . . .

* * *

The sudden explosion tore open the stillness, and Lew saw the dirt at his feet kick up with a black spouting. His eyes jerked up in shocked surprise, and he saw the pistol in Frank's hand and heard the second shot.

Instinctively, he jumped to the side, but the bullet tore up the ground a yard in front of him.

A sudden fire sparked in Lew's brain. He's afraid! he thought in startled wonder.

The third shot came closer but still only blew up a spurt of earth that spattered across his Levi's and boots. And, suddenly, a broad smile appeared on Torrin's face. He couldn't help it.

Almost casually, he clicked shut the watch cover and slid it into his pocket. He saw Frank's face twist and heard the strangled curse flung across the field. Then Frank extended his arm and Lew could actually see the pistol barrel shake as Frank tried to aim.

Without even thinking, Lew dropped his arm, drew the pistol smoothly from his holster, and fired.

Frank cried out hoarsely as the pistol flew from his hand and skidded across the hard dirt. He clutched at his wrist and stared at Lew, a flickering of terror in his dark eyes. Lew started toward him and Frank backed off.

"No," he said. "Don't, Sheriff. Don't kill me!"

But Lew had holstered his gun even before he reached the boy. He walked up to where Frank stood and, grabbing him by his right arm, he drove the back of his free hand sharply across Frank's mouth.

Frank cried out and stumbled back, tripping and slipping to one knee. Lew looked down into the white, contorted face of the young man who had made this day a horror for him. And suddenly all the anger left him completely.

"Go home and get your things," he said flatly. "You have till five o'clock to get out of town. You hear me?"

"Yeah. Yeah, I hear you," Frank said.

"If you're still here at sunset, I'll kill you."

He couldn't help the pleasure he felt at the look of complete terror on Frank's face. I've got it coming to me, he thought.

He stood in the field a long time, watching Frank hurry across the graveyard, and he felt a wonderful, warming relaxation as if, finally, he'd gotten the rest he had needed for so long.

He sighed and bent over to pick up the fallen pistol. As he stuck it under his belt, he looked around. "All right," he said, without anger, "get out of here; the show's over."

When all the men had gone, he took out his watch.

Ten minutes after one. He shook his head. Three hours of agony for ten minutes of victory. He smiled to himself. Well, it seemed odd, but it was worth it.

As he started for his horse he felt a rich, healthy hunger in himself and knew he wanted a walloping dinner.

As he mounted, snow began to fall, the whiteness of it like a clean robe across his town.

The Attack on the Mountain

Glendon Swarthout

Here is Glendon Swarthout at his finest. This rich story, filled with humor, the yearnings of bachelorhood, foreboding, as well as a sense of the ridiculous, first appeared in the Saturday Evening Post *in 1959, and has not been reprinted since its publication four decades ago. In the space of a few pages, Swarthout builds a masterful portrait of the frontier army and its foibles, and also reveals his mastery of all the details of Apache warfare. This is the only short story ever written about the frontier army's heliograph signaling system. Not the least of Swarthout's achievements in this story is the way he makes words dance and the whole English language sing. The author is the winner of two Spur Awards, one for* The Shootist, *which became John Wayne's last film, and the other for* The Homesman. *Several of his stories were turned into films, including "A Horse for Mrs. Custer," which became* Seventh Cavalry, *starring Randolph Scott, and* They Came to Cordura, *which was a Pulitzer nominee. That film starred Gary Cooper. In 1991, Swarthout received the Owen Wister Award for lifetime achievement in the field of western literature. In 1992 he died of emphysema.*

This is about a general and a petticoat and three squaws and a rat roast and a sergeant and some other soldiers and a mutt dog and an old maid and a message.

The general was Nelson A. Miles. He followed George Crook in charge of the military department of Arizona, in which vast command the Apaches, still feisty in the eighties, were accustomed to breaking out of the agencies, stealing horses and cattle, burning ranches, deceasing the settlers, and being beat-all scampish. Tender in the beam, Miles was disinclined to spend much time in the saddle, as Crook had done, preferring to reign over military reviews and fancy-do's in towns with the locals and let the terrain and the latest in tactics conduct his campaign for him.

To this end he scattered his cavalry in troops across that area most pested by the Indians, ready to strike at any raiding band close-range, and also set up the most intricate, cosmographical system of observation and communication ever seen in the West. The finest telescopes and heliographs were obtained from the chief signal officer in Washington. The heliograph consisted of a mirror set on a tripod and covered with a shutter; by means of a lever that alternately removed and interposed the shutter, long or short flashes of light coded out words, the distance depending on the sun's brilliance and the clearness of the atmosphere. Infantrymen were trained at Signal Corps school at Fort Myer, in Virginia, then shipped west and stuck up on peaks so as to form a network. There were twenty-seven stations, not only in Arizona but in New Mexico, and even more were eventually added, reaching down into Sonora, Mexico. The entire system covered a zigzag course of over four hundred miles, a part of it being pieced out by telegraph. It was a monument to science and to General Miles's administrative genius, and it was not worth a tinker's damn.

The Apaches took to moving by night. By day they observed the observers, using their own means of communication—fire, smoke, sunlight on a glittering conch shell. They yanked down the telegraph lines, cut them, and spliced them with wet rawhide, which dried to look like wire, the cuts then being almost impossible for linemen to detect, thus degutting the system.

But whatsoever General Field Order No. 7 establisheth on April 20, 1886, at Fort Bowie must endure. The station could at least transmit messages like the following:

RELAY C O FORT HUACHUCA PREPARE POST
INSPECTION AND REVIEW GENL MILES

So much for the general.

On Bill Williams Mountain, five thousand feet up, set on a ledge, there were five men of the 24th Infantry and two mules and a mutt dog. This was the way they passed their time. Sgt. Ammon Swing was in command. He copied the messages sent and received, made sure there was always an eye to the telescope, and allowed himself only the luxury of an occasional think about Miss Martha Cox. Corporal Bobyne had charge of the heliograph. After two weeks training in the code, he worked the shutter with a flourish, youngsterlike. Private Takins cooked. He never bathed, and over the months built up such a singular oniony odor that they said of him he could walk past the pot and season the stew. The guards were Corporal Heintz and Private Mullin. Reckoning to grow potatoes, Heintz, a stubborn Dutchman from Illinois, hoed and hilled at a great rate while the studious Mullin took up botany, cataloguing specimens of yucca, nopal, and hediondilla. In their brush corral the two mules tucked back their ears and pondered whom to kick next. Their names were Annie and Grover, the latter after Mr. Cleveland, who was then serving his first term in 1886. The mutt dog chased quail and was in turn hunted by sand fleas, who had better luck.

There was no call for the men to be lonely or the mules mean or the dog to mope. Only six miles away, down in the valley, was Cox's Tanks, a ranch from which water was packed up twice weekly on muleback; only twelve miles off, along the range at a pass, was the Rucker Canyon Station; and only thirty-four miles to the south was Fort Buford, whence supplies were hauled once a month. The five men had high, healthy air to breathe, the goings-on over a hundred square miles of nothing to watch, a branding sun by day and low fierce stars by night.

In addition, they could gossip via heliograph with Rucker:

YOU SEEN ANY PACHES? NOPE HEINTZ
GROWED ANY TATER YET? NOPE

But after May and June on Bill Williams Mountain they began to be lorn. In July they commenced talk-

ing to themselves more than to each other. One day
in August the dog turned his eyes heavenward and
ran at full speed toward the top of the mountain and
death. Dogs had been known to commit suicide in
that way hereabouts.

OUR DOG RUN AWAY
SO DID OURN

So much for the mutt.

When they rousted out one September morning
there was smoke columning a few hundred yards
down the ledge. Taking Mullin with him, Sergeant
Swing went out to reconnoiter, snaking along through
the greasewood until they reached a rock formation.
What they spied was a mite insulting. They had
Apaches on their hands, all right, but squaws instead
of braves—three of them, and a covey of kids running about. The ladies had come during the night,
built a bungalow of brush and old skins, and set up
housekeeping. The smoke issued from a stone-lined
pit in which they were baking mescal, a species of
century plant and a staple of the Apache diet. Ollas
and conical baskets were scattered about. The squaws
wore calico dresses, which meant they had at one time
been on an agency, and one of them was missing the
tip of her nose. The whites had not as yet succeeded
in arguing the Apache warriors out of their age-old
right to snick off a little when they suspected their
womenfolk of being unfaithful. But the final indig-
nity was dealt the sergeant when he and Mullin
crawled out of the rocks. Two youngsters, who had

watched their every move, skittered laughingly back to their mamas.

Apaches or not, they were the station's first real company in six months and the men were glad of them. Sergeant Swing was not. He could not decide if he should start an official message to department headquarters and if he did, how to word it so that he would not sound ridiculous.

While he hesitated young Bobyne shuttered the news to Rucker Canyon anyway:

THREE SQUAWS COME SARGE
DUNNO WHAT TO DO

The reply was immediate:

HAVE DANCE INVITE US

When this was decoded, since no one but Bobyne could read Morse, there was general laughter.

"Folderol," the sergeant says.

"You tink dem squaws vill 'tack us?" Heintz asks, winking at the others. "Zhould ve zhoot dem kids?"

Swing ruminated. "You fellers listen. If you expect them desert belles come up to cook and sew for us, your expecter is busted. Where there's squaws there's billy-bound to be bucks sooner or later." He said further that he was posting a running guard at once. He wanted someone on the telescope from sunup to dark. "And here's the gist of it," he concluded. "We will stay shy of them Indians. Nobody to go down there calling, and if they come up here you treat them as kindly as 'rantulas, which they are."

"Dats too ztiff," Heintz protests.

"Sarge, you mean we ain't even to be decent to the kiddies?" complains Mullin.

"Not as you love your mother," is the answer, "and calculate to see her again."

They grudged off to their posts and the sergeant went to sit by a Joshua tree and study his predicament. He was more alarmed than he had let on. The news along the system had for two weeks been all bad. The most varminty among the Warm Springs chiefs had left the agency with bands and were raiding to the south—Naiche and Mangas together, Kaytennay by himself. With their example before him, it would be beneath Geronimo's dignity down in Mexico to behave much longer. General Miles had cavalry rumping out in all directions, but there had as yet been neither catch nor kill. He had heard that the first thing sought by the Apaches on breakouts was weapons. What was more logical than to camp a few squaws and kids near a heliograph station, cozy up to the personnel, then smite them suddenly with braves, wipe out the sentimental fools, and help yourself to rifles and cartridges? Apaches had been known to wait days, even weeks, for their chance. And how was a mere sergeant to control men who had not mingled with humankind for six months?

Had he been an oathing man, Ammon Swing would have. He had in him a sense of duty like a rod of iron. A small compact individual, he wore a buggy-whip mustache that youthened his face and made less New England his expression. Pushing back his hat, he let his gaze lay out, first at the far mountains on the sides of which the air was white as milk, then lower, at the specks of Cox's Tanks upon the valley floor. This brought to mind Miss Martha Cox, with whom he might be in love and might not. The sister of Jacob Cox, she was a tanned leathery customer as old as the sergeant, which put her nigh on forty-four, too old and sensible for male and female farandoles. She ran the ranch with her brother, plowed with a pistol round her waist, spat and scratched herself like a man, and her reputation with a rifle, after twenty years of raids, caused even the Apaches to give the Cox spread leeway. Swing had seen her five times in six months during his turns to go down with Annie and Grover to pack water. Only once, the last trip, had anything passed between them.

"Ain't you considerable mountain-sore, Mister Swing?"

"Suppose I am," says he.

"Seems to me settling down would be suitable to you."

"Ma'am?"

"Sure," says she. "Marry up and raise a fam'ly and whittle your own stick."

"Too old, Miss Cox."

"Too old?"

"Old as you are," says he.

He knew his blunder when he saw the turkey-red under her tan. She squinted at the mules, then gave him a granite eye.

"Mister Swing, if ever you alter your mind, I know the very one would have you."

"Who, ma'am?"

"Annie," says she.

For the next few days Ammon Swing was much

put on. The little Indians soon swarmed over the station, playing games, ingratiating themselves with the soldiers, eventually sitting on their knees to beg for trinkets. Shoo as hard as he might, the sergeant could not put a stop to it. Down the ledge the three squaws went on baking mescal and inevitably there commenced to be visiting back and forth. Takins was the first caught skulking off.

"Takins," says the sergeant, "I told you to stay shy of them."

"I be only humin, Sarge," grumbles the cook, which was doubtful, considering his fragrance.

"You keep off, that's an order!" says Swing, losing his temper. "Or I'll send you back to Buford to the guardhouse!"

"You will, Sarge?" Takins grins. "Nothin' I'd like better'n to get off this cussed mountin!"

Thus it was that the sergeant's authority went to pot and his command to pieces. Men on guard straggled down the ledge to observe the baking and weaving of baskets and converse sociably in sign. The ladies in turn, led by Mrs. Noseless, a powerful brute of a woman, paid daily calls on the station to watch the operation of the heliostat and giggle at the unnatural ways of the whites.

Three days passed. Then a new factor changed the situation on Bill Williams Mountain from absurd to desperate. The supply party from Fort Buford did not arrive. Takins ran entirely out of salt beef and hardtack. Ammon Swing was reduced to swapping with the squaws for mescal, which tasted like molasses candy and brought on the bloat; but the commodity for which the Apaches were most greedy turned out to be castor oil, of which he had only two bottles in his medicine chest. He considered butchering Annie or Grover, but that would mean one less mule to send down to Cox's Tanks for water.

Water! He could not wait on that. But to obtain it, and food as well, would short him by two men. If an attack were ever to come it would come when the station had only three defenders. Worse yet, it was his turn to go down the mountain day after next, his and Takins's, and he wanted very much to go to Cox's again. Why he wanted to so much he would not admit even to himself.

The next morning he traded the last drop of castor oil to the squaws for mescal. In the afternoon the water casks went dry.

At day-die Ammon Swing called Heintz to him and said he was sending him down for water and food with Takins. It was his own turn, but he should stay in case of attack.

The Dutchy puffed his checks with pleasure. "Goot. You be zorry."

"Why?"

"I ask dis voman to vedding. I ask before, bud zhe zay no. Dis time zhe zay yez, I tink."

One end of the iron rod of duty in the sergeant stuck in his crop. "Why?" he inquires again.

"I goot farmer. Zhe needs farmer to raunch. Alzo zhe iz nod much young. Nod many chanzes more vill zhe get. You change your mind, Zarge?"

"No," says Ammon Swing.

As soon as Heintz and Takins and Annie and Grover had started down in the morning Sergeant Swing would have bet a month's pay this was the day. Something in the pearl air told him. He ordered Mullin and Bobyne to stand guard near the heliostat and have hands on their weapons at all times. They would change off on the telescope. No man was to leave the sight of the other two.

The morning inched.

They had not had food for twenty-four hours nor water for eighteen. Nor would they until Heintz and Takins returned. The squaws did not come to visit nor the kids to play.

One message winked from Rucker Canyon and was shuttered on:

RELAY GENL MILES REQUESTS
PLEASURE COL AND MRS COTTON OFFICERS
BALL HEADQUARTERS FT BOWIE 22 AUGUST

By noon they were so thirsty they spit dust and so hungry their bellies sang songs. It had never been so lonesome on Bill Williams Mountain.

Then they had visitors. The three squaws came waddling along the ledge, offspring after them, and surrounded a pile of brush not twenty yards off. In one hand they held long forked sticks and in the other small clubs. Mrs. Noseless started a fire. The soldiers had no notion what the Indians could be up to. When all was ready, the fire burned down to hot coals, the squaws and kids began to squeal and shout and poke into the brush pile. Curious, the soldiers came near.

What they soon saw was that the Apaches had discovered a large convention of field rats. Under the brush the animals cast up a mound of earth by burrowing numerous tunnels. When a stick was thrust into one end of the tunnel, the animal, seeking an escape route, would dart to the opening of another and hesitate for an instant, half in and half out to scan for his enemy. In that split second another Indian would pin the rat down with forked stick, pull it toward him, bash it over the head with his club, and with a shout of triumph eviscerate it with a stroke of the knife and pitch it into the fire. In a trice the hair was burned off, the carcass roasted to a turn, impaled on the stick, and the juicy tidbit lifted to a hungry mouth. Starved and horrified, the soldiers were drawn to the banquet despite themselves. There seemed no end to the victuals or the fun.

A little girl ran laughing to Bobyne with a rat. The young man sniffed, tasted, and with a grin of surprise put down his rifle and commenced to feast. Mullin was next served. Then a squaw bore a plump offering to the sergeant. It was done exactly to his liking, medium rare. He could no longer resist. The taste was that of rodent, sort of like the woodchuck he had shot and cooked as a sprout. He had, however, to keep his eyes closed.

What opened them was the terrible silence immediately smashed by a scream.

For an instant as the food fell from his hands he was stricken with shock and fright. The kids vanished. A dying Mullin staggered toward him, screaming. An arrow transfixed his body, driven with such force into his back that it pierced him completely, feathers on one side, head and shaft on the other.

One squaw ran full speed toward the tents to plunder, holding high her grimy calico skirt.

Like deer, three Apache bucks leaped from their hiding place in the greasewood and sped toward him, letting arrows go from bows held at waist level.

Another squaw made for the heliograph and, giving the tripod a kick, toppled the instrument onto rock, shattering the mirror.

An arrow skewered through the fleshy part of Swing's left leg. He cried out with pain and went down on one knee, reaching for his rifle.

Young Bobyne retrieved his and began to blaze away at the oncoming bucks when Mrs. Noseless seized him from behind in powerful arms and hurled him backward into the fire of hot coals as she might have barbecued a rat, kneeling on him and setting his hair afire and bashing in his skull with her club.

Shooting from one knee, Ammon Swing brought down one of the bucks at twenty yards and another point-blank. But it was too late to fire at the third, who swept a long knife upward from a hide boot.

He had only time to glimpse the contorted brown face and yellow eyeballs and hear the death yell as a bullet slammed life and wind out of the Apache and the buck fell heavily upon him. He lay wondering if he were dead, stupefied by the fact that the bullet had not been his own.

Then the buck was dragged off him by Miss Martha Cox. She took the Indian's knife, knelt, and slitting the trouser leg began to cut through the arrow shaft on either side of his thigh.

"Soldiers and wimmen," she snorts.

"You shoot him?" he groans.

"Sure."

He asked about Heintz and Takins. Dead, the both of them, she told him—ambushed on the way down. When they had not shown at the ranch, she rode up to find out why.

She had the arrow cut off close to the meat now and bound his leg with shirt cloth. As he sat up she said he would bleed a little; what was dangerous was the chance of infection, since the Apaches had as much fondness for dirty arrows as they did for dirty everything else. He was to ride her horse down as fast as he could manage. Her brother would have the tools to pull the shaft piece, and water for the wound.

Ammon Swing saw that she wore the best she owned, a long dress of gray taffeta and high-button shoes. When furbished, she was near to handsome.

"Heintz was intending to ask you to marry."

"I figured it would be you coming down today," says she. "So I got out my fancies. Ain't had them on in ten year."

"Oh?" says he. "Well, help me."

With her arm round his waist he was hobbling toward her horse when he caught the flash from the Mogollon Station, to the south.

"Message." He stopped. "I ain't trained to read it, but it better be put down."

"It better not," says she, bossy.

But he made her fetch pencil and paper from a tent and wait while he transcribed the signals according to length, long and short. When the flashes ceased, he cast a glum look at his own shattered heliograph nearby.

"Ought to relay this," says he. "It's maybe important."

"Mister Swing," says she, "infection won't wait. You army around up here much longer and you might have to make do without a leg."

He did not even hear. He sat down on a boulder and tried to think how the Sam Hill to send the message on to Rucker Canyon. The piece of shaft twinged as though it were alive, the pain poisoning all the way to his toes. There was no other mirror. There was neither pot nor pan bright enough to reflect sun. Miss Martha Cox kept after him about infection, but the more he knew she was right the more dutiful and mule-headed he became. He would not leave with chores undone. Such a stunt would do injustice to his dead. Suddenly he gave a finger snap.

"Making apology, ma'am, but what do you have on beyunder that dress?"

"Well, I never!" says she, coloring up real ripe for a woman who had just put down a rifle after a killing.

"Would you please remove same?"

"Oh!" she cries.

The sergeant gave a tug at his buggy whip. "Govermint business, ma'am."

With a female stamp of her foot she obeyed, hoisting the taffeta over her head. Above she wore a white corset cover laced with pink ribbon and below, a muslin petticoat so overstarched it was as stiff and glittering as galvanized tin, touching evidence that it had been a long time since she had made starch.

"We are in luck, ma'am," says he. "We have a clear day and the whitest unspeakabout this side of Heaven, and I calculate they will see us.

Being most gentlemanly, he escorted her near the lip of the ledge facing Rucker Canyon, took her dress and, reading from the paper, began to transmit the message by using her dress as a shutter, shading her with it, then sweeping it away for long and short periods corresponding to the code letters he had transcribed. And all the while poor Miss Martha Cox was forced to stand five thousand feet high in plain sight of half the military department of Arizona, being alternately covered and revealed, a living heliograph, flashing in the sun like an angel descended from above and blushing like a woman fallen forever into sin. When her ordeal and her glory were ended, and Rucker blinked on and off rapidly to signify receipt, she snatched her dress to herself. To his confusion, a tear splashed down one of her leathery cheeks while at the same time she drew up breathing brimstone.

"Ammon Swing," cries she, "no man has ever in all my days set eyes on me in such a state! Either I put my brother on your evil trail or you harden your mind to marrying me this minute!"

"Already have," says he.

Thoughtfully she pulled on the gray taffeta. "We better kiss on it," says she.

"Folderol," says he. But they did.

Then she helped him on her horse and together they went down Bill Williams Mountain.

So much for the petticoat, the three squaws, the rat roast, the sergeant, the other soldiers, and the old maid.

The signals reaching Rucker Canyon Station twelve miles off were less distinct than usual, but by means of the telescope and much cussing they could be deciphered and sent on:

RELAY COL AND MRS COTTON ACCEPT
WITH PLEASURE OFFICERS BALL
BOWIE 22 AUGUST

So much for the message.

Comes the Hunter

Jory Sherman

*I was drawn to this story because of its breathtaking
and lyrical prose and the spiritual and moral dilemma
it poses. It is the story of an impoverished frontier
hunter who carries life and death, mercy and revenge,
in his hands one sweet morning. Jory Sherman is a
master storyteller, winner of the Spur Award, and
veteran novelist, poet, short story writer, and con-
noisseur of literature. This story first appeared in
audio form, and this is its first printing.*

He looked down into morning. Looked through a
tunnel of pine trees to see it. Heard it come to
the blunt face of Ute Mountain. Saw it dawn over the
rimrock like the soft fire in the complexions of
peaches, listened to it sing in the quivering throats of
meadowlarks, listened to it sigh like a woman loved,
like a wind rising from the upper Rio Grande del
Norte, roam moaning through his Lost Creek Valley,
carrying with it the echoes of copper-red men and ar-
rowheads of flint and obsidian, of moccasins padding
on sandstone trails, of his grandparents in rattling
wooden wagons pulled by brawny oxen, of mules
with whip wounds and the bloodscrawls of horseflies

and sweat bees on their hides. Saw it all splash through the quivering aspen and the shy young willows along the creek, on the tops of evergreen hills and make sounds that only he could hear, because he saw it all and thought of all the times past and the time upon him now in the fine Colorado morning when spring takes in its breath and just before summer comes through the canyons like a padding visitor surging with heat and the sweat of sun on cottonwood leaves and skin.

He saw the morning, heard it. Felt it pulse in his veins like Taos Lightning, burning into him, becoming part of him, part of the sad, angry light in his blue Teutonic eyes.

"Jess," she said, "you go easy now. Walk keerful."

"Um," he breathed, turned his head to look at her in the doorway of the cabin. His broad chest filled with the scented air of morning. His face crinkled with a smile as he looked at the spruce trees, the tall, stately firs stretching to the sky on the mountain slopes, the patch of tall pines like an orchard left standing for game cover beyond the quarter-acre garden on the cleared slope still soaked with the nightdew, destined to steam in the summer boil from a blazing star just rising majestic as a god over the far snowcapped peaks of country once roamed by the Ute and the Arapaho, the fur trappers, one of whom had spawned him thirty-odd years ago.

"Ah," he sighed.

It wasn't only that Katie was beautiful, it was that she still bore the tiny freckled coppers of childhood on her face, and that her long hair was freshly braided like a Crow woman's, glistening with a bright purple-black sheen, and that her belly was swollen with child. His child. Theirs. Their firstborn. She stood, flat-footed, leaning backward slightly, so that her stomach jutted proud, so that she carried their baby easy as could be, in a mother's intricate sling, a delicate hammock of seawater and blood stretched across the twin bone frames of maternal thighs.

"I mean it, Jess, now you hear. Keerful.

He loved to listen to her talk, to the soft patter of her voice on his ears, like the music in the dulcimer's box she played after supper on evenings when they sat on the porch and watched the rugged land gentle and flicker with the falling sun's light and the fireflies wink on, like floating lights of prairie wagons going west through high grasses, in the dark, before the moon rises cold on the brawny backbone of the Rocky Mountains.

He loved so many things about her that they all became tangled up in his mind until he felt his mind could not breathe nor sort through them for explanation. There were times when he wanted to explain to her the love in his heart, and when he would open his mouth, she would smile and he would see those white teeth, so perfect, so shining pure that he just choked on the words, felt his neck skin tighten down on his Adam's apple so that his speech was shut off plumb and square.

So he would just reach out with his jumbled thoughts and touch her with his heart and clench his lips in frustration until she frowned and made him want to kiss her and never stop kissing her. Ever.

At such times, he wanted to pray, but could never find words. And, too, he thought that it might be wrong to pray in praise of a woman, but his skin tingled, just the same, and what he couldn't say became a ringing song in his big, jutting jug ears until they turned red as cherries with a kind of simple shame.

"Oh, Katie," he said, "don't go on so. I'll be keerful, ya know."

But the rifle in his hands pulled his arm down so that his shoulder socket hurt. And he could feel her eyes on the rifle, on his veined hand and wrist sticking out of his chambray sleeve. The two brass-cased shells in his shirt pocket burned hot against his breast. There were only three bullets left. One nestled in the chamber of the single-shot rifle, a rifle old enough to have lost its bluing, old enough to be pitted along the barrel, the receiver. A single-shot, bolt-action Henry .44-70, with an octagonal barrel, given him by his daddy before he passed on, before "all of them shirttail relations paw over my things."

Katie's eyes took on a kind of whimpering light, and Jess saw it, felt the coldness of morning rise up again, flow through him, jolt his bones like Granny's "arthuritis."

He swallowed air to keep the bile in his stomach down, threw a hand in the air.

"See ya 'fore long," he said, knowing the words were wrong. These were not the words he wanted to say, meant to say. Ah, his throat was tight, his chest cloudy still with the nightdamp, fogged in like the deep canyons where the ribbon of creek ran, the giant, boulder-strewn gorge where the Rio Grande flowed beneath the ghostly plateaus of old Ute campgrounds, under the haunting evergreens standing like dumb sentinels, rooted to the earth, scarred with certain parts of its history, old blazes that marked a trapper's trail, notches axed in by long dead Mexican sheep-herders.

He could almost hear Katie say "be keerful" again, and he knew he could hear her stifled sob.

At the top of the road he had cut and graded with the mules five years before when it was still a game trail, where mist still hung in the chokecherry brambles, he turned, looked at her again. And the sob he heard was his own.

When he turned back to the road, he stepped into his father's footsteps, his grandfather's. He walked over silted footprints left by Utes over a century ago. He thought of the old Lancaster County flintlock back at the house, Grandpa's, its wood eaten away by time, its frizzen balled up now with a thick spiderweb he hadn't the heart to ream out, its ramrod frozen against the stock, swollen by moisture, its brass discolored, ravaged by corrosive rust. Heavy as a hickory limb with its long, big-bored barrel, its German lock stiff-ened into a kind of metallic death, its graceful lines marred by the wounds in its maple stock, its patch-box dulled by a hundred years of disuse and neglect.

And the rifle in his hand turned heavy as any Penn-sylvania flinter, weighted him down until his shoulder ached.

Jess smelled the scent as he knew he would. A giant paw seemed to wipe away all thoughts of Katie and the babe she carried in her swollen womb.

He stepped off the road, onto a trail where the deer crossed from ridge to ridge, down through a shallow draw, leaving their rubs on saplings, their musk scrapes in soft loamy earth. Leaving their shadows among the fallen skeletons of leaves, their hoofprints sunk deep in the hillside like cuneiform messages.

But the scent of bear was strong in his nostrils, and the fear, too, like a cloying fragrance of deep woods where the blue clay spring eked from the rocks, where the land had not been timbered off and the evergreens grew thick on steep slopes that rose to the high ridges.

The bear had murdered both of his beagle hounds the night before. Black bear. Old bear probably. Mean bear certainly.

Jess followed scent, down trail and through thin, second-growth brush, above the wide meadow fed by a spring trapped into pools by the beaver, where last fall he had shot a six-point buck through the heart, feasted on deer meat all winter. He had smoked haunches and ribs over a slow hickory fire, hung the carcass in the springhouse until nothing was left but the skeleton.

The beagle pups, Skipper and Patsy, had chewed bones and sucked marrow until the bear had come, slaying them with mighty paw swipes until there was nothing left of them but the shrill echo of their yelps and their crumpled black and tan hides holding only broken bones and jellied, pulpy flesh.

He still found it hard to believe the dogs were dead. They had been fearless. Many's the time they had chased old man Sisco's prize bull down on the flat, or neighbor Wakefield's pigs, including Lord Randall, the meanest Poland China boar along the big river. Maybe he should have trained them better. He might have taught them not to attack a full-grown bear.

Jess's eyes stung when he thought of the pups, and

his stomach knotted when he thought of the outlaw bear.

Outlaw? This high country of the Rio Grande headwaters had known Zeb Pike and Apaches, Kiowa and Pawnee raiders, Mexicans from Taos and Santa Fe, trappers from Bayou Salade, the upper Missouri, traders from St. Louis and Chihuahua. There was blood on the land, and it had soaked through time, left its smear on every sunrise and sunset so that the people would never forget the dark riders who had roamed these mountains with knife and rifle and tomahawk, the gold seekers, the hunters, the scalpers, the cheats and cardsharks, the traders, the dreamers.

The fear built up in him and he wondered if he could do it, could even find the bear, and if, when he found it, kill it without thought of meat or survival, but only for revenge, only for payment in kind for the deaths of two beagle pups.

"Skippoozer," he said to himself, a baby-talk name for Skipper. When he thought of little Patsy, Skip's sister, he choked up, could not say her name.

She had been the bold one, always getting Skipper into trouble. Why, once she even treed a young painter up on the rimrock, and when it finally got fed up with the barking and jumped out of the gnarled, windbent juniper to attack, Patsy skedaddled for her hiding place under the house, leaving Skipper to fight off eighty pounds of clawing cat. More than once, Skipper had wound up with the rattlesnake bite when Jess knew that Patsy had started the fight. Maybe she had tackled the bear first this time, too, and hadn't gotten away in time.

He walked very quietly now, the bear smell strong

in his nostrils. He stayed downwind, following the contour of the mountain, where the spring tumbled into a deep, miniature gorge, running off a sheer chunk of rock so that it made a lacy waterfall so pretty he wished sometimes he could freeze it, take it home to Katie.

She had never come here. The climb was too steep in her condition. But he would bring her here some-day. If the bear didn't kill him. That was the trouble with a rogue bear. It had killed two dogs, senselessly. Swiped them with huge claws as if they were gnats or mosquitoes. Such a bear would as soon kill a man. It had come close to home, and that wasn't natural. Maybe it had come to the smell of meat, a dead por-cupine the dogs had dragged close to the cabin. He should have checked around back for sign.

He heard the jays. But they weren't squawking at him. They were thick in the willows and cottonwoods that grew near the beaver ponds. He moved toward the lower end of the gorge, where it was open. The brush was thick in there. It would be like going into a box. If the bear got behind him, he would be trapped.

He saw the jays then, dozens of them, flapping like blue and gray flags through the trees, perched on spruce branches above the tangled chokecherry bushes. He heard, too, the crashing of a large animal in the underbrush. There had been a fire here once, and the big trees had burned to ashes. Now second growth fought for dominion in the boxed canyon. Berries would grow in profusion all summer, and it was here that the bear fed on grubs in the rotted trunks of burned trees that lay scattered among the bushes.

Jess moved to the open throat of the small canyon, treading softly. Brambles tore at his overalls, scratched at his hands. The jays screamed. Then, as if at a signal, they rose from the ground and from the small trees, filling the air with the whuffing sound of their flight.

It was suddenly still. Jess's heart froze. He stopped moving, listened.

He peered intently up the draw, looking for a black shape.

The silence seeped through him, raised the hackles on the back of his neck. He shivered with a sudden bleak chill.

To his right, the ground rose, a small hogback of earth that was higher than where he stood. He stepped carefully through the briars, making his way toward higher ground. The steep walls of the gorge rose above him. He heard the waterfall, saw it glisten like a silver veil in the sun.

On high ground, he saw the trampled path the bear had made. In the center of the open canyon, the brush was not so thick, but open, rocky.

The bear rose up, then, its back to Jess. It looked, he thought, its rounded shoulders hunched, like an old woman in a fur coat. He dropped down, his hands shaking, his thoughts charging his senses with fear. He levered a shell into the chamber of the old Henry rifle. The faint scrape of metal boomed loud against his eardrums. But he knew he had not made much noise. He hoped the little sound would not carry.

The bear grunted as Jess eased himself up out of his crouch. He measured the distance. Fifty yards, perhaps. Less than a hundred.

He brought the rifle to his shoulder, moving like a mime in slow motion. The barrel waved. Sweat trickled down his face, drenched his eyebrows. Salt stung his eyes, but he dared not brush them.

The barrel steadied as he pulled the rifle hard against his shoulder. He brought the sights into alignment on the bear's back. He took a breath, held it.

It was then that he saw the cubs. They came boiling out of the bushes above the she-bear, hit the open spot like a pair of furry medicine balls. The first one tripped, went tumbling end over end. The one following bumped into its brother and floundered backward.

Jess saw the bloody slashes on their muzzles.

In that instant, a picture flashed in his mind. He saw the beagles, Skipper and Patsy, ragging the little fellows, nipping at them. He saw the cubs fighting back, heard them squealing.

He looked at the bigger bear again.

This was no rogue bear, but a mother, devoted to protecting her young against all enemies.

A most dangerous bear.

For a long moment, Jess considered following through. His finger caressed the trigger. The she-bear, upwind, had not scented him. Instead, she was intent on watching her cubs. They sat up, engaged in a mock battle, batting each other with their paws. Jess could almost hear them laughing.

He felt bad about the dogs. They had not known about the mother bear. She, seeing her cubs in jeopardy, had probably rushed up with fire in her eyes, swatted them. His heart tugged at the thought of Skipper and Patsy locked in combat with the powerful she-bear.

Slowly, Jess brought the rifle down. He drew in a breath. He had stopped shaking. He eased the hammer down.

There was no vengeance in him. Killing the mother bear would not bring back his pups. Rather, such an act would be a subtraction from life. This was the bears' country, not by choice, but by natural design. They belonged here, just as much as he did.

He backed down to the mouth of the gorge. Behind him, he heard the three bears thrashing in the berry bushes. Their scent was overpowering, smelled of earth and rotted, burnt trees, grubs and carrion.

The cubs had wandered off, of course. Explored new territory. That was their nature. It was too bad the pups had seen them. But he couldn't change what had happened. It just had.

He backed out of the hollow, hunched over like a mendicant, quiet and careful where he stepped.

The rifle was light in his hands. He put it on his shoulder, walked upright down the gentle slope. He didn't care whether he made noise or not. These were his mountains, too. The bears would just have to get used to him, or move on. They would, he knew. The cubs would grow, establish their own territories.

He reached the game trail to his road, walked to the place where he could see his house. He stood there, for a long time, looking down at it. Smoke from the woodstove lazed from the chimney like a child's charcoal scrawl.

For a moment, he forgot that the pups were gone. He expected them to run up the road, barking at him, scolding him for leaving them behind. He looked at the towering mountains rising like walls around him, saw his place below, the cattle feeding down by Lost Creek and in a pasture by the Rio Grande, the horses lit by sun, their coats already shedding winter hair, glistening as if lit by the golden light of a lantern. He drank in the beauty of the scene, drew clean cool air into his lungs.

Katie emerged from the springhouse, looked up at him. She lifted her hand in a tentative wave.

Jess waved back, his heart suddenly swollen in his chest.

He worked the lever on the Henry, spilled the bullets on the ground. Then he held them up triumphantly.

He began to stride down the road, letting the gravity pull him faster and faster until he was in a lope, hurrying to take Katie in his arms.

Long before he reached her, she started to run, too, and her arms were outstretched in a lover's welcome.

As he rushed up to her, he saw the bright tears brimming in her eyes. They shone, he thought, like the sunlight on the waterfall. Someday, after their child was born, he would take her up there on horseback, to the small gorge, to the birthplace of the spring that filled their pails night and morning.

Maybe they would see the cubs, too, and their mother, feeling contented in the wild deep private canyon that was their home.

The Face

Ed Gorman

This Spur Award–winning short story was published by Swallow Press in The Best Western Stories of Ed Gorman, *in 1991. It is the most haunting study of men at war that I have ever read. It brims with horror and beauty and darkness and evil. Gorman is primarily a mystery and suspense novelist, but turns occasionally to the western field, and is the author of several distinguished western novels. Novelist Bill Pronzini calls Gorman's stories "western noir" because so many of them deal with the aftermath of crime. His most recent is* Storm Riders, *from Berkley.*

The war was going badly. In the past month more than sixty men had disgraced the Confederacy by deserting, and now the order was to shoot deserters on sight. This was in other camps and other regiments. Fortunately, none of our men had deserted at all.

As a young doctor, I knew even better than our leaders just how hopeless our war had become. The public knew General Lee had been forced to cross the Potomac with ten thousand men who lacked shoes, hats, and who at night had to sleep on the ground without blankets. But I knew—in the first six months in this post—that our men suffered from influenza, diphtheria, smallpox, yellow fever and even cholera; ravages from which they would never recover; ravages more costly than bullets and the advancing armies of the Yankees. Worse, because toilet and bathing facilities were practically nil, virtually every man suffered from ticks and mites, and many suffered from scurvy, their bodies on fire. Occasionally, you would see a man go mad, do crazed dances in the moonlight trying to get the bugs off him. Soon enough he would be dead.

This was the war in the spring and while I have here referred to our troops as "men," in fact they were mostly boys, some as young as thirteen. In the night, freezing and sometimes wounded, they cried out for their mothers, and it was not uncommon to hear one or two of them sob while they prayed aloud.

I tell you this so you will have some idea of how horrible things had become for our beloved Confederacy. But even given the suffering and madness and despair I'd seen for the past two years as a military doctor, nothing had prepared me for the appearance of the Virginia man in our midst.

On the day he was brought in on a buckboard, I was working with some troops, teaching them how to garden. If we did not get vegetables and fruit into our diets soon, all of us would have scurvy. I also appreciated the respite that working in the warm sun gave me from surgery. In the past week alone, I'd amputated three legs, two arms, and numerous hands and fingers. None had gone well, conditions were so filthy.

Every amputation had ended in death except one and this man—boy; he was fourteen—pleaded with me to kill him every time I checked on him. He'd suffered a head wound and I'd had to relieve the pressure by trepanning into his skull. Beneath the blood and pus in the hole I'd dug, I could see his brain squirming. There was no anesthetic, of course, except whiskey and that provided little comfort against the violence of my bone saw. It was one of those periods when I could not get the tart odor of blood from my nostrils, or its feel from my skin. Sometimes, standing at the surgery table, my boots would become soaked with it and I would squish around in them all day.

The buckboard was parked in front of the General's tent. The driver jumped down, ground-tied the horses, and went quickly inside.

He returned a few moments later with General Sullivan, the commander. Three men in familiar gray uniforms followed the General.

The entourage walked around to the rear of the wagon. The driver, an enlisted man, pointed to something in the buckboard. The General, a fleshy, bald man of fifty-some years, leaned over the wagon and peered downward.

Quickly, the General's head snapped back and then his whole body followed. It was as if he'd been stung by something coiled and waiting for him in the buckboard.

The General shook his head and said, "I want this man's entire body covered. Especially his face."

"But, General," the driver said. "He's not dead. We shouldn't cover his face."

"You heard what I said!" General Sullivan snapped. And with that, he strutted back into his tent, his men following.

I was curious, of course, about the man in the back of the wagon. I wondered what could have made the General start the way he had. He'd looked almost frightened.

I wasn't to know till later that night.

My rounds made me late for dinner in the vast tent used for the officers' mess. I always felt badly about the inequity of officers having beef stew while the men had, at best, hardtack and salt pork. Not so bad that I refused to eat it, of course, which made me feel hypocritical on top of being sorry for the enlisted men.

Not once in my time here had I ever dined with General Sullivan. I was told on my first day here that the General, an extremely superstitious man, considered doctors bad luck. Many people feel this way. Befriend a doctor and you'll soon enough find need of his services.

So I was surprised when General Sullivan, carrying a cup of steaming coffee in a huge, battered tin cup, sat down across the table from where I ate alone, my usual companions long ago gone back to their duties.

"Good evening, Doctor."

"Good evening, General."

"A little warmer tonight."

"Yes."

He smiled dourly. "Something's got to go our way, I suppose."

I returned his smile. "I suppose." I felt like a child

trying to act properly for the sake of an adult. The General frightened me.

The General took out a stogie, clipped off the end, sniffed it, licked it, then put it between his lips and fired it. He did all this with a ritualistic satisfaction that made me think of better times in my home city of Charleston, of my father and uncles handling their smoking in just the same way.

"A man was brought into camp this afternoon," he said.

"Yes," I said. "In a buckboard."

He eyed me suspiciously. "You've seen him up close?"

"No. I just saw him delivered to your tent." I had to be careful of how I put my next statement. I did not want the General to think I was challenging his reasoning. "I'm told he was not taken to any of the hospital tents."

"No, he wasn't." The General wasn't going to help me.

"I'm told he was put under quarantine in a tent of his own."

"Yes."

"May I ask why?"

He blew two plump white perfect rings of smoke toward the ceiling. "Go have a look at him, then join me in my tent."

"You're afraid he may have some contagious disease?"

The General considered the length of his cigar. "Just go have a look at him, Doctor. Then we'll talk."

With that, the General stood up, his familiar brusque self once again, and was gone.

*   *   *

The guard set down his rifle when he saw me. "Good evenin', Doctor."

"Good evening."

He nodded to the tent behind him. "You seen him yet?"

"No; not yet."

He was young. He shook his head. "Never seen anything like it. Neither has the priest. He's in there with him now." In the chill, crimson dusk I tried to get a look at the guard's face. I couldn't. My only clue to his mood was the tone of his voice—one of great sorrow.

I lifted the tent flap and went in.

A lamp guttered in the far corner of the small tent, casting huge and playful shadows across the walls. A hospital cot took up most of the space. A man's body lay beneath the covers. A sheer cloth had been draped across his face. You could see it billowing with the man's faint breath. Next to the cot stood Father Lynott. He was silver-haired and chunky. His black cassock showed months of dust and grime. Like most of us, he was rarely able to get hot water for necessities.

At first, he didn't seem to hear me. He stood over the cot torturing black rosary beads through his fingers. He stared directly down at the cloth draped on the man's face.

Only when I stood next to him did Father Lynott look up. "Good evening, Father."

"Good evening, Doctor."

"The General wanted me to look at this man."

He stared at me. "You haven't seen him, then?"

"No."

"Nothing can prepare you."

"I'm afraid I don't understand."

He looked at me out of his tired cleric's face. "You'll see soon enough. Why don't you come over to the officers' tent afterwards? I'll be there drinking my nightly coffee."

He nodded, glanced down once more at the man on the cot, and then left, dropping the tent flap behind him.

I don't know how long I stood there before I could bring myself to remove the cloth from the man's face. By now, enough people had warned me of what I would see that I was both curious and apprehensive. There is a myth about doctors not being shocked by certain terrible wounds and injuries. Of course we are but we must get past that shock—or, more honestly, put it aside for a time—so that we can help the patient.

Close by, I could hear the feet of the guard in the damp grass, pacing back and forth in front of the tent. A barn owl and then a distant dog joined the sounds the guard made. Even more distant, there was cannon fire, the war never ceasing. The sky would flare silver like summer lightning. Men would suffer and die.

I reached down and took the cloth from the man's face.

"What do you suppose could have done that to his face, Father?" I asked the priest twenty minutes later.

We were having coffee. I smoked a cigar. The guttering candles smelled sweet and waxy.

"I'm not sure," the priest said.

"Have you ever seen anything like it?"

"Never."

I knew what I was about to say would surprise the priest. "He has no wounds."

"What?"

"I examined him thoroughly. There are no wounds anywhere on his body."

"But his face—"

I drew on my cigar, watched the expelled smoke move like a storm cloud across the flickering candle flame. "That's why I asked you if you'd ever seen anything like it."

"My God," the priest said, as if speaking to himself. "No wounds."

In the dream I was back on the battlefield on that frosty March morning two years ago when all my medical training had deserted me. Hundreds of corpses covered the ground where the battle had gone on for two days and two nights. You could see cannons mired in mud, the horses unable to pull them out. You could see the grass littered with dishes and pans and kettles, and a blizzard of playing cards—all exploded across the battlefield when the Union army had made its final advance. But mostly there were the bodies—so young and so many—and many of them with mutilated faces. During this time of the war, both sides had begun to commit atrocities. The Yankees favored disfiguring Confederate dead and so they moved across the battlefield with Bowie knives that had been fashioned by sharpening with large files. They put deep gashes in the faces of the young men, tearing out eyes sometimes, even sawing off noses. In the woods that day we'd found a group of our soldiers who'd been mortally wounded but who'd lived for a time after the Yankees had left. Each corpse held in its hand some memento of the loved ones they'd left behind—a photograph, a letter, a lock of blonde hair. Their last sight had been of some homely yet profound endearment from the people they'd loved most.

This was the dream—nightmare, really—and I'd suffered it ever since I'd searched for survivors on that battlefield two years previous.

I was still in this dream-state when I heard the bugle announce the morning. I stumbled from my cot and went down to the creek to wash and shave. The day had begun.

Casualties were many that morning. I stood in the hospital tent watching as one stretcher after another bore man after man to the operating table. Most suffered from wounds inflicted by minié balls, fired from guns that could kill a man nearly a mile away.

By noon, my boots were again soaked with blood dripping from the table.

During the long day, I heard whispers of the man General Sullivan had quarantined from others. Apparently, the man had assumed the celebrity and fascination of a carnival sideshow. From the whispers, I gathered the guards were letting men in for quick looks at him, and then lookers came away shaken and frightened. These stories had the same impact as tales of spectres told around midnight campfires. Except this was daylight and the men—even the youngest of them—hardened soldiers. They should not have been so afraid but they were.

I couldn't get the sight of the man out of my mind, either. It haunted me no less than the battlefield I'd seen two years earlier.

During the afternoon, I went down to the creek and washed. I then went to the officers' tent and had stew and coffee. My arms were weary from surgery but I knew I would be working long into the night.

The General surprised me once again by joining me. "You've seen the soldier from Virginia?"

"Yes, sir."

"What do you make of him?"

I shrugged. "Shock, I suppose."

"But his face—"

"This is a war, General, and a damned bloody one. Not all men are like you. Not all men have iron constitutions."

He took my words as flattery, of course, as a military man would. I hadn't necessarily meant them that way. Military men could also be grossly vain and egotistical and insensitive beyond belief.

"Meaning what, exactly, Doctor?"

"Meaning that the soldier from Virginia may have become so horrified by what he saw that his face—" I shook my head. "You can see too much, too much death, General, and it can make you go insane."

"Are you saying he's insane?"

I shook my head. "I'm trying to find some explanation for his expression, General."

"You say there's no injury?"

"None that I can find."

"Yet he's not conscious."

"That's why I think of shock."

I was about to explain how shock works on the body—and how it could feasibly effect an expression like the one on the Virginia soldier's face—when a lieutenant rushed up to the General and breathlessly said, "You'd best come, sir. The tent where the soldier's quarantined—There's trouble!"

When we reached there, we found half the camp's soldiers surrounding the tent. Three and four deep, they were, and milling around idly. Not the sort of thing you wanted to see your men doing when there was a war going on. There were duties to perform and none of them were getting done.

A young soldier—thirteen or fourteen at most—stepped from the line and hurled his rifle at the General. The young soldier had tears running down his cheeks. "I don't want to fight any more, General."

The General slammed the butt of the rifle into the soldier's stomach. "Get hold of yourself, young man. You seem to forget we're fighting to save the Confederacy."

We went on down the line of glowering faces, to where two armed guards struggled to keep soldiers from looking into the tent. I was reminded again of a sideshow—some irresistible spectacle everybody wanted to see.

The soldiers knew enough to open an avenue for the General. He strode inside the tent. The priest sat on a stool next to the cot. He had removed the cloth from the Virginia soldier's face and was staring fixedly at it.

The General pushed the priest aside, took up the

cloth used as a covering, and started to drop it across the soldier's face—then stopped abruptly. Even General Sullivan, in his rage, was moved by what he saw. He jerked back momentarily, his eyes unable to lift from the soldier's face. He handed the cloth to the priest. "You cover his face now, Father. And you keep it covered. I hereby forbid any man in this camp to look at this soldier's face ever again. Do you understand?"

Then he stormed from the tent.

The priest reluctantly obliged.

Then he angled his head up to me. "It won't be the same any more, Doctor."

"What won't?"

"The camp. Every man in here has now seen his face." He nodded back to the soldier on the cot. "They'll never be the same again. I promise you."

In the evening, I ate stew and biscuits, and sipped at a small glass of wine. I was, as usual, in the officers' tent when the priest came and found me.

For a time, he said nothing beyond his greeting. Simply watched me at my meal, and then stared out the open flap at the camp preparing for evening, the fires in the center of the encampment, the weary men bedding down. Many of them, healed now, would be back in the battle within two days or less.

"I spent an hour with him this afternoon," the priest said.

"The quarantined man?"

"Yes." The priest nodded. "Do you know some of the men have visited him five or six times?"

The way the priest spoke, I sensed he was gloat-ing over the fact that the men were disobeying the General's orders. "Why don't the guards stop them?"

"The guards are in visiting him, too."

"The man says nothing. How can it be a visit?"

"He says nothing with his tongue. He says a great deal with his face." He paused, eyed me levelly. "I need to tell you something. You're the only man in this camp who will believe me." He sounded frantic. I almost felt sorry for him.

"Tell me what?"

"The man—he's not what we think."

"No?"

"No; his face—" He shook his head. "It's God's face."

"I see."

The priest smiled. "I know how I must sound."

"You've seen a great deal of suffering, Father. It wears on a person."

"It's God's face. I had a dream last night. The man's face shows us God's displeasure with the war. That's why the men are so moved when they see the man." He sighed, seeing he was not convincing me. "You say yourself he hasn't been wounded."

"That's true."

"And that all his vital signs seem normal."

"True enough, Father."

"Yet he's in some kind of shock."

"That seems to be his problem, yes."

The priest shook his head. "No, his real problem is that he's become overwhelmed by the suffering he's seen in this war—what both sides have done to the other. All the pain. That's why there's so much sorrow on his face—and that's what the men are responding to. The grief on his face is the same grief they feel in their hearts. God's face."

"Once we get him to a real field hospital—"

And it was then we heard the rifle shots.

The periphery of the encampment was heavily protected, we'd never heard firing this close.

The priest and I ran outside.

General Sullivan stood next to a group of young men with weapons. Several yards ahead, near the edge of the camp, lay three bodies, shadowy in the light of the campfire. One of the fallen men moaned. All three men wore our own gray uniforms.

Sullivan glowered at me. "Deserters."

"But you shot them in the back," I said.

"Perhaps you didn't hear me, Doctor. The men were deserting. They'd packed their belongings and were heading out."

One of the young men who'd done the shooting said, "It was the man's face, sir."

Sullivan wheeled on him. "It was what?"

"The quarantined man, sir. His face. These men said it made them sad and they had to see families back in Missouri, and that they were just going to leave no matter what."

"Poppycock," Sullivan said. "They left because they were cowards."

I left to take care of the fallen man who was crying out for help.

In the middle of the night, I heard more guns being fired. I lay on my cot, knowing it wasn't Yankees being fired at. It was our own deserters.

I dressed and went over to the tent where the quarantined man lay. Two young farm boys in ill-fitting gray uniforms stood over him. They might have been mourners standing over a coffin. They said nothing. Just stared at the man.

In the dim lamplight, I knelt down next to him. His vitals still seemed good, his heartbeat especially. I stood up, next to the two boys, and looked down on him myself. There was nothing remarkable about his face. He could have been any of thousands of men serving on either side.

Except for the grief.

This time I felt the tug of it myself, heard in my mind the cries of the dying I'd been unable to save, saw the families and farms and homes destroyed as the war moved across the countryside, heard children crying out for dead parents, and parents sobbing over the bodies of their dead children. It was all there in his face, perfectly reflected, and I thought then of what the priest had said, that this was God's face, God's sorrow and displeasure with us.

The explosion came, then.

While the two soldiers next to me didn't seem to hear it at all, I rushed from the tent to the center of camp.

Several young soldiers stood near the ammunition cache. Someone had set fire to it. Ammunition was exploding everywhere, flares of red and yellow and gas-jet blue against the night. Men everywhere ducked for cover behind wagons and trees and boulders.

Into this scene, seemingly unafraid and looking like the lead actor in a stage production of *King Lear* I'd once seen, strode General Sullivan, still tugging on his heavy uniform jacket.

He went over to two soldiers who stood, seemingly unfazed, before the ammunition cache. Between explosions I could hear him shouting, "Did you set this fire?"

And they nodded.

Sullivan, as much in bafflement as anger, shook his head. He signaled for the guards to come and arrest these men.

As the soldiers were passing by me, I heard one of them say to a guard, "After I saw his face, I knew I had to do this. I had to do this. I had to stop the war."

Within an hour, the flames died and the explosions ceased. The night was almost ominously quiet. There were a few hours before dawn, so I tried to sleep some more.

I dreamed of Virginia, green Virginia in the spring, and the creek where I'd fished as a boy, and how the sun had felt on my back and arms and head. There was no surgical table in my dream, nor were my shoes soaked with blood.

Around dawn somebody began shaking me. It was Sullivan's personal lieutenant. "The priest has been shot. Come quickly, Doctor."

I didn't even dress fully, just pulled on my trousers over the legs of my long underwear.

A dozen soldiers stood outside the tent looking confused and defeated and sad. I went inside.

The priest lay in his tent. His cassock had been torn away. A bloody hole made a target-like circle on his stomach.

Above his cot stood General Sullivan, a pistol in his hand.

I knelt next to the cot and examined the priest. His

vital signs were faint and growing fainter. He had at most a few minutes to live.

I looked up at the General. "What happened?"

The General nodded for the lieutenant to leave. The man saluted and then went out into the gray dawn.

"I had to shoot him," General Sullivan said.

I stood up. "You had to shoot a priest?"

"He was trying to stop me."

"From what?"

Then I noticed for the first time the knife scabbard on the General's belt. Blood streaked its sides. The hilt of the knife was sticky with blood. So were the General's hands. I thought of how Yankee troops had begun disfiguring the faces of our dead on the battlefield.

He said, "I have a war to fight, Doctor. The men— the way they were reacting to the man's face—" He paused and touched the bloody hilt of the knife. "I took care of him. And the priest came in while I was doing it and went insane. He started hitting me, trying to stop me and—" He looked down at the priest. "I didn't have any choice, Doctor. I hope you believe me."

A few minutes later, the priest died.

I started to leave the tent. General Sullivan put a hand on my shoulder. "I know you don't care very much for me, Doctor, but I hope you understand me at least a little. I can't win a war when men desert and blow up ammunition dumps and start questioning the worthiness of the war itself. I had to do what I did. I hope someday you'll understand."

I went out into the dawn. The air smelled of camp-fires and coffee. Now the men were busy scurrying around, preparing for war. The way they had been before the man had been brought here in the buck-board.

I went over to the tent where he was kept and asked the guard to let me inside. "The General said nobody's allowed inside, Doctor."

I shoved the boy aside and strode into the tent.

The cloth was still over his face, only now it was soaked with blood. I raised the cloth and looked at him. Even for a doctor, the sight was horrible. The General had ripped out his eyes and sawed off his nose. His cheeks carried deep gullies where the knife had been dug in deep.

He was dead. The shock of the defacement had killed him.

Sickened, I looked away.

The flap was thrown back, then, and there stood General Sullivan. "We're going to bury him now, Doctor."

In minutes, the dead soldier was inside a pine box borne up a hill of long grass waving in a chill wind. The rains came, hard rains, before they'd turned even two shovelfuls of earth.

Then, from a distance over the hill, came the thunder of cannon and the cry of the dying.

The face that reminded us of what we were doing to each other was no more. It had been made ugly, robbed of its sorrowful beauty.

He was buried quickly and without benefit of clergy—the priest himself having been buried an hour earlier—and when the ceremony was finished, we returned to camp and war.

The Anniversary

Win Blevins

Novelist and short story writer Win Blevins has made a name for himself in the realms of fur trade literature and novels dealing with American Indians. His biographical novel about the Sioux war leader Crazy Horse, Stone Song, *won the Spur Award for Best Novel of the West along with other honors, and is widely regarded as the finest study of Crazy Horse ever written. His nonfiction* Give Your Heart to the Hawks *is considered one of the bibles of fur trade lore. But there is more to Win Blevins than his specialties. His interest in the American West is protean, and includes the twentieth century as well as the earlier West. Here, he writes fascinatingly about the trick riding, rodeo, and Wild West shows that became an American phenomenon in the decades before World War Two. Amazingly, this story is set in New York, where the West has been brought to Madison Square Garden by gifted daredevils who would do anything with a horse to win a gasp from the crowd. This piercing story is notable for its great tenderness and sensitivity.*

Lew watched Robert Burns McTavish cross the street headed west. Mac walked at a brisk pace, with the confident sort of gait that fit a big man, hefty but no more than fifty, in the prime of life physically, and duded up like a prosperous capitalist. Which was what the boss was, sole proprietor of McTavish's Wild West Show and Rodeo.

Lew Evans slipped along behind. Difference between your Scot, he thought, and your Welsh-Indian. The Scot strides, commander of all he surveys. The Welsh-Indian slips, hoping not to be seen.

Headed west. But where?

All he'd said was, "Run-through tonight."

That was when Lew realized: Today was the anniversary. Lew had forgotten because today's show was a matinee, and last year's had been at night. But today was the one-year anniversary, for sure, November 2.

Mac crossed a street, Lew had no idea what one. Mac had left Times Square one avenue to the east. Besides that and Fifth Avenue, Lew, who knew every crick of the Bear Paw Mountains, didn't know a single street name in New York. They stayed in a hotel next to Madison Square Garden, so he didn't have to.

A bum sat propped against the traffic light on the far side. His face raised to Mac's, and his lips moved. Lew could almost read the words, the refrain of the Great Depression, which would be ended by the coming war, everyone said—some deal for the common man. "Brother, can you spare a dime?"

The boss turned and stared at the bum. Lew stood sideways behind an anonymous fellow in a suit. The Welsh-Indian cowboy was thin, thin enough that Mac probably wouldn't glimpse enough of his shape to know it, even if he looked straight this way. And Lew had left his broad-brimmed hat behind, which made him feel naked.

The boss reached into an inside pocket of his Norfolk coat and Lew stiffened. Pistol? He carried one. No, a wallet. Mac drew out a bill and tossed it at the bum's lap. What was wrong with the Scot? He didn't pay some of his help a dollar a day. Mac turned on his heel and walked away. So. He might give a fellow something material, Lew thought, but feeling, never.

Mac strode down the street like he owned it, not looking to the right or left—step purposeful, look purposeful. He scarcely glanced at the neighborhood, which was rough. Young toughs hung around on the steps of the slum houses and in front of the bars. Irish, Lew would guess from the look of them. But it wasn't an Irishman that was going to get Mac today, if anybody or anything did.

Lew slipped along Indian-like. His grandfather Sees Twice, a Piegan, had taught him how to move without letting people see you. But that was on the plains, not the streets of some big city. According to Sees Twice, the same thing got every man or woman, every mortal. The north wind. It came and frosted you, like it did the plants. In Lew's childish imagination it carried you back to the north pole, where you lay forever crusted in ice.

Lew would see if the north wind came for Mac today. He would also see if he'd learned from his grandfather to follow a man without getting spotted. After Mac went across a lot of them avenues, he crossed under some overhead roads and over some railroad tracks and tramped like a fool across private property and walked out a long wharf or whatever they called it and stood above the river. Lew had trouble working his way even half close, to see what Mac would do. Lew didn't even know which river it was, though he knew it was tidal, as much salt water as fresh.

The boss smoked a cigarette.

Mac pulled out the pocket watch on its gold fob, popped the cover, and studied the time. Lew couldn't imagine why he cared about the time. This last year he hadn't cared a whit for time, or money, or the people who worked for him. And not much of a whit for the last friend he had left, Lew Evans. Lew remembered when he'd been a softer man.

Mac stood at the very end of the dock and stared down. Lew didn't look down at the river. He could hear it, sloshing against the piles, gray and cold, and with a tide that would suck out to sea like . . .

This is it, Lew thought. He'll jump and I won't be able to do a thing. It was twenty feet or more to the water, and nothing like a ladder, just pilings that could never be climbed. Mac's heavy woollen clothing would take him straight down anyway. Probably what he wanted.

Suddenly, the boss spun and walked smartly back toward land. Lew slipped into the doorway of a shed. As Mac passed, the boss said, "Kinda far from the hotel, ain't you, Evans?" and kept walking.

Lew felt a proper fool. How long had Mac known? Lew caught up with him. "Care for a drink, Mc-

Tavish?" Meaning whiskey, of course, which to a Scot meant Scotch, preferably single malt. It was odd. These two men once had been the inseparable Mac and Lew. They'd come out of Montana and had walked the same road for twenty years, as competitors, as true friends, and finally as owner and top hand. Now they called each other by their last names.

Mac just shook his head no. No drink, no talk, no nothing, not the boss, not anymore.

Lew walked along, not sure whether he was alongside or just a little behind. Either way, he knew he occupied no part of Mac's mind. Not on the one-year anniversary.

Robert McTavish was wondering if he could stand it any longer. Well, yes, he would do a run-through. It was like wanting a woman when your wife was dead. Though Fannie had never been his wife, he corrected himself. It built up and it built up and finally you couldn't stand it any longer and you rented some woman and made the gesture. But that left you emptier than before, and self-disgusted besides.

Hardly anyone knew about the run-throughs, just Evans and two or three others. They didn't understand. No one had ever understood anything about him. They hadn't understood how his people were poor and he wanted to own a business. Didn't understand how he longed to make his the biggest show of all, Buffalo Bill's Wild West Show gone wilder and woollier and more fun. Didn't understand his love for Fannie. Didn't understand his passion for his daughter by Fannie. For a long time they didn't understand his pride. Now they didn't understand his guilt. So they didn't understand his shadow run-throughs.

He thought of Evans, half a step behind, once a friend, now just a loyal dog. He remembered Fannie, who'd liked him, and liked other men just as well. No one knew you, or cared to. You walked alone. He had understood that for a long, long time.

There was no one he wanted to have a drink with.

Maybe this anniversary run-through will be the last, Lew was thinking. November 2, 1941, and no more. He sighed. At first Mac had done run-throughs every Sunday evening, just like he and Jillie had always done. After a month that had stopped. Now they all needed to stop.

He was standing in the ramp, the dark, concrete tunnel under the thousands of seats. Right hand poised, he looked to the middle of the arena at Mac. Some months ago, he remembered for no reason, Mac had asked Lew to address him as Mr. McTavish in front of the other employees. What struck Lew hardest then was that the word "employee" was damn funny for your top hand, and a fellow you'd known your whole grown-up life.

Mac's hat brim snapped down and back up—that was the man's signal. Lew slapped the white mare on the rump and she started easy, like always, cantering down the ramp in the shadows underneath the grandstand. Since she was an old pro, she hit the end of the tunnel at a hard run. When she galloped into the glare of the bright lights, she flashed like an angel horse, just like her name. Riderless, she sported black reins and saddle with silver trim.

In the tunnel Lew heard Mac's amplified roar, for he did his own PA work in all shows and rehearsals. "Ladies and gentlemen, cowboys and cowgirls, the world's finest trick-riding mare, A-A-ANGEL!"

Silence, of course. The afternoon crowd was in the safety and warmth of their homes now. Mac always did the run-throughs late at night, when the hands were done with the work and in the hotel, or out on the town. Just the boss and old Lew to help out. And Jillie.

On the cue word "Angel" Lew spanked her mate, an upside-down twin for the white mare, also fourteen hands, likewise short-coupled. But this was a stallion, and black as . . .

Lew didn't know as black as what. He watched the powerful animal sprint away—he wasn't big, but he was strong and fast and quick, and too damned dangerous. Uncut, he was, and Lew had never been able to believe Mac let the show's star, not to mention his own daughter, trick-ride a stallion. Damn few trick riders had ever used a stallion, and no women. Lew had seen 'em all: Faye Blackstone, Midge McLain, Nancy Bragg, Barbara Huntington, and the best men riders, too, especially Dick Griffith, still World's Champion Trick Rider in Lew's mind, though no rodeo was running trick-riding competitions anymore, just exhibitions.

The PA system boomed, "Ladies and gentlemen and boys and girls, does, bucks, and cute little fawns, the world's *only* trick-riding stallion, D-E-E-E-VIL." The first time around Mac always pronounced it to rhyme with *evil.* "The star of McTavish's Wild West Show and Rodeo—AND ONLY OUR STAR—is dar-

ing enough to trick-ride a proudly uncut horse, this
handsome black, DEVIL"—now it sounded like level.

Down the tunnel, from darkness into bright, Lew
watched the stallion sprint out and turn toward the
station. He would pound to a dramatic stop right next
to Angel. The horses knew the routine perfectly. The
big black's saddle and reins were white, the trim gold,
real gold. The showman and his star spared no expense.

Lew clomped down the ramp, headed for the arena
himself. He had to get the gear ready for the last trick.
His feet hurt, though—too many years in cowboy
boots, the doc said. But that was dumb. He was just
stove up from riding bulls and saddle broncs in the
great days, then sticking around trying to earn a few
bucks at team roping, and finally doing clown work.
When he couldn't move quick enough to be around
rough stock close at all, only forty years old but feeling old bones, Mac gave him the title Manager. Sometimes Lew wondered whether Mac really wanted to
keep him around. Too many memories. But maybe
Lew was his last link to the human race.

The third announcement started. Mac himself
would be opening the far gate, the one beneath the
VIP box. "Ladies and gentlemen, bulls and cows,
dudes and dudettes, McTavish's Wild West Show and
Rodeo presents the Women's World Champion Trick
Rider, Miss JILL LA JOIE!"

Means "joy" in French, a bulldogger said sugges-
tively within Mac's hearing once, and Mac promptly
coldcocked the man, gave his entry fee back, and ordered him to stay away from McTavish's Wild West
Show and Rodeo. Jillie had made the name up her-

self, and when she was flirting, she herself would say "means 'joy' in French, but it's pronounced LAE-ZHWAH."

She flirted a lot. She was on the wild side, like her mother. Fannie Mulhall had been a wild one for sure, first woman ever to win Best All-Around Cowboy at a big show. Even when Mac got her pregnant—at least they both said it was him—she wouldn't marry Mac and settle down. Jillie McTavish was raised at the Mulhall family ranch in Montana. After Fannie died, Jillie grew up traveling with her dad, in the cabs of pickups, the backs of horse trailers, the dust of chutes, the boozy haze of honkytonks, and on the backs of rough stock. Mac never doted on any grown woman any more, not the way he did his daughter.

The only woman he'd ever wanted, to Lew's recollection, was Fannie. She'd been fond of him. "Bobbie Burns," she'd always call him, the only person Lew ever heard use Mac's first name, "my poet." But one man was never enough for Fannie.

Clomping down the dark ramp, Lew could see Jillie making her circuit of the arena in the hippodrome stand in his mind's eye, holding high an American flag. It looked sort of like she was standing on the saddle, but her feet were in the loops of the hippodrome strap, below the forks. It was one of the simplest riding tricks, the one lots of cowboys learned first, but the big, waving flag got a rise out of the crowd.

Mac always introduced her as the world champion, for she did win it the last year the Turtles awarded one. That was the rodeo riders association. They didn't have a trick-riding champion anymore due to lack of competition.

In private Mac always bragged she was the best of all. Lew agreed, of women trick riders. Two or three of the men were ahead of her, though. He had seen Dick Griffith do 109 tricks with Tex Austin's outfit in one two-week run over in London, England, the finest display Lew had ever witnessed. Never repeated any trick but one, and he ended every show with that— the only trick judges ever gave 95 points for, back when there were still competitions—going between the hind legs from above. Mac hadn't seen Dick Griffith them two weeks in London.

But she was tops among the women, and Mac was proud. He'd done almost all he bragged of, taught her himself, trained her careful, gave her every secret, helped her get way better than her mom. Plus he was the one who put the *show* into her show, using horses of three colors, even if one was a stallion. He helped her work out the costumes, and the three styles of trick riding: western, circus, and Cossack. And yeah, Mac got her to do the Roman riding leap through the ring of fire to climax the show. Jillie had resisted that one at first. It worried her. But Mac had a newsreel fella shoot film of her jumping those three horses through that fiery ring. When Jillie saw it, she was sold forever.

Lew stepped into the arena. He blinked in the glare of the big banks of light. Across the way he heard the rhythmic hoofbeats. Though the big lights blinded him, in his head he could see horse and rider, the mount a grulla mare, the color the oddest he'd ever seen, a light blue that always transformed under the big lights, glowing so luminous it seemed almost as bright as the flag, and the mare looked like a magic creature, a spirit horse.

That was perfect for Jillie, because what she had on her own, what neither Mac nor anyone else had taught her, was an airy style, like she was spirit, weightless, able to float and maybe fly, not made of flesh and bone and organ, but fairy stuff.

Mac's voice reached a climax on the PA as the grulla left the circuit and galloped toward the station. "Miss LaJoie rides the champion trick-riding horse in all the world, the winner of more points from the Turtles than any other, SPI-I-I-RIT OF THE WEST!" Now the grulla would come hard between the white and the black, make a leg-jolting stop, and the flag would droop.

He didn't look in that direction. He couldn't stand to.

The very oddest thing about these run-throughs after the shows, Lew always thought, was not hearing the band strike up "The Ride of the Valkyries," her anthem. Like the audience, the band was gone home.

He clomped on across the arena. He should be checking the rough stock in the trucks, making sure of feed and water, and listening to every cowboy's little problem. Tonight, though, he had to keep every curious hand and even a couple of rival rodeo owners out of the stands, and he had to get the gear ready for the firejump. And avoid watching.

He wondered if Mac would want a drink afterwards. Or if maybe this anniversary run-through was the time for Lew Evans to quit this job. If he could quit, and leave Mac all the way alone.

When Jillie burst into the arena with the flag, Robert McTavish revelled in the music. One of his special touches of showmanship was to hire musicians for the big arenas—Madison Square Garden, Boston Garden, the Cow Palace in San Francisco, and in Fort Worth, Reno, and Cheyenne.

For this first go-round Jillie wore his favorite outfit—red western shirt with white fringe on the bodice and back, and a pleated, red skirt so short that she wore cheerleader briefs ornamented with rhinestones in flashy patterns on her bottom. Yeah, it was his favorite—it was American, it was Montana, like he was, no matter where his grandparents came from. The Cossack outfit was . . . foreign, what else could you say, and the circus costume was too foofaraw for him. Though he'd toured Europe with his show, had his clothes made in London, and could order wines in the best restaurants, he was a man of Montana first and last.

Once he had resisted the short skirt and cheerleader briefs—women trick riders had worn nothing but riding pants until then. But Jillie showed him that the skirt couldn't get hung up, because the tricks she would do in it didn't bring the hem near any rigging. When he saw how crowds loved the rhinestone display, he was won over. His Jillie could win him to anything. Now he looked at her on the grulla, and felt his heart squeeze.

He liked to call the run-throughs over the PA, a good way to tell her what he wanted her to do next, and it added to the fun, the illusion of making a show for a crowd, which he thought was good for horse, rider, and himself.

They'd taught the three horses different tricks. All a western trick-riding horse had to do during a stunt was to sprint straight ahead without guidance, and not shy, veer, or change lead, gait, or pace regardless. It wasn't easy, because the horse had to learn not to respond to the rider's weight flying all over the place, and not to flinch when touched in unexpected and perhaps intimate places. The mares, for instance, were used to having Jillie go under their bellies and even between their hind legs. Mac wouldn't let her try that with the stallion. On the other hand, the stallion was strong in the hindquarters, and his rump rose powerfully on the canter and gave more lift for the somersaults.

Mac walked to Jillie at the north station, carrying the gear she didn't use all the time—his grandfather's Confederate saber, the pick-up strap, the wooden block, the surcingles, and other props. He would hand each to her for its trick and then take it back.

As the applause began to wane, Mac announced the first stunt, the Lay Over the Neck. Jillie started the grulla.

It was an easy trick, but made a fine display. Mac watched as Jillie did it smoothly. She stepped out of the left stirrup, grabbed the saddle horn with her right hand, and stood on the right of the horse. Then she leaned backward over the grulla's neck, grabbing the mane with her left hand for a steadying hold. When she was secure, she kicked her left leg straight toward the sky and held it. The *oooh* was for the rhinestone display on the briefs. Mac didn't need the actual *oooh*, or the hand-clapping or whistling or the foot-stomping—they were all there in his mind.

She made a wide, smooth swing back into the saddle and stopped at the far station, the one on the south end. Mac always felt misgivings when she was at the other end of the arena.

"Ladies and gentlemen," he boomed electronically, "Miss Lajoie now executes the Sprinter's Crouch Stand in the Saddle. Watch the somersault she finishes with!"

It was another easy trick, worth only 20 points in competition, but the somersault was spectacular and worth 65. Jillie came toward him at a sprint. He watched her stand left-legged on the saddle, holding horn and cantle, and raise the right leg into the air. The audience was mostly waiting to be excited, as always. Jillie always did things with a floating quality no other rider could approach, and now she showed it. With leg still raised, she dived forward facedown, flipped her feet over her head backwards, kicked off the ground, and somersaulted onto the horse's neck, facing the rear.

The audience exploded—wild, mad, almost lunatic with excitement.

When you've captured their hearts, he thought, you can do with them as you will.

She smiled down at him as she turned the grulla at the station, a true angel's smile.

Ah, lass, you've captured your father's heart, he thought with a pang, and it's yours forever.

She grinned and whispered, "Elder Drag."

Oh, she was feeling in fine fettle tonight. After the first down and back, some choice of tricks was hers, according maybe to where she ached or didn't, or according to how high was her highlander spirit. The drag invented by Ted Elder was a declaration, and a little fun with her father, for it was dangerous.

He handed her the wooden block. If she was choosing the drag, he was selecting a safer trick back to the home station.

She smiled at him—had ever a lass smiled at a father like that?—and fixed the block to the horn, meaning she wasn't going to debate it with Dad. She spun backwards in the saddle and started the grulla. He started the PA pep talk.

Jillie grabbed the crupper handholds, special holds behind the cantle, started up onto them like heading for a handstand, then suddenly let her feet go straight on over to the ground.

The audience gasped. A plume of dust spurted from behind the horse, churned up by her dragging feet.

Mac grimaced. This trick didn't seem to him fitting for a lady, since the rider's face got buried between the hind legs of the mount.

Jillie flung her legs upward, came down backwards in the saddle, and threw her arms high to accept the accolades. Adoration, it seemed to Mac. Certainly her father's adoration. It bubbled in his veins like champagne.

Before the cheers subsided—his Jillie knew how to work a crowd—she had turned around, slid back to the rump, kicked the grulla forward, put her head on the block, and raised to a headstand.

Though his Jillie was a wisp of a thing, she was muscular. The neck had to be strong for this trick. The little girls in the audience, especially, were screaming as Jillie rode. But this one was not so risky, it was a sop to the old man.

"Jillie LaJoie, ladies and gentlemen, boys and girls," Mac roared. "The world champion woman trick rider, Jillie LaJoie." He gave the round-the-world hand signal, and the grulla sprinted past the station toward the exit to the ramp. She knew the routine perfectly. Jillie held the headstand until the darkness of the hole snatched horse and rider away.

Lew knew Mac would finish the run-through just the way Jillie always finished the rodeo, with the ring of fire, a fine climax that would send the audience into the streets of New York all gaga, raving in front of folks who might buy tickets. It was Lew's job to make the fire.

In the ramp he could hear Mac announcing the circus tricks. She did most of these bareback on the black stallion, then added Angel for two-horse tricks, and finally the grulla, Spirit of the West.

This part of the act for a while had been a sore point between father and daughter. She ran away with the circus, just like a kid and damn well like her mother, when she was about eighteen. And just like most teenage girls, her reason was a good-looking man, in this case one of the boys of the famous Cristiani bareback-riding family. When she came back, she showed her father all the stunts she had learned in the circus style, bareback acrobatics on a horse that cantered slowly in a circle. Lew had heard she showed some of the cowboys some other stunts she'd learned in private from Lucio Cristiani, or maybe his brothers. Anyway, Mac opposed the circus stuff at first, but

Jillie won him over. It looked great, and it was something the other rodeos didn't have.

Well, the whole truth was, one night Jillie had
showed Lew some of those private tricks, too, maybe
all of them. Never had again. After that, Lew was always a little in love with her.

Devil, the stallion, trained up well as a ring horse,
a *voltige* or rosin-back, as they were called. Lew could
see him in his mind's eye now, circling imperturbably
at the slow canter; his big hindquarters got a wonderful lift on every upward thrust, giving Jillie plenty
of height above the horse. Lew and Mac had tried to
throw the big horse off gait, making banging noises
during rehearsal, and once even turning a stray dog
loose in the ring, but Devil never missed a step. This
was essential if Jillie was to have a landing place when
she ended her flights.

She began simply, with pirouettes and jetés on
Devil's back. In her diaphanous, floating tutu, balle-
rina tights, and toe shoes, she looked grand.

Then she started into the somersaults, from easy to
hard—the backward somersault, the forward-forward,
and the really hard one, the back-backward.

As Mac announced these somersaults, Lew started
tying the burlap bags onto the ring of fire. This last
trick had never been dangerous, not in his mind. What
made the audience gasp was the flames, but wood alcohol made a cool fire. If he'd used oil, that would
have been different. As far as the jump was concerned,
Jillie could get any horse to do whatever she wanted
it to any old time. As far as human-horse relations
went, she was the ultimate diplomat, the ambassador
plenipotent-whatever-it-was.

Lew could hear that Jillie was coming to the climax of the circus routine now. From the arena came the hoofbeats of all three horses clattering, clattering, clattering in that steady lope. First she would somersault from Angel backward to Spirit of the West, then Spirit of the West backward to Devil. Then she would apparently cap the stunts with a double somersault, from Angel to Spirit of the West to Devil without stopping. As the crowd was clapping madly, she would sprint across the ring and do a trick performed only by Lucio Cristiani himself until Jillie matched him, the first woman even to try it. She would get up on Angel and somersault entirely over Spirit of the West onto Devil's rump.

Ah, yes, she was the most agile and graceful creature Lew had ever seen, a right sprite, and an acrobat divine. He supposed he had been too old for her, that was why.

Odd, though he'd watched her in rehearsal a hundred times, he'd never gotten to see her do the circus routine in front of a big house, and he regretted that. He was always getting the ring of fire ready. All day he'd been soaking the feed bags in wood alcohol. Now, the last ten minutes before the jump, he tied them onto the metal hoop. Then he wrapped another bunch around a two-by-four, picked up his can—the kind that railroad engineers used—grabbed the ring, and waited for the roars and cheers and hand-clapping and whistling and foot-stomping that spurred Jillie around the arena one more time, her arms raised, head back, and blond hair streaming as she accepted the adoration of the world. She was like her mother—one man would never be enough for Jillie either.

Lew watched from the shadows as Mac ran her through the Cossack tricks patiently, lovingly, getting the most out of each one, bringing up the band, working the crowd, sculpting each trick of his lovely daughter with the perfect words. Crazy, was what it was. No wonder he didn't let anyone but Lew see one of these run-throughs.

For these she wore the Cossack costume that Americans had fallen in love with at the Chicago World's Fair in 1903—flowing silk shirt in sky blue, baggy pants of silver stuffed into black boots. One of their tricks Lew really admired, the Lazyback Roll Back. Jillie sat sideways on the left side of the saddle, holding the horn with right hand and the saddle strings with left hand. Then she lowered herself and leaned back until the small of her back was on the saddle. Then she seemed to defy gravity and all of God's laws. She flipped her legs up and over the horse (and over her head), hit the ground with her feet, and bounced back onto the saddle. The people in the stands loved it. The riders in the know admired it even more.

Just out of sight in the ramp, ready with the ring, Lew waited.

Mac called the last trick of the Cossack routine, the Russian Drag, also referred to as the Suicide Drag. It was easy but dangerous, and she and Mac had added a fine touch. She put her right foot through a drag strap near the right cinch ring and threw herself off the left side of the horse, arms over her head, left foot pointing to heaven. It always looked like she was going to bounce her skull off the ground. Then Mac stuck his grandfather's Confederate saber in the ground. Jillie snatched it and put it between her teeth.

People shrieked and thundered. "The Suicide Drag," Mac repeated over the PA. "Ladies and gentlemen, Jillie La Joie in the Sui-cide Drag!"

That was Lew's cue. He pushed the ring into the arena. He didn't need to look at the center to see what was happening. Mac was starting the buildup for the Roman-riding trick over the PA system. Angel, Devil, and Spirit of the West, white, black, and grulla, were standing close together at the north station, and Jillie was putting surcingles on them and tying them together with harness straps.

The surcingles and harness were the linchpin of this trick, and Mac insisted on supervising the way she did it. Other riders would have resented his intrusion, but Mac said he meant to make sure for his own daughter.

Roman riding—riding astride two or three or up to five horses—wasn't so hard, not for skill or technique or balance or strength, not in Lew's mind. It could go wrong, though. The three horses had to stay exactly together. It was the surcingles encircling the withers, the heartgirth of all three horses, and the harness straps between horses that kept one from getting in front of the others, or behind. Any of them might get out of place, in Lew's mind—the grulla he'd never trusted, or the stallion Devil, or even white Angel. The grulla ran in the middle, and Jillie's spread feet were on the other two. She held three sets of reins in her hands.

She had to keep the three horses on the same lead

foot, and on the same stride, so the backs and rumps would rise and fall together. That way the horses would come to the ring on the same footing, and be ready to take to the air off their hind legs at the same time. The rider's skill, unlike other riding tricks, was not in the rider's own balance or strength or acrobatic ability but in using the reins to get those horses into the air at the same moment. Actually, Jillie had trained them so beautifully they could do the jump alone, without a rider.

The twelve hoofs began their drumbeat, and Lew knew Angel, Devil, and Spirit of the West were on the first circuit. Mac's voice lashed at their rumps, and whipped up the audience at the same time. "Roman riding dates back all the way to the Roman Empire, ladies and gentlemen. The brave gladiators had three great sports: They fought to the death with swords, they raced chariots at daredevil speeds, and most exciting of all, they rode standing astride two or even three horses at once!"

As many as five horses, Lew thought, looking at the expectant faces in the crowd. Jillie would be using the long reins to whip the horses to speed now. The lights were on for this first ride around the arena.

Suddenly Mac dropped his voice, his low tones making the audience listen eagerly. "Ladies and gentlemen, McTavish's Wild West Show and Rodeo presents Miss Jillie La Joie Roman-riding three horses through the ri-i-ing of fi-i-ire!"

All the banks of lights in the Garden went out. The arena was black, except for two follow spots. One was on Jillie, Devil, Angel, and Spirit of the West; the other one on Lew and the ring.

Lew was a showman, too. Though the bags on the two-by-four torch were wet with alcohol, he lifted the black engineer's can high and squirted plenty more on. Then he took a big wooden kitchen match and struck it on his boot sole. He touched it to the torch. *Humph!* went the flames, red with heat and black with smoke. The spot on him went out, so that only the torch showed. He held it in the air and made a 360-degree turn, pointing the torch at every member of the audience. Then he touched it to the ring.

WHUMPH! went the ring of fire.

"A-A-A-A-H-H," breathed the audience.

In Lew's mind the band struck up the familiar bah-BAH bah-bah-BAH-bah, the trombone theme of "The Ride of the Valkyries," horse-charging music if ever Lew had heard it.

On that signal the horses brought their speed to its peak. Finishing their second circuit of the arena, they swung around the ring of fire, and galloped toward battle, toward victory and defeat, life, and death, the glory that belongs only to warriors who go to the Valkyries. Female demigods, Lew had heard they were, who escorted warriors to Valhalla. Jillie was a warrior, a true one.

"Into the valley of death rode the six hundred," intoned Mac. "Miss Lajoie rides alone into the ri-i-ing of fi-i-ire."

Lew stole a glimpse at the three horses at the far end of the arena, the light man keeping that follow spot right on them. He supplied the music in his head, and imagined the awed silence of the audience, getting perfectly quiet, every mind and heart on the leap, on the rise into the fire, on the secret question in each heart—Is it a leap into the black silence of eternity?

Where is the step that launches me into that dark leap?

Mac repeated in reverential tones, "Into the valley of death."

Angel, Devil, and Spirit of the West galloped through the darkness of the far straightaway and into the last turn. As they straightened for the last time, their pounding hoofs rose to a crescendo. Their heads were toward Lew now. Jillie was always invisible, low down, her legs spread wide enough to get footing on Angel and Devil, the outside horses. Lew had never been able to catch even a glimpse of her head over the heads of the mounts as they charged headlong toward the flaming ring, like she was ethereal, she was their spirit, the true Spirit of the West.

Lew didn't turn his head until the horses got close enough to smell. The drumbeat was throbbing inside his head. He watched them take the last few sprinting steps, legs churning, tendons stretching, muscles pulling, lungs heaving, eyes wild. He watched the three horses make the riderless jump, their thousandth leap through the ring of fire from mortality to the heroic afterlife.

Most nights in his dreams he also saw it, and at every one of these shadow run-throughs. He saw all of it. He looked in pity and terror on just what had happened that mortal night a year ago today.

It was simple. The grulla, Spirit of the West, refused the jump.

Who could ever know why a horse balked? A well-trained mount would make a certain jump without hesitation a thousand times and then refuse it at the Olympic games, costing some rider the honor he or she wanted most in life. Maybe because a sound scared it. (The band's "Ride of the Valkyries" was supposed to cover surprise noises.) Maybe because it smelled something and remembered danger. Probably because it was a horse, and horses were the most lovable and most perverse animals the gods ever made.

On November 2, 1940, here in Madison Square Garden, the grulla locked her front legs, trying to stop. But the three horses were at a full sprint in tandem, and bound by the surcingles and harness straps.

The straps snapped like ladies' sewing thread. The outer two horses, Angel and Devil, jumped through the ring of fire, but not quite together. Jillie flipped over the grulla's head and landed right on the flames.

Lew moved like a demon. He dragged her off the ring. Her tutu was burning wildly, and the tights and top were already in flame—rayon caught quick and burned like dry straw. She was screaming, and the screams swirled around Lew's head like howling winds, voices of the north winds, of death.

He tried to jump right on top of her, full length, wanting to smother the flames with his body while he slapped at them with his hands. But Jillie writhed away from him, screaming, elusive, beyond his grasp.

He grabbed. He snatched at air. He got hold of her hair.

I will win! That was the wild thought that came to him. I will win, I will save her. His heart swooped up.

Then her hair burst into flame. Her face was in a

ring of fire, and he looked into her eyes and saw what there was to see, and knew all there was to know of life, and death, and loss, and grief.

But that was what had happened a year ago. This time, ridden only by a ghost, the three horses made the jump impeccably, and cantered off . . .

Lew didn't even look toward them. He would have to get hold of them, take the surcingles off, get the saddles and bridles put away, put the horses into the trailers and make sure of their feed and water, then get the ring of fire and other equipment stored. But he was looking at Mac.

All right, he decided, this time I will be bold, even rude. I'm going to walk right up and look you in the eye.

Mac was sitting in the dust by the north station, splatted down. Lew had to walk around in front of him to see.

Mac was weeping. Silently, motionlessly, but a flood of tears. When they'd taken the rodeo to Alaska, Lew had seen a flood of water like that, flowing out of the butt end of a glacier. Melted ice, it was.

Embarrassed, Lew backed away.

In a few minutes, Lew was leading the horses off. Out of the corner of his eye, he saw Mac get up and walk unsteadily through an exit.

Lew knew where to find him.

Robert McTavish—Bobbie Burns, she had called him once—stood on the end of the wharf. It was dark now, and he could distinguish only a murky, gray nothing of cold river, a river that carried everything to sea, and to oblivion.

He raised his light hand and flipped the cigarette into the murk. It sailed through the air, hot and bright, then went out, doused as sudden as a life.

He lit another. Beneath the click of the lighter he heard boots clomp on the wharf behind him. Lew Evans.

He drew, inhaled, drew again, and flipped the cigarette into the void. A red arc, then blackness.

No Valkyries came to take you to any Valhalla. You just extinguished.

He wondered what he should do about Lew.

He lit another cigarette, flipped it without even a drag, lit another, flipped it. You just went out.

He looked into the gray and dark and he couldn't see a damn thing.

But he felt something close behind him. Someone. He guessed he was glad.

Mac knew he was there, Lew could even see it in his stance. But the boss, the capitalist, the man who never got the wife he wanted, the man who lost the daughter he loved, this man didn't acknowledge Lew, not even with a sideways glance.

Lew gave him the respect of standing off a few steps, waiting. He wished he could find a way to be a friend.

Mac's legs looked steady, but he was standing on the very end, feet half into the air. Lew worried about the wind. Not that there was anything he could do. Except witness.

Mac sailed one more cigarette into the river. The

Hudson, someone had told Lew it was. Then he turned and stepped away from the end. He looked directly at Lew.

Lew took the chance. The words nearly caught in his throat. "You want a drink, Mac?"

Robert Burns McTavish nodded. Twice. Nodded yes. Three times. "Guess so."

They fell in stride together. After a few yards Mac spoke. "Lew." The first name came out stumbling, but Mac was looking straight into his eyes. "It won't make no difference, Lew."

The two men held each other's eyes, the same bleakness in each of their hearts.

Bleakness, and something else in Lew's.

Lew said, "No, Mac, it won't."

He was thinking, Maybe it will.

Sue Ellen Learns to Dance

Judy Alter

This marvelous short story by Judy Alter won the Spur Award in 1998. It is about sin, or at least how the children and grandchildren of settlers perceived their ancestors. Alter writes: "I saw a book of photographs of Texas and Texans during the Great Depression, and one woman stuck in my mind. Lean and gaunt and hopeless, she was a true picture of despair. I wanted to write about her, but somehow when I did, the story became mixed with that old western motif about the old lady who remembers one brief moment of great joy in her life; often that moment has to do with an outlaw or something outside the pale of accepted behavior." In particular, Dorothy Johnson's "Laugh in the Face of Danger" inspired this story. Judy Alter is a prolific novelist, winner of multiple Spur Awards, and editor.

"Sue Ellen!" He cut the engine on the clattering Model A truck, in 1934 some ten years old and threatening always to fall apart. When he raised his voice again, impatience rang in it. "Sue Ellen!" He stayed in the car and waited.

She came to the door carrying a child on her hip,

though the child was plainly old enough to walk on his own. Still, his arms encircled his mother's neck with a tenacity that indicated he would not easily be put down. Sue Ellen Flett was a lean woman with lank hair, faded to the pale yellow of corn silk. She wore a shapeless cotton dress and over it, an apron that clearly said "Burrus Flour Mills" across the front. With her free hand, she pushed her hair behind her ear. The other hand held tight to the child.

"What is it, Alvis?" Her voice was soft and tired, lacking the life of his impatience.

"Ma says Grammy's dyin' and we got to go to Kaufman."

"Go to Kaufman?" she echoed. From where she stood, on the slanted porch of a rough board and batten shack near Eden in South Central Texas, Kaufman, beyond Dallas, deep in East Texas, might as well be as far as the moon. Then, though, she said softly, "Your grammy's dying?"

He scoffed. "She won't die. That woman's got too much sin stored up in her. She'd go straight to Hell, and she knows it."

"She's not a sinful woman," Sue Ellen said mildly. She looked at him. He was thirty, looked fifty and, she often thought, acted sixty. When she married him, he was twenty-two and stood straight and tall, his eyes sparkling with laughter. But that was before the rain stopped and all of West Texas turned to dust that blew away if you looked at it, and the bank took their farm up to Kaufman, where they'd both been raised. Now they sharecropped a tiny, worthless piece of land. Konrad Schwartz, the German farmer who owned the land, provided a tractor, fuel, and seed, and they farmed on halves. The parcel of blown-away land was all mesquite stumps and rattlesnakes, and they made a poor crop. She worried about the children, who went too many days without meat and milk, and she worried about Alvis and herself, who were cross, tired, and hopeless most of the time.

At least, she told herself ten times a day, they lived in a house. Not much of one—a shack some would call it, with slanted floors and cracks so large between the siding boards that she could look out at night from her bed and watch the stars. But there were folks in this region, she knew, who'd lived in half dugouts not more than ten years ago. No, Sue Ellen counted herself lucky to have a house.

"Well," she said, looking at him, "I reckon Grammy Flett can't put it off forever. If it's her time, it's her time." She barely got the words out before a young girl of six banged through the screen door, letting it slam behind her and ignoring the precarious way it bounced on its hinges.

"Don't slam the door," Sue Ellen said automatically, while the girl asked, "Who's got sin in their soul, Papa?"

Sue Ellen gave him a long, hard look and then said to the girl, "No one, Marisue. Your papa didn't mean that."

"My grandmother's dyin'," he told the child, ignoring that he had made his wife unhappy and that the child would instantly know it was his grandmother who had sin in her soul.

"Is she goin' to Hell when she dies, Papa?" Marisue asked.

He opened his mouth, but Sue Ellen spoke too

quickly for him. "Of course she's not goin' to Hell, Marisue. How you do talk. You remember Grammy Flett. She always gave you candy, and you used to like to sit on her lap when you was little."

"I disremember," Marisue said.

"Well," Sue Ellen said, turning her back on her husband and leading the children inside, "it's been a long while since you saw her. Grammy Flett's old, near ninety I think."

"Are we going to see her?"

Sue Ellen sighed. "I guess we'll have to." Turning, she asked over her shoulder, "Where's Albert?"

"I left him in town, swamping out Tubbs's store. He'll walk home."

She turned without another word. It was, she knew, a long walk for a child of eight to make alone, but no harm would come to him. And she'd save back a potato for his supper.

That night, to Alvis's back, because now he always turned away from her in bed, she said, "I hope to heaven that rickety truck will make it to Kaufman."

"It'll have to," he muttered.

She wanted to reach out and touch him, rub his back, riffle his hair, but she knew he would flinch and pull away. "Can't feed no more babies," he'd told her the last time she'd tried to touch him in his privates. Instead, she asked, "Why do you say she's so sinful her soul's goin' to Hell?"

He groaned, a sure sign he didn't want to talk about it. At last, after a long moment, he spoke. "Ma told me. She . . . she was . . . you know . . . one of those women, back when cowboys were the law in West Texas. She . . ." It was obviously hard for him to bring the words out. "She . . . danced in saloons in Fort Worth, that kind of thing."

"Grammy Flett?" Sue Ellen sat straight up in bed, barely remembering to pull the covers up to hide herself. She thought this was surely the most astounding news she'd ever heard . . . and the very thought of Grammy Flett dancing in a saloon somehow lightened and lifted Sue Ellen's mood. But she could never tell Alvis that.

"Family's been ashamed ever since," he said stiffly. "We don't talk about it."

"Your family's still ashamed about something that happened . . . what? Fifty, sixty years ago?" She could never give voice to the thought that was really on her mind, for it was almost envy . . . envy of Grammy Flett and the good times she must have known.

"Don't do to have bad blood," he said, muffling his voice in the pillow.

"Well, I'll be!" And with that, Sue Ellen lay back down in the bed, pulled the covers to her chin, and lay with wide-open eyes half the night.

The truck ground to a stop short of Fort Worth. From Eden, they'd gone north to Ballinger, then angled over to Brownwood, on to Comanche, and finally to Cleburne, all the while bouncing over rutted roads so rough that Sue Ellen ached in every bone in her back and bottom. Dust blew in at them, but Sue Ellen had been covered by dust for so long now she paid it no mind. Her skin had turned a nut-brown color, and fleetingly she sometimes thought of her mother's admonition to always wear a poke bonnet, lest your skin acquire an unbecoming darkness. Hers had, and it was too late to worry about it.

The baby in her arms cried, and in the back, supposedly resting on a pallet, Marisue whined about needin' to use the rest room and wantin' to sleep and when were they gonna get there. Albert sat stoic, staring over the boards of the pickup bed at the passing dry land.

Sue Ellen looked at her children, their faces wary and unsmiling, their clothes soiled with ground-in grime that would not come out no matter how hard she scrubbed, their feet bare and dirty. She sighed and turned back to stare sightlessly at the road before them.

When the children finally slept, Sue Ellen said, "She wasn't sinful, you know. Grammy Flett's one of the best persons I ever met. I wouldn't have a problem lettin' my soul follow hers."

He gripped the wheel tightly and stared straight ahead at the rutted road. "You can send your soul wherever you want. I know I'm obeying the Good Book."

"It says," she whispered, "love thy brother . . . and that means thy sister . . . and thy grandmother too."

Alvis didn't answer.

They were just beyond Cleburne, some thirty miles from Fort Worth, when they hit a deep rut in the road, bounced badly, and heard a clattering sound. In seconds, the car died.

"What'd you do?" Sue Ellen asked.

"I didn't do nothin'," he said angrily. "The thing just stopped." He got out to study around the car. Finally, at a loss to do anything else, he crawled under it. After what seemed forever to Sue Ellen, Alvis emerged, holding up a squarish metal pan—something, she thought, she might have baked in if she ever could bake again.

"Oil pan," he said. "Guess it got bounced off."

"What's that mean?"

"Means the engine ain't got no oil, and it's froze up. Probably ruined."

"We might just as well walk back to that last town," Sue Ellen said, "get something for the children to eat." Her own stomach gnawed at her, but she would not eat.

"What you gonna buy it with?" he asked. "Your good looks?"

She wanted to tell him there was no call to be mean, but she kept quiet.

"No sense goin' backward," he declared. "We'll hitch to Fort Worth."

Leaving the car that much farther behind, she thought.

Hot and dusty, they waited by the side of the road for a ride, the baby crying all the louder when Alvis took him to relieve her, and Marisue whining all the more, saying she'd just sit in the shade and wait for them to come back for the car.

"What shade?" Albert asked, scorn in his voice.

Finally a farmer in a Model A stopped for them. Alvis sat in the front, while Sue Ellen and the youngsters crowded into the back. The farmer made laconic conversation about car trouble and having a passel of kids, and it was plain to see he was glad he was not part of this pitiful family. In Fort Worth, he let them out at a garage where he personally recommended the honesty of the owner.

"Lost the oil pan?" The man snorted. "Ain't no use to go look at it. Bet you ruined the motor."

Alvis nodded sagely. He thought so too.

Sue Ellen protested. "Can't you at least go see if you can fix it?"

"Lady, you want me to charge you thirty dollars for telling you what I already know? The engine's burnt out, running with no oil, even for a little bit."

Sue Ellen stared off at the concrete around her and clutched Marisue to her.

The mechanic took them to a church with a soup kitchen for the homeless, and they were fed the best hot meal they'd had in months—soup, corn, potatoes and fresh homemade bread—and Sue Ellen tried to ignore Alvis's mutterings. "We ain't like these people. Don't need no charity."

Finally, she poked him hard in the ribs and said, "Without it, we wouldn't be eatin'. I ain't too proud to feed my children on charity if I got to."

When their plight was made known to the pastor of the church, bus tickets to Kaufman shortly appeared.

"Don't know when I can repay you," Alvis muttered.

"No matter," the pastor said. "It is our mission to help those in need. Go with God."

They rode to Kaufman, Sue Ellen holding the baby, Albert staring out the window, and Marisue dozing in her seat.

"You gonna be nice to Grammy Flett?" Sue Ellen asked Alvis.

" 'Course I'll be nice. She's my grandmother, ain't she?"

"You think she's sinful . . . and I, well, I just think it's sinful you feel that way."

"Who's sinful?" Marisue asked shrilly. "Are you talking about Grammy Flett again? What'd she do?"

"Hush and go to sleep," her father told her. "Don't be tellin' everyone on this bus our family business."

There were three other passengers, none of whom appeared to have heard the outburst.

From Kaufman, it was no trick to find a ride to the Flett family farm.

Mama Flett greeted them at the door, hugging the children and telling Alvis, "It's good you got here, son."

"Thought you might need me," he muttered, and that was as close to affection as the two of them came.

But Sue Ellen got a hug and a murmured, "I am glad to see you, child. You're lookin' thin. I got chicken and dumplings on the stove."

Sue Ellen knew that, from the smell that filled the rambly old white clapboard house that had belonged to Alvis's grandparents and had stayed in the family by hook or by crook all these years. Alvis's father was gone now, some five years—just up and left he did one day, Mama Flett had told them. Nobody knew if he'd run off, though that seemed unlikely, or if he'd hurt himself back in the wilds of the piney woods, hunting alone in some place so remote that nobody had yet stumbled on his body. His huntin' dog had come home three days later, but he hadn't been real communicative about what had happened to his master.

Sue Ellen didn't understand—and never would—how Mama and Grammy lived, beyond that truck garden in the back of the house, but they survived nicely, much more nicely than she and Alvis and the children.

While Marisue clamored for dinner and Albert stood staring hungrily at the stove, Mama Flett reached for the baby. "She's in there," she said to Alvis, motioning with her head toward a room off the kitchen that had apparently been turned into a sickroom. "But she's outta her head, talkin' strange, she is."

With a finger to the lips to caution the children to be quiet, Alvis led his family into the sickroom. Grammy Flett barely made a bump under the thin coverlet spread over her. She lay on her back, eyes wide open and staring at the ceiling, hands folded over her chest as though she were anticipating death and willing to save the undertaker at least the chore of arranging those hands with their paper-thin skin.

"She's singing," Marisue stage-whispered, and Alvis drew back a hand as though to cuff her.

But Marisue was right. A weak, high, reedy sound came from the bed, and looking close, Sue Ellen could see the thin chest rise a little and the pinched mouth moving ever so slightly.

Alvis was clearly disconcerted. "How're you doin', Grammy Flett?" he asked in a voice so loud and hearty that even Albert jumped a little.

Her eyes turned slowly, as though making an effort to focus on this new person. Then, smiling ever so slightly, she said, "I been dancin'. You know, at Uncle Windy's in Fort Worth . . . in the Acre." Her voice was whispery.

"Hush, now," he said too harshly. "We don't want to be hearin' about that."

She paid him no mind and went back to her singing.

Back in the kitchen, Albert carefully asked, "What was she talkin' about? Uncle Windy's and the acre?"

"Nothin' for you to know," his father told him harshly, and Albert subsided, but not before Sue Ellen saw the resentment in his eyes. Had it been up to her, she'd have filled Albert with the little knowledge she had: Grammy Flett had been a dance hall girl in Fort Worth before the turn of the century, when Hell's Half Acre was the flourishing sin district in that town. Oh, Grammy had never been a whore—Alvis had made that point clear and Sue Ellen chose to believe it. But Alvis did not want his son to know even the varnished truth.

They ate mightily of chicken and dumplings, fresh tomatoes off the vine, green beans that had cooked their way to mushiness the whole day and a blueberry pie. "I'm sorry I ain't got no cream for the pie," Mama Flett apologized.

"Is she all right at night?" Sue Ellen asked as she dried the dishes for her mother-in-law.

Mama sighed. "I been mostly sleeping in that chair in her room. Don't sleep too good, but if I was to come and find her gone some morning, I couldn't live with myself."

"I'll sit with her tonight," the younger woman volunteered.

"Land's sake, you had that hard trip. I'll hear no such thing."

"I want to, I really want to." And Sue Ellen found that she did want to, indeed was almost desperate for time alone with Grammy.

"You sure?"

"I'm sure."

And so, by ten o'clock, they were all packed off to bed, even the baby whom Mama Flett took to sleep with her. Albert, feeling big and manly, took a blanket and went to the loft in the barn, and Marisue curled into a big double bed all by herself. Alvis chose to sleep on the sofa, lest he be needed in the night, so he said, but Sue Ellen knew after that big dinner she wouldn't be able to rouse him if she needed him.

She took a last cup of coffee and went to sit by Grammy's bed in a big old rocker. Setting her coffee down, she reached for one of those thin, frail hands that were all bone and no flesh and held it in her own browned and roughened hand. "Sing to me again, Grammy."

Grammy had been dozing, but she roused now, turning her head ever so slightly toward Sue Ellen and staring at her. Then the thin voice raised in a song Sue Ellen knew was not a hymn. Sue Ellen closed her eyes and let her mind drift, holding that hand and listening to the weird music.

"We danced, you know," Grammy said, suddenly stopping her singing.

The sound of her talking voice startled Sue Ellen awake. "Yes . . . yes, Grammy, I know you danced. . . . I . . . I think it must have been wonderful."

"Not always," she said, "but sometimes . . . not

when you were dancing for pay with men you didn't like. But when we'd dance for ourselves . . . and the music made you feel free and alive . . . and I wasn't beholden to no one then . . . no parents, no husband, no children, just me!" She paused to catch her breath.

"I was young . . . and pretty"—it seemed not to shame her to admit that openly—"and I had lots of young men courtin' me. I've carried those memories all my life."

"Were you . . . Grammy . . . did you do anything sinful?" Sue Ellen bit her lip, knowing she'd over-stepped the bounds with the question.

Grammy snorted. "Sinful? Not on your life. I was raised Baptist and dancing was sin enough . . . but no, I was never wicked."

And they both knew what she meant.

"Tell me," Sue Ellen said, "about the music again and how you've heard it all your life."

And so, late into the night, Grammy Flett—spurred by an energy nobody thought she had any longer—talked about life in the city. And sometimes she'd stop talking to sing awhile. And then she'd talk again.

Listening, her eyes closed, Grammy's hand still clutched in hers, Sue Ellen ever so briefly felt that she too heard the music and that she was free and young and beautiful and happy. And she knew that Grammy was giving her a dream that she would carry through her life.

In the morning, Mama Flett found Sue Ellen sound asleep in the rocker. Grammy Flett had gone to her reward, her hand still clutched in Sue Ellen's and the corners of her mouth lifted as though she were smil-ing . . . or singing.

*   *   *

Sue Ellen and Alvis never went back to Eden. Abandoning the car outside Fort Worth and the furniture and clothes in their shack at Eden, they stayed in Kaufman, where Alvis farmed and eventually, when the Depression wore itself out, became a man of some small means, free of debt at least, though he never lost his dour and pessimistic streak . . . and he never liked to talk about Grammy Flett. Sue Ellen fixed chicken and dumplings and blueberry pie for her children and grandchildren and tended the truck garden and kept the house . . . but sometimes, they'd find her staring off out the window, singing a strange song none of them recognized. And when they'd call her back to the present moment, she always had a smile.

I Never Saw a Buffalo

Frank Roderus

An outlaw seen through the eyes of a little boy is not the man whom adults see. In this gentle story, Spur Award–winning novelist Frank Roderus describes a chance encounter with an outlaw being taken to prison on a train, with unexpected results. Roderus is a veteran novelist of the West and two-time Spur Award winner. He lives in Florida.

I was five that summer. I remember because I already knew my letters and all my numbers way up past forty and soon I would learn to read. I hated not being able to read words and things, like the signs on all the places we were passing through. I didn't like having to ask Mama where we were all the time, but I couldn't help it. It was all so exciting. So new and grand and special.

That was the summer, you see, that we left the city. For all my life we'd lived in the city; in a fifth-floor walk-up in a neighborhood where the other ladies were all fat and wore black dresses and wouldn't talk to Mama. We didn't speak Russian or Yiddish or Polish and maybe that's why none of the neighbor boys wanted to play with me. Not that I cared about those boys. Mama and me did just fine together.

She had a job in a factory during the day, and at night she would pull the Murphy down and make it up with fresh-smelling sheets and tuck me into bed, and she would sit on the other side of the room with a hood covering the side of the gas lamp so the light wouldn't glare in my eyes while she sewed.

At night to make some extra she sewed doll clothes. She'd cut pictures out of catalogs and magazines and make pretty gowns just like in the pictures but small so they could be put onto little girls' dolls. The hiss of a gaslight still makes me feel all warm and safe and drowsy.

All that was until Mama saw an ad in one of the magazines she got her pictures out of, and she answered it, and then for that whole winter she wrote back and forth to a Mr. Berg in Nevada. She showed me on a map where Nevada was and showed me some pictures of the Wild West. Somewhere she got a poster advertising Colonel Cody's true-to-life exposition of life in the West, and it had wonderful pictures on it of Indians and buffalo and cowboys. I've never seen Colonel Cody's show, but I hope to someday.

Anyway, after they'd been writing back and forth for months and months, early that summer Mr. Berg sent Mama tickets for our passage to Nevada, and it was the most exciting thing that ever happened to anybody.

We saw big fields and real mountains and just miles and miles of plants in rows—farms those were—and after that miles and miles of grass. Just miles and miles and *miles* of it, so much it scarcely seemed possible.

And in Nebraska we saw Indians. They were near as dark as Negroes and had black, thick, coarse-looking hair—but straight—all shiny with grease, and they dressed funny and never smiled. I was afraid one of them would come over and start fingering my hair to see did he want to take a knife and scalp me, but Mama held me close by her side, and if any of the Indians had any such thoughts they didn't do anything about it.

There were supposed to be buffalo all over the plains. Mama showed me the pictures. But I never saw any. I hung out the windows looking for them until my eyes burned from the dry wind of the moving train and my nose got all black and sticky inside from the coal smoke, but I never did see any buffalo.

We left Nebraska into Wyoming and stopped in Cheyenne where we got off the train and walked around and Mama bought me an ice cream at a store not far from the station. There were no motorized carriages in Cheyenne, not that we saw, but there were electrified lights and trolley tracks. That was kind of disappointing.

Then in Bosler City late in the same day we left Cheyenne the man got on the train.

I was half asleep, leaning up against Mama and moving with the lift and fall of her breathing, and I felt her go stiff. I think I mumbled something and she said, "Oh, no, that looks like . . ." and then she stopped herself from saying anything more. She clamped her lips shut real tight, and when I looked up at her I could see that she was pale.

She was staring up the aisle toward the front of the car, so naturally I got wide awake and sat up and looked in that direction too.

Two men had come onto the train there, and even I could tell that one of the men was set up just frightfully handsome. He looked . . . special. It wasn't that he was so tall, really. He was half a head shorter than the man who was with him. But he looked tall. He was dressed neat and tidy in a brown suit with a brown-and-white check shirt that had a celluloid collar attached and a chocolate-brown necktie with a small knot that was twisted just a bit off center. He had one of those wide-brimmed hats like you always see in pictures of the West, and I kind of expected to see a gun belt under his coat.

He wasn't wearing one of those, but I felt a thrill of excitement when I saw that what he was wearing instead was a pair of steel manacles connected by a chromium-plated chain about a foot and a half long.

It was the other taller and not nearly so nice-looking man who had a gun in a leather pouch at his waist and a badge—it wasn't really star shaped like in the pictures but round—pinned to his coat.

The two of them came down the aisle to the only vacant bench in the coach and sat down right next to Mama and me, immediately across the aisle from us. The one with the badge unfastened one handcuff and slipped it through the iron seat arm and refastened it onto his prisoner, locking the gentleman to the seat so he couldn't go anywhere.

The man in the chains saw Mama and me looking at him. He nodded to Mama and dipped his head low so he could reach his hat even though his hands were

chained to the seat. He touched the brim of the hat
and lifted it just a fraction of an inch in a gesture of
respect to Mama. Then he looked me in the eye and
smiled just a little. "'Lo, button," he said.

I suppose I should have been scared being so close
to a dangerous prisoner, but I wasn't. I didn't feel
there was any danger from this man.

The tall sheriff or whoever looked at Mama too,
but not in the same nice way that the prisoner had.
I didn't like the way the sheriff looked at her, and I
didn't like that he laughed when he turned away and
leaned down to whisper something to the man with
the chains on him.

Mama made a point of looking out the windows
on our side of the coach, and the man with the chains
tilted his hat forward over his eyes and made himself comfortable for a nap. That gave me a chance to
study him close without him knowing it, and of course
I did.

By then we'd been traveling in the West enough
that I'd seen a lot of fancy boots, most of them with
tall heels and pointy toes and colored stitching deco-
rating the sides. This man wore simple boots, black
and plain and with an ordinary heel and round toe
but freshly blacked and brushed. His boots and his
hat, all his clothes, looked elegant and awfully well
taken care of, like he was a tidy sort of person. So
did the rest of him. His mustache was fluffy and
trimmed and carefully tended, although a stubble of
beard showed that he hadn't been able to get to the
barber's yet today. There were bits of gray in the
brown hairs of his mustache, I noticed. And his eyes
were pale. So pale they looked almost unnatural. But

not scary. Not at all scary. I didn't think there was anything about this man that would scare me.

I wondered if Mama's friend Mr. Berg would have so fine an appearance. I hoped so.

The train jerked and clanked ahead from Bosler City, and I got to daydreaming about all sorts of wild crimes and such as might have brought our train coach neighbor to this state. I can't remember what any of those ideas were, but I know they were wonderful to speculate upon.

Later that afternoon the train stopped at another station—I don't know where we were then because I never thought to ask Mama—and a man in a blue coat with shiny buttons came through and said we'd be stopped there for a spell because there was a repair crew working somewhere ahead. That sort of thing had happened a couple times on our trip before so it wasn't worrisome.

The other passengers kind of grumbled and complained but of course there wasn't anything to be done about it, and pretty soon everyone got up and stretched and wandered off the train to walk around some on solid, motionless ground while they could.

The sheriff checked his prisoner's manacles and chain to make sure they were secure, then muttered something about being back soon and for the prisoner not to go anywhere. He laughed after he said that.

I thought Mama would want to leave the coach for a while too but she didn't. She seemed distracted and kept giving the prisoner looks that she tried to keep me from seeing. It was like she didn't want to keep looking at him but couldn't help herself. I didn't know why at the time but I think maybe I do now. Anyway she stayed where she was.

I hoped maybe she would buy me another ice cream or a candy and after a minute asked could I have something. She made me promise to be careful and not to talk to strangers—which didn't make much sense really because how could I buy a candy if I weren't allowed to talk to the stranger who would be selling it—and gave me a penny so I could go see what I might find.

As I was leaving the coach, which was empty now save for Mama and the man in chains, three men were getting on.

They were cowboys, I think, but there wasn't anything romantic or wonderful about them. They were rough-looking men with heavy gauntlets stuck behind their belts and big pistols hanging in pouches at their waists.

Their hats and boots were dusty and unkempt, and none of them had shaved in days and days.

When they passed me there was that warm, humid smell of liquor on them along with the scents of sweat and smoke and other things that I wasn't sure of.

They had been drinking, I was sure, and their voices were loud and hard and sounded strained. I drew aside so I wouldn't be in their way when they went by and hurried down the steps to the cinder-covered ground.

When I looked back up into the coach I could see two of the cowboys leaning close to whisper and snicker, and I began to get worried. They were all three looking toward the back end of the coach, and

the only people there were the man who was chained
to the seat and Mama.

And of those two I was pretty sure it wouldn't be
some man chained to a seat arm that had their interest.

The thought of a candy wasn't so attractive just
then, and I ran back along the outside of the car to
the steps leading up into the next car back and crept
back aboard the train where those men couldn't see
me.

I don't know what I intended. There wasn't anything I could have done to three armed drunks if I
had to. But I wanted to be close in case Mama needed
me. Didn't want to be where those men could see me
though. Not unless I had to.

I crossed forward into the end of the car and
crouched down just back of the door where I could
hear what was being said. Some of it anyway. And
some of what I did hear I didn't understand.

The cowboys were laughing and saying bad things
and pretending to be nice while they invited Mama
to walk out with them. They didn't say where.

She tried to ignore them, but they wouldn't stop
and wouldn't stop and the sounds of their voices were
starting to make me scared. The things they were saying got uglier and uglier, and that made me all the
more frightened.

That was when the man in the chains said something to them and they got quiet so that after that I
could hear better.

"You're Joe Harvey, aren't you? That would make
you Cleve? Or you?"

"I'm Cleve," one of the cowboys said.

"Which makes you William."

"That's right."

I raised up a little so I could peer through the glass. The oldest of the brothers—I guessed they were brothers after what the prisoner said to them—looked pleased, like he was proud to be recognized.

"And you know who I am," the prisoner said in a soft, gentle voice. He wasn't bragging. Just making sure.

"That's right," the oldest of the Harveys said.

"I think you boys better leave now," the prisoner told them, still speaking soft and nice. "Real quiet. Real polite."

"Oh now, and why should we do that?" It was one of the other ones but I didn't know which as I hadn't been looking when the prisoner was figuring out which one was which one.

"Because the lady doesn't need this." He smiled. "And because I asked you to."

"We don't have to pay no attention to you, y'know. You're no threat."

The other of the younger brothers added, "Everyone says you won't ever walk out free again. There's not one damn thing you can do. Not now."

The prisoner just smiled. "I'm betting my life I'll walk free again, Cleve." The smile became brighter and his voice even softer. "Are you willing to bet yours that I won't?"

Joe Harvey blanched and gave his brothers a hard look.

"Apologize to the lady and say good-bye, boys. There won't be no hard feelings." The Harveys had guns in their pouches and the prisoner was shackled to an iron chair arm, but there wasn't any doubt about which of them had the stronger will or who it was that was in control.

Joe took his hat off and bobbed his head a couple times and choked out an apology of sorts. He was speaking to Mama but it was the man with his hands chained to the seat that he was looking at. Joe elbowed his brothers and made them do the same, and the three of them turned tail and scurried off the train.

Mama tried to say something to the prisoner, but he dipped his head low to his chest and closed his eyes and pretended like he was falling asleep. He never answered her nor so far as I could tell looked in her direction again.

I snuck off that end of the train and ran back to the front of our car and came aboard again where Mama could see that I was all right. For some reason I didn't want her to know I'd overheard. That seemed better somehow than letting her know that I'd heard the sort of language those men used toward her. It would have embarrassed both of us.

I completely forgot about the candy I'd wanted so badly just a little while before.

After a while the passengers returned to the car and the conductor in the blue coat came through and half an hour or so after that the train was moving again.

I fell asleep leaning tight up against Mama, and when I woke up in the morning we were in Utah and the sheriff and the man in the chains were gone. Mama said they'd gotten off somewhere back in Wyoming.

Mama had been crying during the night. I could

see the dried tear tracks on her cheeks until she went back to the water closet and washed them off.

I didn't then but now I think I know why. Not for the prisoner. For the man who looked so much like him.

It's funny, but I think maybe that prisoner had as strong an effect on Mama as my father had, in his own sort of way.

We finally did get to Winnemucca, and Mama fell in love with the place and I guess so did I.

Mr. Berg was there waiting for us. He was a decent enough looking man, tall and with a scraggly mustache. He smelled of pipe tobacco and horses and harness leather and looked like he had more than enough money for comfort.

"I've made arrangements to board the boy, Naomi. There's no school close to the place, but you can see him when we drive in on weekends."

"There is no need for that, Mr. Berg."

"Of course there is. I grant you there is no school during the summer months, but there is no proper facility at home for—"

"You misunderstand me," Mama said, her chin firm and voice steady.

"Come again?"

"I apologize for your inconvenience, sir, but I shall repay you the cost of our transportation. Not immediately but as soon as I can manage."

"But . . ."

"I am sorry, Mr. Berg. I shan't be marrying you. I simply can't."

"I don't understand."

I guess he never did.

It was pretty rough for a while, but I didn't mind. I had Mama and she had me, and that was enough for both of us.

She found a job clerking in a store and a place for us to rent, and at night she still makes doll clothes except now she has to sew by the light of a coal oil lamp as there is no gas where we live in Winnemucca.

Me, I'm big enough to help out some by running errands or doing odd jobs. And I can read good now.

As for the man on the train, someone told me after that he was convicted of ambushing and murdering a fourteen-year-old boy and was hanged by the neck until he was dead.

I don't believe that. Oh, someone did a murder and someone was hanged for it.

But not the man who was on the train with us that time. That man would never do such a thing. Not in a million years.

I still look for him whenever a train pulls in and the passengers unload to go running for coffee or crullers. Someday maybe I'll see him again. Or else the man who Mama says looks so much like him.

Whether I meet him again or not there's one thing sure.

When I grow up I want to be like him.

The Indian Summer of Nancy Redwing

Harry W. Paige

*This tender story about a modern Indian woman's
small joys and painful choices reaches powerfully into
the reader's heart. It won the short fiction Spur Award
for literature published in 1989. Harry Paige is a pro-
fessor at Clarkson University, and the author of several young adult novels, nonfiction books, essays, and
short stories, many of them dealing with the Sioux.
His work has won numerous prizes. This one was
first published by Doubleday in* The New Frontier:
The Best of Today's Western Fiction, *in 1989.*

It was the Moon of Falling Leaves, the white man's
November. Nancy Redwing sat on the ash-gray,
timeworn steps of her tar-paper shack and watched
the sun drip like honey through the fragile lace of
leaves that still clung to the only shade tree for six
prairie miles.

It made her heart sad to see the brittle leaves waiting to be taken by the wind. She had watched her
flowers close like velvet fists against the early-morning
cold. She had watched the prairie turn to a stubbled
yellow. She had watched the moving sky change from
a turquoise blue to a cold, gray flannel. Soon the white

shroud of winter would unfold itself over the empty miles and tuck itself in at the distant place where the earth and sky met. And then the long, gray time would begin and her hours would be spent by the spitting wood fire quilting for the next summer's tourists while the wind charged the hilltop cabin and snow seeped through the mud chinks and gathered delicately in the dark corners.

Her heart was heavy, too, because it was her thirty-fifth birthday and her husband had not remembered. She knew it was a little thing: Indians, especially poor ones, did not make the white man's fuss over the day of one's birth. She remembered that her grandmother could not even name the day she was born. It was sometime in the Moon of Cherries Reddening, in July, but the old woman with the spiderwebby lines in her dark face could not recall the day. It was written somewhere in the church records perhaps, but she had not even bothered to find out. Yes, truly, it was a little thing.

Birthdays were for children, she told herself. The little ones who wandered knee-deep in summer and did not count the falling leaves. But even as she told herself these things there was a pain that closed like a cold fist on her heart.

Summer dies slowly, she thought, watching still another leaf break from the tree and waltz to earth. A leaf at a time. Yet the sun was warm and tender on her face—like a remembered kiss from a faraway time. And the breeze was gently warm as it played in the dark waterfall of her hair. It was enough to make the heart glad, this Indian summer. Even if thirty-five winters had passed and your man had not remembered to add them with you.

As she watched the nearly bare branches score the falling sky a cloud of dust rose beyond the tree and she knew that a car was climbing the hill to her home. She watched it stop and pass through the cattle gate, knowing the visitor must be a stranger when the car did not stop again to close the gate. The car was shining and new so she did not recognize it but she watched as it gleamed through the churning dust.

In a few minutes the car pulled into her yard in a hail of flying stones and a flurry of squawking chickens. A white woman, neat and attractive, got out of the car and approached her.

"Hello there," she called in a friendly drawl. "Are you Mrs. Redwing?"

Nancy Redwing rose from the step and nodded, holding out her hand shyly to the strange woman.

The white woman took the rough, worn hand in her own slim, manicured fingers. "I'm Helen Wingate from Valentine," she announced professionally. "I'm your district Gentry Lady."

"Gentry Lady?"

The white woman smiled patiently. "Maybe you've seen our ads on television—" She stopped herself suddenly, noticing that no wires ran into the tar-paper shack. She sounded a quick, nervous laugh. "Maybe you've heard of us from friends then?" She waited and when there was no answer, she continued: "The House of Gentry is your own private cosmetologist."

The dark, liquid eyes of Nancy Redwing gave no indication that they understood.

"Cosmetics," the white woman explained.

"Makeup to bring out the beauty that is already yours." She pantomimed the action of applying makeup.

Nancy Redwing nodded, momentarily lost in the white woman's smell that was like a field of summer flowers on the wind. She had rubbed herself with sage a few hours before but the smell of the white woman took it away.

The white woman took a deep breath like a diver about to plunge into the water. "Now, you appear to be a woman of about my own age." She giggled, running a thin scale of laughter. "Heaven knows I wouldn't tell that to anybody but a good customer." She lowered her voice and bent down secretly. "Well, I'm forty-three years old. Most people refuse to believe it, but that's what I am—forty-three. People take me to be ten years younger. And that's because I take care of myself, you know. Diet, proper exercise, plenty of sleep—and the scientific assistance that's available, especially for me at the House of Gentry."

Nancy Redwing smiled and the smile followed the hard creases in her face like gentle rain following the rough furrows in the land. She watched another leaf fall from the tree and flutter down through the branches with a lonely, scratching sound. She noticed too that a few clouds had started to gather in the west.

The white woman excused herself, went to her car and removed a suitcase and a handful of color brochures. "Do you mind if I show you a few things in our new line of products?" She held out a small jar decorated with flowers. "But first here's a free sample of our new Luxura 100 face cream that makes wrinkles vanish like magic and deep-cleanses the pores like all get-out."

Nancy Redwing took the flower jar in her thick, spade-shaped fingers. She smiled and her dark eyes crinkled and were lost. "*Pilamiye*," she said softly. Then, embarrassed, she added quickly: "Thank you."

The white woman brushed off the step with paper tissue and sat down. "Let's have our little chat out here, shall we? It's such a lovely day and there won't be many more, now will there? This will probably be my last trip to the reservation until next spring. The roads are so bad—and everything."

She lay the suitcase at her feet and opened it, her words coming faster and dripping over the display of bottles and jars set like jewels in the black velvet of the case. . . .

After the woman had left, Nancy Redwing hurried into the house and looked at her new face in the cracked mirror that hung from a nail in the kitchen. She stared at her reflection as though it were a ghost. It was hard to believe that lotions, creams and paints could take away the years so! She had tried the old herbs and potions of Emma Black Bear, the medicine woman from out near Box Elder Creek. She had taken tobacco and several of her best quilts to the old woman in exchange for her knowledge of the young-looking medicines. But it had done no good. The seams of her face were still as creased as leather and the feet of many crows gathered around her eyes. Her breasts still sagged like half-empty pouches and her hips continued to spread.

She smiled at her image and the painted lips cracked and the white teeth shone against the burnished, mahogany skin. Her eyes had become dark pools shining like a fawn's against the lighter background of the eyeliner. Doe eyes, she thought, looking out from a snow bush. The lashes were longer too—heavier and swept upward. The stray tufts of hair had been plucked from her cheeks and her mole had been painted over like a mistake in a picture. She smiled again. Truly, she was a different woman! She even smelled different: The perfume from behind the ears and the V of her loose, calico gown seemed to fill the room and take away the bread-frying smell and the smell of the kerosene lamp that hung from one of the exposed beams.

When she thought of the twelve dollars and sixty cents her smile faded and a worried look crossed her face like a dark shadow. Even with all of her quilt money she had taken from the coffee can she still had been forty-two cents short, but the good-smelling white woman had told her to forget about it. She said that she would make up the difference herself, out of her own pocket.

But the chill of having no quilt material for the winter showed in her face until she smiled again and there was a thawing that started in her heart. She was younger and prettier and her eyes shone where the tiredness had been. It was like looking at an old photograph and seeing the way she used to be before the loneliness and hard times had come.

And today was her birthday! It was a reason to take away some of the years with paint. It was an unexpected gift—like Indian summer. To make her know the faraway times again and throw her tiredness into a cracked mirror.

She would leave the paint on her face and surprise her husband. She would tell him about the sweet-smelling white woman with the presents called samples. But she would not speak of the quilt money that was gone and could not buy material for the winter quilting.

She brushed at a tear that had welled crystal in her eye suddenly, as though it had been squeezed from her by memory. She watched as a single tear coursed down her cheek, washing away the paint and leaving a dark delta near the corner of her mouth. She daubed at it with the hem of her gown and then touched up the streak where the tear had come down. It was strange how the sadness came even as she smiled. Even as she looked at her presents lined up on the kitchen table. Even as she smelled the smell of many flowers blowing in the wind.

She would go outdoors and wait for her husband on the steps. She would spend this last, golden day like a coin on remembering the good things—the son who was away at school, the husband who was a good man and the pains that had made her smile into a glass.

But when she stepped outside the tears came again, this time from both eyes. The weather had turned around in a cruel joke. Dark clouds boiled up in the west and the wind was a cold knife. The tree rattled and shook down its dry and wrinkled leaves. The sun was gone, swept behind a cloud. Shadows spread across the prairie like a stain, drawing dark designs. Where Indian summer had been there was only a sad, gray November day that promised a winter moon.

Nancy Redwing went back inside, shivering. She

gathered up the flowered bottles, put them into a paper sack and stuffed them into the bottom drawer of her ancient sewing machine. Then she filled the washbasin, using a tarnished dipper to carry the water from a twenty-gallon oil drum. She got a fresh bar of brown soap and lathered her hands. Then she leaned over the basin like a priest at a baptismal fount and patted the harsh suds on her face. In a few minutes the strong soap took away the perfumed smell of flowers.

Several times during the washing she stopped and straightened up to listen as the blowing leaves scraped across the roof with a forlorn and desperate sound—like something trying to get in.

The Big Two-Shoot Rifle

R. C. House

*This is a poignant and tender story about the dreams
of an orphaned and rejected boy, Two Shoot, who has
nothing in life but his hopes. It is also a classical
story of marksmanship, and the contest of skilled
combatants for the greatest of all prizes. It was published in American Rendezvous Magazine in
1982, and is here reprinted for the first time. House
is a Spur Award finalist, and a past president of
Western Writers of America. He lives in southern
California.*

Two Shoot had come of age. It was the time of life
now, he knew, that he should take a woman. For
a long time he also knew he wanted Dove Wing, the
Indian woman.

In the village that Two Shoot so often visited to be
near Dove Wing, her brother, Many Elk, was chief.
He would be very demanding before he would re-
lease Dove Wing to be a white man's bride.

Still Two Shoot knew that the time was now—or
soon. To the best of his knowledge, he had seen twenty
summers, probably more. Others he knew who had
seen twenty summers had their Indian wives, their

lodges, bartered their annual catch of furs for more horses and more of the good things of life. Also, these same white men were quickly becoming men of influence and stature in the Indian villages where they had chosen to live. Two Shoot yearned to become one of them.

Everything Two Shoot knew had come from watching others, seeing where they had succeeded and where they had failed. When he saw another succeed, he studied on that success and tried to apply it to his own life. When he learned of failures, he determined where and why a venture had gone astray and how he could profit from another man's folly.

Two Shoot was not unduly dismayed that others his age were already wed and were proud with squalling young ones in papoose racks in their lodges. His life had had such a slow start that he had calmly resolved not to allow the experience of another to be a tally stick for his success or failure.

Still, deep urges grew strong within him. His mind was filled with reality and fantasies about the day Dove Wing would become his woman.

It was time. It had been for a long time. Two Shoot had not grown up quickly or particularly well.

He remembered little of it. His infancy and childhood were a blur, something perhaps best forgotten. Coming into the wild, untamed West to live the life of a trapper among the Indians had been Two Shoot's way of closing the book on that chapter of his life.

Charitably it had been said he was an orphan, but at a tender age the suggestion of something more sinful came with the jeers of two taunting bullies. For years the specter and the word "bastard" haunted Two Shoot.

He hid his sadness even from old Rosa, the fat, toothless, raven-haired crone who had raised him in her hovel at the edge of the frontier settlement. Though sluggish, indolent, and totally without means, Rosa owned a heart sufficiently large to adopt all manner of wayfaring dogs and cats, the dregs of male society, and even the tiny boy infant. To her dying day, Rosa did not reveal where Two Shoot had come from. She assured him only that he was not her child.

His earliest recollections were of being cradled to the point of near suffocation between her enormous breasts, and looking up at the pink and toothless gums as she chanted a lusty lullaby in a mannish baritone that had been tuned to everlasting huskiness by the cheap whiskey she consumed in greater quantities than any food.

Rosa was French and soon after adopting the waif, had named him Touissant, but never with the benefit of a last name. Because of his clouded background, he became known in the town, to the men and young boys, as "the bastard Two Sins." For a few years, until he left the dirty and sordid frontier town to strike out on his own, he thought his name might be "Tucson"— the same, he had learned, as an old, old Mexican town far to the southwest.

At times, when he was very small, he wondered if his real parents might live in that town and in fantasies vowed to go there and seek them out. It was this urging that at first caused him to move west. Secretly, though the urge was not strong, he went west thinking someday he would find his way to Tucson and the parents who had somehow forsaken him.

It was from one of the many "uncles" who frequented Rosa's hovel that Touissant got the big two-shoot rifle, a long-barreled piece with a fine polished walnut buttstock and crescent of German silver for him to cup his shoulder against when he fired. It was a marvel of the gun maker's craft.

The big two-shoot rifle had two barrels, one atop the other. When a small button ahead of the trigger guard was depressed, the barrels could swivel, the bottom one aligning perfectly under the percussion hammer with the mere twist of the wrist.

Outwardly, both barrels appeared the same. The rifled one took a patched ball which measured a half inch across—a .50 caliber, Two Shoot was to learn later. The other barrel, unrifled, was larger, designed to accommodate a larger powder charge, wads instead of patches, and tiny lead shot designed to scatter in a wide pattern, as opposed to the single bullet of the rifled barrel.

When he first saw the two-shoot gun, Two Shoot was still Touissant, the long bean sprout with fair skin, blue eyes, and a shock of unruly blond hair, whose legs jutted awkwardly out of the bottoms of his breeches, and whose shirtsleeves were never long enough.

An uncle named Al lugged it in on one of his visits to stay a few days in the aging shanty Touissant and Rosa called home.

The parade of uncles through Rosa's shanty was something Touissant grew accustomed to as part of the way of life in his growing-up home. To their faces, they were addressed by Rosa by their first names. When she spoke of them to Touissant, they were uncles. Uncle Al, Uncle Hank, Uncle Bill, and Uncle John all fused together in Touissant's memory, a composite of filthy men, bearded and unkempt, but men with good hearts and prodigious appetites where the buxom, toothless Rosa was concerned.

These were the men who kept her in cheap whiskey and fresh meat. They would come with their jugs and their haunches of odorous meat, often dripping with blood. While Touissant found things to occupy himself in the tiny, two-room frame cabin, the uncle and Rosa would sit at the crude table, passing the jug until nearly senseless. Then Rosa would stir herself with a bass sort of whiskey cackle and statement of purpose and get busy fixing the meat as steaks or a roast over the open fire in the cabin's hearth. With the meat barely warmed through, and with a generous slab served up tenderly for Touissant, the adults would gorge themselves at the table, the meat filling their bellies serving to revive spirits dulled by their enormous quantities of whiskey.

Shortly the table chairs would scrape and Rosa and whatever uncle was visiting would lock arms over each other for support and, chuckling, guffawing, and murmuring little obscenities to each other, make their weaving, clumsy way through the door into the shanty's lean-to, which was Rosa's sleeping quarters.

It was the uncle named Al who toted in the great two-shoot gun, along with a jug and a haunch of fresh meat.

"Rosa," the uncle said, settling heavily at the table

and thumping down the full jug, "I brang somethin' for the boy."

Rosa pulled the stopper from the jug and took a long draw on the contents. "He don't need nothing," she said, hauling down the jug and rasping the back of her hand across her lips.

The uncle ignored her. "A man got stabbed and robbed down to the landing last evenin'. They figured there was no call to waste time buryin' him with the river so close, so they th'ew him in. He'll smell it up down Holt's Crossing way, I'll wager."

"You men," Rosa said.

"His rifle set away back up in the dark agin a tree. When the rest of 'em went off, I moseyed up there and took it. It'd of been foolish leaving it there for somebody else to cart off."

"Well, I s'pose the boy could use a gun," Rosa said. "Sometimes it's a long spell we ain't got fresh meat in the house."

"Oh, she's a dandy! Two bar'ls. Top 'un is rifled and the underside 'un is a scattergun bar'l, er he can shoot punkin balls in 'er. I got me a good enough piece and I'm set in my ways, so I figured to let the boy have 'er."

"I don't know nothin' about guns. He'll have to learn her for hisself. But Toosun is a sharp boy. He catches on quick."

"Well, she's his if he takes to the notion. He's a strappin' boy, and time he was earnin' his keep puttin' game on the table."

"I s'pose you aim to stay a few days with me, Al. Figger the gun for the boy buys you a night's lodging, and the meat gives you leave to stay longer."

"You take objection to that, Rosa?"

"This jug'll be dry come mornin'."

"There's more where that came from. Meat, too."

"Well, then, have you a pull on the jug, Al. Toosun, stir up that fire and fetch some wood to show Uncle Al your appreciation for your nice new shootin' piece. I'll fix us up a real nice meal with that meat directly."

Touissant pulled himself up from his cot in the corner where he had been sitting, listening.

"Thank 'e, Uncle Al," he said.

"Learn to use 'er good, son, and she'll stick by you in the good times and the bad."

"I'm obliged, Uncle Al." Touissant went out to the wood yard where he had a pile chopped and split put by that might see him and Rosa through most of the winter. He loaded up his arms.

Later, after Rosa and Al had reeled off to the lean-to, Touissant quietly studied the rifle in the waning firelight, learning to swivel its barrels and testing the strength of the hammer spring.

Another button on the toeplate under the butt released the catch on the graceful long silver lid of the patchbox; the inlaid box plate was edged also in German silver with ornate and delicate scrollwork and piercings.

By the time Touissant took the big two-shoot rifle and lit out for the West, his frame, once gangly and spare, had thickened to a fine masculinity. His neck and shoulders filled and muscled out, and he'd become stout through the chest. He owned uncommonly strong arms, and his thighs threatened to split every pair of breeches he wore.

In the end, it was the loss of Rosa that brought it

all to pass. She sickened—some said it was "the pox"—and began to fail. Something for sure had darkened their door; no more would the "uncles" come to stay the night or for several days. Touissant took his big gun and hunted, putting meat on the table and trading the worthwhile hides for whiskey to ease Rosa's long and pain-filled days.

Her once enormous frame melted by the day, causing Touissant great alarm. The whiskey laugh no longer filled the cabin. One morning Touissant called softly into the lean-to. He knocked, and getting no response, entered.

Rosa lay sprawled, gaunt and lifeless, across the tiny pallet where she had entertained so many uncles. Her eyelids were veined with bluish purple against the sunken eyes, her lips furrowed and puckered and drawn back against the toothless gums. The tone of her skin had the dull texture of window putty, deeply etched and wrinkled. Her hands, which he clasped lovingly over her once pendulous breasts, were delicate and white as fine china and traced with large blue veins.

Touissant sat a long time with her and his grief.

Remembering the dead man thrown in the river the night before he got the two-shoot rifle, Touissant vowed a decent burial for Rosa. He told of it in town, but no one, not even any of the uncles, came by when he tenderly lowered the once ponderous frame into the deep hole he'd chopped in the ground.

The sun was well past its zenith, coasting like a wafer against some low haze when he got the burying place fixed to his satisfaction. He went into the shanty, tied his few meager belongings into a rolled blanket, took down the two-shoot rifle, and went outside.

He took a sight on the sun floating softly in its westward course, and started after it. Where it was going, he knew, was a big, wide-open country where he could forget he was a bastard commonly known as Two Sins, and be someone. He intended to go there and achieve mightily. Somewhere out there, too, was that other name, Tucson.

As he always had, Touissant learned by watching and by listening. He attached himself, finally, to a brigade of trappers, signing on to handle camp chores, to help with the skinning and curing, and to do whatever hunting was needed with his two-shoot gun. It was during this time that his name was changed by his trapper friends to Touissant Two Shoot. Later that was changed to Two Shoot.

The following season he had saved enough for a few traps, owned two horses—one to ride and one on which to pack his belongings—and took up the free trapping life.

Many Elk's village came to the next annual trappers' rendezvous, to trade their furs as the white men did, for goods freighted all the way from Missouri. Two Shoot was bargaining a pack of prime beaver pelts for some more traps when he chanced to look up and see the girl, Dove Wing, standing shyly in a circle of Indians and white trappers in the trading area. She appeared to have been watching him intently before he caught her eye. Embarrassment registered in her face, and she turned her head away.

But in the glance, Two Shoot sized her up. She was a substantial woman with a good neck and shoulders and breasts, a narrow waist, and strong-looking hips. She owned a build that in a white woman would be the mothering kind, turning out a flock of healthy, full-of-the-devil young ones.

Black hair parted in the middle was plaited in two strands that hung to her shoulders, wreathing her dark, oval face. The features Two Shoot saw in his quick glance were delicate. The woman's dark eyes were large and lustrous, timid-looking now, but promising a glow of smoldering fire, as well as lively sparkle.

Later in the day, his curiosity drew him on a stroll through the cluster of lodges that marked Many Elk's camp for the chance of another sight of her. As he strolled through, he saw her before a lodge, preparing some meat for a meal. Aware of someone passing, she looked up, recognized him, smiled, and quickly turned back to her work.

As he lay in his buffalo robes that night, his mind fought to recreate her image for his thought-visions to cherish.

In the morning, Two Shoot went back. Dove Wing was walking to the stream with two skin sacks for water. He hurried to catch up with her. "Here," he said, reaching for one of the sacks. "Let me help you."

"It is woman's work," she said. "You will be laughed at."

"I have been laughed at before."

"Very well," she said, giving up one of the sacks.

"By what name are you known?"

"Dove Wing, sister of Many Elk."

"Dove Wing," he repeated, liking the feel of the sound against his tongue and lips.

"And you are called Two Shoot for the gun that shoots twice."

"You know of me?" Two Shoot reddened. He hadn't imagined anyone in the entire rendezvous camp had taken notice of him. Still he was flattered that she knew.

"Men in Many Elk's village speak of the gun that can talk twice and of its owner, Two Shoot. The squaws hear this talk and repeat it to the women. In this way I have learned of you."

Together they knelt at the stream and filled the sacks with water and trudged back toward the distant lodges. Two Shoot walked in silence. The woman offered nothing unless spoken to.

"Have you a man?" he finally said, coming sharply to what had been on his mind since the day before.

The woman was also direct. "I am the sister of the chief of my village. Our father died in battle long ago. Many Elk will require many horses and much tribute before I may be spoken for as a wife."

Two Shoot sensed some of the old helpless feelings that he had known when he was merely the bastard Two Sins. Nothing, no marked achievement, no significant worth would ever be his. He owned nothing more than a string of iron traps, a pair of horses, and a special kind of shooting gun.

His heart felt vacant knowing he would never possess anything as precious as this woman at his side. And just now he wanted her more than any rifle, any horse, any traps. But they were simply not enough. By the time he could amass such wealth to tempt Many Elk for her hand, Dove Wing would long have been another man's woman and the squalls of two or perhaps three small ones would fill their lodge.

Still, life had taught him that there was always hope where there was possibility. Over two seasons, he kept close track of the movement of Many Elk's village. Careful to avoid any outward signs of haunting or dogging them, he found, each time, the best fur country near these Indians.

The obsession filled him that he must have Dove Wing for his woman; his mind allowed no other notion.

He found occasions to visit, to spend time with the village, getting to know them, and to get on friendly terms with Many Elk. He hunted alone to bring fine feasts to Dove Wing's lodge; rarely would he hunt with Many Elk, a superior bow hunter.

A scheme hatching in his mind, Two Shoot was always careful only to use the rifled barrel of the two-shoot gun when he and Many Elk did hunt together.

He often thought of Rosa and how, despite being ugly and fat, she had used weakness and vulnerability to lure in uncles who provided her with meat and her beloved whiskey.

Though he knew himself supremely skilled with the rifled barrel of the two-shoot gun, he contrived hunting situations to miss or wound the game, giving Many Elk the opening for the killing shot with the arrow.

He knew Many Elk to be a vain and proud man, one who would gloat over his superiority, and tell in the village of the white man's lesser skills. Still, Two Shoot made enough clean kills to challenge the young chief.

Two Shoot had also become a skilled trapper. He knew that too much of the scented medicine bait on a stick over the trap jaws could spook the animal, driving him away. He looked upon Many Elk now as his quarry, baiting the chief with hints—only enough to keep his interest. Two Shoot was careful not to overstate his case.

At length, late one evening in Many Elk's lodge, as Dove Wing busied herself with the final chores of cleaning up after the meal and readying the lodge for the night, Two Shoot baited his medicine stick and set and cocked the jaws of his trap for Many Elk.

"Two Shoot would ask Many Elk to grant him Dove Wing as his woman."

A superior smile flitted across the young chief's face. "Does Two Shoot have horses Many Elk does not know of?"

"Many Elk has seen all of Two Shoot's horses. I have but two."

"Already others have come with twenty horses and been turned away. What of robes and blankets?"

"Many Elk knows of my possessions. My horses, my traps, my blankets and robes are the tools of my work, nothing more."

"Two Shoot is a fool to come with so little."

"Has it no meaning that Dove Wing has feelings to be Two Shoot's woman?"

Many Elk glanced at his sister. She was watching, listening. Seeing her brother's eyes on her, she turned back to her work.

"That Dove Wing should be a happy woman is important to me. Also there is the tradition of my people. To give her for a few traps and worn blankets and broken-down horses would diminish me in their eyes."

"Many Elk's village would honor a contest of skill. There could be no shame in that. A shooting contest. The two-shoot rifle against Many Elk's true bow."

A brief smile again softened Many Elk's face. "'White men are always fools. You would chance such an uneven contest to win Dove Wing?"

"It is all I have. If I lose, I will wish Dove Wing a happy life and leave Many Elk's lodge and not return."

Many Elk's gaze drifted back to his sister, still busy with her chores, trying to ignore the conversation now. Then he looked back to the blue eyes and fair features of Two Shoot.

"Done," he said. "Then she will take one of my people for her man and make many brave children. Not weakling half-breeds as she would as the woman of Two Shoot."

Two Shoot almost spoke in anger at the insult. Victory, he felt, was nearly in his grasp. After a long pause, he spoke.

"Then you are prepared to abide by the results of the shooting contest? If I win, Dove Wing will become my woman . . . and no more talk of weakling children?"

"It shall be. My subchief, Stolen Horse, will judge the contest."

In the morning, Stolen Horse, having been advised, prepared the slabs of thick bark with great Xs marked in charcoal. Two Shoot, who had slept in his buffalo robes away from the camp, cleaned his rifle at daybreak and carefully charged both barrels. The village was alive with anticipation, a crowd already gathered at the shooting place when he strode up. Many Elk was waiting.

"One more condition, my brother," Many Elk said.

Two Shoot, warmed by being called brother, still wondered. He said nothing, waiting for Many Elk to continue.

"If you lose, you will give the great two-shoot rifle to Many Elk."

Suddenly confident that he had baited his trap properly, Two Shoot paused as though weakening. When he spoke, he spoke slowly, as with great reluctance.

"Agreed. Has Stolen Horse set up the contest?"

"Yes. Fifteen shots at three targets. Best score between the two-shoot gun and my bow wins. All shots at fifty paces."

Inwardly, Two Shoot chuckled. When hunting outside the frontier town for meat for Rosa, and later for the trapping brigade, he had placed killing shots where he intended at much greater distances. He had fired good targets from longer ranges.

Still, Many Elk was skilled—a formidable adversary.

"Are you ready, my brother?" Many Elk's voice brought Two Shoot's thoughts back to the here and now.

"Many Elk may have the first shot."

The chiefs first arrow was off the X, but only slightly. The understanding was that they would shoot five times at each target, peg the holes, and measure around the pegs with string. Of the three targets shot for a total of fifteen, the one with the shortest string would be declared winner.

After the first target, Many Elk was clearly the leader, his string an inch shorter than Two Shoot's. On his shots at his second target, Two Shoot brought his group in tighter. With the second set, his string had shortened markedly.

Many Elk studied the strings and Two Shoot. "My brother has a good eye this day. And the two-shoot rifle aims true. You may have the first shot at the last target."

Two Shoot stepped up to the line and sighted down the long barrel, feeling the silver crescent comfortably nuzzling his shoulder, his cheekbone pressed lightly against the raised walnut rest of the stock's left side. Following the example he had seen in other good shooters, he exhaled, held it, and drew his sight down keener, slowly tightening his squeeze on the trigger.

The ball carved a hole exactly where the two charcoal lines intersected. A soaring thrill of confidence surged through him. Many Elk, too, took his time with his aim; his left arm forcing the bow to full tension without a tremor, he brought his hooked fingers holding the arrow against the string strongly back to his right cheek. With a twang of bowstring, his target, too, was broken at the crossing of the X. An appreciative sigh went up from the villagers crowding around, watching.

For each shooter, these targets were the best. The holes bored by the big .50 caliber balls of the two-shoot gun touched one another at the X mark.

Many Elk's arrows did the same. In the end, Stolen Horse pegged the holes, measured them with string, studied them, and declared the match a draw. Villagers crowded close to see.

"We will shoot again," Many Elk said. "Another target to decide."

"Wait," Two Shoot said, feeling his trap jaws closing on his victim. "The hawk that circles the camp for food thrown out after meals. Even now he soars and dips down in his search for meat. He is close enough to make a good target. Let that shot be the deciding round."

Many Elk studied him, and the hawk. "Only a great marksman could shoot a bird on the wing. Very well. I have before brought down birds with my bow. You make the final decision easy for me, my brother."

As the crowd intently watched Many Elk bring up his bow, Two Shoot, also watching, dipped his gun toward the ground and slowly pushed the button and rotated the barrels.

"Lead him well, my brother," he said just before Many Elk released the arrow. "The arrow is slower than the rifle ball."

The sharp angle of bowstring flattened with a loud twang. All eyes traced the arrow's flight toward the soaring hawk; the two appeared on a collision course.

The arrow whizzed by the unsuspecting bird so close as to startle it. The hawk broke its easy glide in panic, and with wings beating a retreat, began an upward flight from the danger that had so suddenly loomed.

Confident his ruse had worked, Two Shoot swung up the gun and gasped. Instead of the single quick front sight of the scattergun barrel, sure to bring down the bird, he looked over the notched rear and blade front sight of the rifle barrel.

In his overconfidence and self-assurance at the dare to Many Elk, he had absentmindedly pivoted the barrel twice! It was too late now to change, and surely Many Elk would suspect a trick.

Never say die, a voice within him shouted. A beautiful life with Dove Wing, the only thing he had ever loved, hung in a decidedly lopsided balance.

Still, he calmly took his sight on the disappearing hawk, already much too far away. Knowing the rifle's range, he led the bird as he had told Many Elk to do. The big gun erupted with a roar of smoke and sound.

One of the hawk's wings, lifted in flight, buckled. His heart pounding, Two Shoot watched broken feathers flutter away. A great wave of emotion poured over him. He had done the impossible.

Amid a roar of cheers from the gathered Indians, the great bird crashed to earth a hundred yards from the village. As the Indians raced to the hawk to snatch feathers and thus count coup and take strength from the great feat, Two Shoot brought down the rifle with a bemused sigh and looked into the disbelieving eyes of Many Elk.

Two Shoot realized he was trembling violently.

He felt a soft warm hand close over his palsied one, the fingers seeking to intertwine with his. He looked down to see Dove Wing at his side, eyes looking down, but with great joy shining in them.

She was his woman.

Never again did Two Shoot have thoughts of going to Tucson.

Just as I Am

Joyce Gibson Roach

*This 1990 Spur Award–winning short story by Joyce
Gibson Roach deals with a Texas girl's mixed feelings about revival meetings earlier in this century.
She discovers that those who attend revivals aren't
necessarily kind and merciful Christians. Joyce Roach
is the author of both fiction and nonfiction literature
dealing with the American West, and especially Texas.
Her article "A High-toned Woman" won the short
nonfiction Spur Award in 1987.*

The words came sweet and soft and oh, so familiar to my fourteen-year-old ears. They were playing my song.

> Just as I am, without one plea
> But that Thy blood was shed for me,
> And that Thou bidd'st me come to
>   Thee,
> Oh, Lamb of God, I come, I come!

The long call of revival commenced. The locusts of
summer buzzed. The June bugs flew with a whir of
wings and landed with a thud on the backs of be-

lievers who set their teeth against the onslaught of stickery legs that clung to the cotton material of shirts and dresses. Women and children who usually cried out at the attacks of such creepy-crawly things murmured not. My skin shivered a bit. Maybe one landed on my stockings when I wasn't looking and was climbing up my leg right now. No, you always felt the hit of a June bug. They didn't creep up on you and they didn't sting you. They were honest bugs.

Swarms of lesser insect creatures hovered by the hundreds around the bare lightbulbs hanging on the tops of tall creosoted poles and departed from time to time to trouble the members of the congregation. Fans moved furiously.

A blister bug got down the collar of Brother Martin's shirt. His wife went after it with quick fingers. Blister bugs were dishonest bugs but no match for a good wife's hands. Invitation hymn or not, a blister bug's got to be attended to. Mrs. Martin would have probably fainted or at least stifled a scream, for which she was famous, if a blister bug got down her dress, but she just dove right down Brother Martin's shirt without a thought. She was a Christian.

I was waiting on another verse of the invitational hymn and although my head was down in an attitude of prayer, I could see a lot of what was going on. It was hot as hell, in the biblical sense I mean. I do not use profanity unless it is in a religious context.

Tears poured down my cheeks. The sweat poured off my forehead and mingled with the flow from my eyes. I was getting pretty wet, fixing to make my move down the grass aisle toward the wooden platform at the front of the arbor. The tears were instant. I'd been working on the sweat part since early afternoon.

I thanked the Lord for allowing me to be ofttimes convicted of my sins, for being as blameless, contrite and perfect as a fourteen-year-old girl could be in His eyes. Then I bolted down to the altar to demonstrate to the assembled sisters and brothers that the power of the Almighty had seized my life, my all, for the sixth time that very summer. I come, I come; oh, yes, Sweet Jesus, I come. Then I went. That's all there was to it. Afterward, a lot of people shook my hand or hugged me. Some said, "Bless you, child. Bless you." Then everybody went home.

August! There was nothing like it in the whole year. I live way out in West Texas at Toad and that place has never been known for riotous or sinful living not either in August or any month. The Horned Toad Cafe and my mother's table provided some memorable meals, but neither food nor entertainment ever came close to orgy in Toad. Farmers and ranchers and those who obliged their needs made up most of the population. Working hard for the grown-ups and school for the young folks was practically all a person could hold up to. Many, not just me, looked to the church for entertainment and edification and the church was not found wanting either—none of the churches, not just mine.

August was the time for summertime revivals, and, judging from the numbers as each denomination took its turn, better than half the town got a real religious pleasure in revivals. Mid July through August was the season, the time, to gather Lukewarm Christians, Backsliders and New Material into the fold. We were made up of sprinklers, dippers, drenchers and dunkers, but at revival time only a round of loud gospel singing, hellfire preaching from someone strange at least thirty miles away and a soaking, dripping, all-the-way-under baptism, usually performed in Old Man Tubbs's stock tank on the edge of town, could hold us through the fall, winter and spring without faltering, doubting, backsliding and grace-falling.

I looked on the first revival of each summer just like a debutante in Dallas looked to her coming-out party. You see, revivals had a strange effect on me. I do not know whether it was the music or the preaching or just a combination of things, but whatever the cause, the results were the same. Yes, I do know. It was the music, not the other stuff. At the first call by the minister for rededication, I plunged down the aisle every summer, at every church, at every opportunity to give my heart anew to the Lord Jesus Christ, my Savior, and to whatever cause He had pending. Sometimes I gave myself to Christian nursing in the darkest jungles of Africa, sometimes as a gospel singer in the slums of some big town, sometimes as a missionary to teach sewing to the Indians in Oklahoma. Everybody knew I couldn't medicate, educate, sing or sew a stitch, but I knew, even as I am known, that the Lord would fill in the gaps, that His eye is on the sparrow and I know he watches me.

The summer of my fourteenth year was, in a way, the high point of a very successful revival career. I'll never forget it as long as I live, never.

It was the same year the blister bug went down Brother Martin's shirt. I was tall, had stopped wearing my hair French-braided so tight that the skin around the outsides of my eyes was in a bind, and, for the first summer of my life, felt relaxed. Jesus, what a relief! I had a whole different visual experience with my eyes finally out of traction. Headaches were gone and I quit grinding my teeth, which I had always done in trying to free my scalp from such intimate acquaintance with my hair. Boys were beginning to look at me, without contempt at least, although without any marriage interest. Knowing I was too young for any real interest from men, I could still feel their eyes on me especially when I left my pew to make the flight to the altar. I do not think they understood my deep religious conviction while they were looking.

But wait, I'm leaving out the best part, the Genesis that led up to the Exodus to the altar. I heard a preacher use that line once; use the first two books of the Bible to talk about the beginning of a journey that the Israelites went on and I've worked it into my own talking ever since.

Oh, yes, and my name is Nancy Ann MacIntyre and I am an only child. You ought to know that, at least. I always get ahead of myself. I should have told you my name right up front. I mention the "only child" part because it helps explain all kinds of peculiarities. People sometimes said, "Well, she's an only child, you know." They used it to excuse some of my transgressions—which were mighty few, by the way. I worked at being a Christian every single day.

Well, like I was saying, there was a certain order to things. There's always order to being a Christian. That's one of the benefits when comparing it to heathenism. Nobody ever heard of orderly sinning, for Jesus' sake!

Religious matters began for the young folks of all denominations an hour before regular revival services. Mostly we had sword drills which commenced when the leader read out a scripture and then said, "Go." The first one to find the scripture was the winner. All the churches did it the same way. A person such as myself had to go to all the revivals as well as two or three more in other communities close by. A person had to make choices about some of them, but even if you missed one or two you got pretty good at knowing the Bible.

There was another game we played with Sister 'Lizabeth, who was one of the leaders at her church. Elizabeth Morris was a maiden lady, whatever that means. She started out revival season just loving us young folks to death and ended the season by predicting that we were all going to hell, which had to be OK because Sister 'Lizabeth insisted that she wouldn't be there. The game that caused her to make such predictions about our future was called "Fill in the Scripture." She gave a topic and we found appropriate verses just quick as we were able. For instance, if she said find a scripture about love, there was God is love, God loveth a cheerful giver, Love thy neighbor as thyself.

But there were other scriptures that someone always happened across, such as "Let him kiss me with the kisses of his mouth; for thy love is better than wine." Solomon 1:2. We were off and running then and the more times we played the game, the more familiar we became with the unusual answers. Sister

'Lizabeth would move on faster and faster. "Sports," she said. "Who can tell us about Bible sports?" Bubba Ray Andrews jumped up. He was ready with Genesis 26:8. "Isaac was sporting with Rebekah his wife."

To cover up quick, she went on to animals. Bubba responded with a line about asses. "Women," she shrieked and Bub jumped in with a plum about whores. That did it. Sister Elizabeth Morris hit the door running to tattle on us to our parents and shouting about the evils of our wicked generation. Nobody acted like that except Bubba and it wasn't as if she didn't know he wasn't going to, but we all got the blame too. Sometimes it is a Christian's lot to be persecuted for His name's sake and we accepted Sister 'Lizabeth's prediction as our burden.

There was a little space of time between sword drills and regular service, and we girls would stand around in little clusters talking, checking to see that we had fresh hankies and that the bows on our dress sashes were tied right. The topic of the big house across the road from Mount Zion Church came up, and that was good for several minutes' speculation. Mount Zion was a funny name for a church in such a flat place. It's an Israelite word.

The church ladies referred to the place across the road as "the house of ill repute." We didn't know what ill repute was. The house did need paint, and its two stories looked pretty spooky at night. So a dark house in need of paint was what a house of ill repute meant to us. The house faced the opposite direction from the church so we couldn't see anything but the back side with mops and buckets and the clothesline showing.

I particularly never connected anything very bad with the place because I had a good friend living there. Texanna was her name. Texie, as I knew her, bought baked goods from me two or three times a year, and I made a pile out of that one house. I sold cookies and cakes and pies baked by the church women for missionary causes. Because of Texie's house, I raised the most money of anybody. All the churches let me sell for them and they were really proud of my efforts, and I saw no reason to let anybody else in on my territory by telling them where I did such a good business. Surely, that wasn't a sin—just keeping my mouth shut.

Mother knew of my acquaintance with Texie. She never said any thing about her, but she told me never to go inside the house. It was hard on me not to go in because Texie was such a good and mysterious person, and a child or someone such as myself always loves a good and mysterious person the best of all. Anyone would have loved my friend if only they'd known her. She was tall like me, and pretty, which I wasn't yet but planned on being.

I asked Mother once how old she thought Texie was, and Mother said she was probably in her late twenties or early thirties. I knew she was considerably older than me because she had bosoms which I was just beginning to get. I hoped mine would be as nice as hers. I cannot bring myself to say "breasts" for bosoms. Breasts is a loathsome word contained in the Song of Solomon. The deacons and elders met once to see about having the Book of Solomon removed from the Bible, at least in Toad. Since having the book removed seemed too large an undertaking even for all the brethren in town, they just decided not to ever teach or read from it and to instruct young people not to use the vile words contained in it. But you will get my meaning when I use the word bosoms.

Well, back to Texie. She had jet-black hair which framed her pale, white face. Her eyes were dark too. Sometimes she'd sit on the rail of her porch that went all around the front and sides of her house. Another porch went all around the front and sides upstairs; a gallery, they called it. If I found her sitting like that, I'd go up and talk to her. I think sometimes she'd sit out of an evening knowing that I'd pass by about the same hour on Wednesday and Sunday. I could spend a little time with her without anyone seeing that I was on the front of the house. We just talked about pleasant things; about me, mostly, and what I was doing at school or at church. She'd ask me what I wanted to be when I grew up and was I going to go away to school or to work or had I seen the *Lady's Home Companion* for the month or how did I stand the heat in the summertime. She never talked about herself and I never asked anything. Anyone's common sense tells them not to ask questions of a good and mysterious person.

She told me about her name and how she was named for Texas and her mother, Anna: Texanna. She was my friend and I was hers and I counted myself lucky. I always asked her to come to church and assured her that she would not have to sit alone, that I'd sit with her. Sometimes I would do my missionary duty and quote scripture or sing her a song. The one we liked to sing together was her favorite and mine too, and it was the one that got me started down the aisle the quickest. Texie had a rich alto voice and we could do the nicest harmony:

> *Just as I am, and waiting not*
> *To rid my soul of one dark blot,*
> *To Thee, whose blood can cleanse*
> *each spot,*
> *Oh, Lamb of God, I come, I come!*

It was so nice sitting on Texie's porch singing the sweet songs of salvation and thinking religious thoughts about God's mercy and goodness and how He loves us all. Well, I was doing all the talking but Texie seemed like she enjoyed listening. At least she smiled at me a lot.

But back to revivals. I have this problem in talking. I always lose my place and start telling things that don't need to be told. Well, anyway, when we girls visited awhile longer and told what we were going to wear the next night and about how the stupid boys were still stupid, yes, and mean, and how they didn't really feel religious at all, we would follow the gathering crowd to the arbor at the back of the church buildings. Every single church had one and every single church did the same things.

First thing, we'd choose fans, you know, those cardboard kind with a stick glued on it like a handle. The funeral parlor, which was located in the furniture store on the east side of the square, provided fans to advertise their business. It was a natural connection, you know, churches and dying, embalming and preaching. My favorite picture was Jesus praying in the Garden of Gethsemane. You could even see the sweat as drops of blood on Jesus' brow. Bubba Ray usually got in a snatching match over Jesus in the Garden and he'd tell everyone that I was the only person in the world he'd ever seen that sweated as much as Jesus in the Garden. I hated that boy.

The schedule of events was fairly regular regardless of denomination. You could count on things being the same everywhere. There was the gathering, the singing, the praying, the testifying, the edifying, the exhorting, the inviting and the rededication. I liked it all, but the testifying was my favorite part even if I never got to participate. When the special music and the amens that followed died away, we got ready for the testifying. The preacher planned ahead of time for one person to come to the front and start it, and then anyone the spirit moved arose to enumerate his past sins and his present cleanliness because Jesus had washed his sins away, in blood, of course. Like I said, we young people never testified, naturally, because we were too young to know about hard sinning, but we could tell from the testifying that we had a lot to look forward to.

Preaching was always the same. The invitation was too. After a verse or two to gather any new material at the altar, the preacher called for prayer, during which time he wanted "every head bowed and every eye closed" while he made an appeal for Christians to rededicate their lives. They'd sing,

> Just as I am, though tossed about;
> With many a conflict, many a doubt;
> Fightings and fears within, without,
> Oh, Lamb of God, I come, I come.

Then I'd go. I didn't really have any fightings or fears either within or without, but that was my cue and it was time to heed the call. By the time every head was raised and every eye opened, there I stood, all tears and sweat. Afterward, there was a lot of handshaking and crying. Then we all went home to rest up for another night.

Well, like I was saying, the affairs of my religious life came to a head that very summer. One Wednesday evening after the midweek service, all the churchmen in town met to plan for a special, all-church revival in late August after everybody had taken their turn.

Because somebody knew somebody who knew somebody's brother, probably, the preachers in one accord with the elders, deacons and leaders decided to invite an evangelist, a professional revivalist! The man was going to bring a tent, a tent big enough to hold everybody. And, the man was coming in an automobile! Oh, I had seen automobiles. They were beginning to come through a time or two a month, maybe, but none ever stayed. It was rumored that Old Man Tubbs was getting an automobile out at his ranch and that it was coming in on the train soon, but it was just a rumor from Marvalou at the post office at the back of the grocery.

When the evangelist pulled up to the big field by the Mt. Zion Church late that summer in his automobile, everybody in town rushed over to see. The man had his wife along too. The men and boys swarmed all over that automobile, but we women were looking at the man and the woman. He was wearing a red plaid jacket and his wife had blond hair. White hair is nearer the truth. Mrs. Edwards said she had to be using something besides lemon juice. One fact was abundantly clear: They ought to be able to tell us about the wages of sin because he looked as if he'd been in the middle of a bunch of it and on a regular basis. The man had a real sweet face, but his hair was plastered down with some shiny stuff and—well, he looked cheap, that's all, cheap. After the men got over the automobile, they were grim. There was nothing to do, though, but go through with it. The town had invited them, and we had to go through with it.

My daddy, who was one of the leaders and planners who had voted for the pair, talked about it more than he should, but only at home. Lord, we were embarrassed. Daddy went about apologizing.

It wasn't working out quite like the town had planned. What they thought was that after the usual round of the usual events in the usual order at the usual time, our church, which has holding the big event because there was the big field next door, would get the Best Revival Award or something like that. That's the way I had it figured.

The man and his wife were staying at the old parsonage near Mount Zion Church. It was vacant and used for special guests. Sometimes visiting preachers stayed in the homes of the congregation, but it was just as well that provisions had been made ahead of time to offer the extra little house. Nobody would have taken them in.

They had come two days early to "get everything ready," whatever that meant. There was a stir up and down the road. The pair found some help to put up the tent and bring in extra pews. More light poles were set up, and you could smell the creosote all over town. It looked like a circus, just like a circus.

On the first Sunday evening, people gathered early. Everybody knew and everybody was coming. Brother Tobias, who was in charge of the Love Offering plates, which was the way we always paid revival preachers, was heard to mutter and then go get some straw baskets. He said we'd need extra for sure, but that is only a bit of hearsay I'm repeating. I never heard it myself, but only overheard it when my daddy repeated it to another man.

I may as well get right to business in telling about that preacher and what happened. The evangelist's services were really something. Would you believe that instead of the special music being sung, the preacher blared it out on a trumpet while his wife accompanied him by playing the piano like she was in a saloon. The community quartet was standing by and ready, but they never made it to the platform. Boy, fans were whipping back and forth like everyone was trying to cool down Hades. Tongues were wagging.

Feelings were running high. Other than the music, nothing out of the ordinary happened, but from what I could gather from listening to grown-ups, the man was just warming up.

The second night was better than the first! I had never seen such a sight in my life. That preacher was drawing them in.

A good hour before the opening hymn, I went by Texie's house. She was sitting on the rail just like she was waiting for me. I nearly ran up the steps. I had walked as carefully as I could so as not to sweat more than usual, but I forgot all about it when I saw her.

"Texie, have you heard about the preacher and his wife?" I squealed. "You never saw anything like it. She's got white hair, white! And she can play that old black piano faster than anybody I ever heard. She pats one foot and keeps up the pedal with the other."

Texie laughed at my excitement. "Nancy Ann, it can't be that bad. Haven't you ever seen lightened hair before?"

I said, no, I hadn't, and I'd sure never seen one who jumped up and down on a piano bench and smiled and shook her head while she played. And I told her I never heard such a horn played by a preaching man before. I put in all the motions when I detailed how he wet his lips and pursed them and how he spread both feet apart and then raised the silver horn higher than his head and then let out with "When they ring those golden bells for you and me."

"But you didn't say if you liked it or not," said Texie.

Did I like it? "Oh, Texie, if it's done any better in the big city than here, then I'm willing to be cheated.

"Oh, Texie, come on over. You've never been before. Please come. God might touch you. You might get saved. Then you could come regular and you could sing in the choir and help with the mission offering and everything. And I know the sewing circle could use you."

Texie didn't reply right away. "I've seen them both over at the little house. I talked to her just for a few minutes. She came over to borrow a little sugar Friday night and she invited me to come . . . and . . ."

Texie didn't say any more, but what little she said surprised me some. She just sighed and squeezed my hand and told me to go on or I might not get a seat up close and near an aisle. "I can hear what goes on from here," she said.

Have you ever noticed how things can change in ever so short a time? It's like rain in August. Nobody ever expects it.

But suddenly, the clouds are there and—wham—it rains. Well, that's the way the meeting was. It didn't take me any time to get used to the change in services and I liked it a lot, just like rain out here when we need it so bad, like "showers of blessing" in the song. But just when things got so good, they didn't stay that way.

Things got awful, terrible. But I think it was only because I got to thinking and really listening to what the man had to say. Brother Roland, that was his name, preached in a different way. He didn't shout much or pound the podium, or snap his fingers the way the other preachers did. Instead he said whole poems by heart, or he whispered, or he hissed and one time he actually cried.

His sermons always mentioned hypocrisy. When he went into detail about the hypocritical disease, he called it, I knew I had been an unsuspecting sufferer from it. God forgives the unknowing, of course, that is provided once a person knows, a person repents, confesses it and then resolves to actively and openly not be a hypocrite, or whatever, again. The plan was the same no matter what the sin. I already knew the plan, but in my mind, the plan always called for a person to go down the aisle, but I was beginning to

think I might not ought to go down the aisle anymore
since that seemed hypocritical, two-faced. And knowing that I shouldn't go down the aisle anymore nearly
killed me. God would be so disappointed. The congregation would be disappointed. It was wrong to go.
It was wrong not to go. Oh, what was wrong and
what was right? Nobody had a right to make me question what had always been right in my religious life.

The preacher confused me worst of all when he
quoted a verse from the song instead of letting us sing
it. He made us quit singing! He said, real quiet, "Just
as I am, poor, wretched and blind. Sight," and he
pointed to his heart and not his eyes at all, "riches,
healing of the mind. Yes, yes, all I need in Thee to
find. Oh, Lamb of God, I . . . me . . . me . . . I come."

He whispered the part about blind. Was he talking
to me? Well, if I was blind, wouldn't I be the first to
know?

By Wednesday I hated that preacher, and the hatred was multiplied tenfold because I knew he was
right. In just three days' time everything went from
white to black, from excitement to sick to my stomach. To make matters worse, Bubba Ray and two more
boys warted me every night. They talked ugly so I
could hear.

It wasn't anything I hadn't heard before. I knew
all those words even if I didn't use them. But they
kept looking at me in places they shouldn't have, and
I sure didn't know what to do about it or even what
it meant.

It wasn't just me that was bothered. Everybody was
stirred up and acting awful. I tell you, I've never been
so miserable in my life. I had to make up my mind

about what was going to be done the last evening. Was I going down the aisle or wasn't I? What if the preacher named off some new cause? What if God meant for me to do a great religious work, maybe in China instead of Africa, where I had already signed on? Could I refuse and maybe miss the opportunity of a lifetime to spread the word and minister to the sinners overseas?

I thought of going to talk to Brother Roland ahead of time. Maybe he'd let me in on what he would be calling on people to do on the final night. I couldn't bring myself to do it, though. That man's services weren't anything like what we were used to. And he hadn't asked anybody to do one thing on any of the other nights except let the love of Jesus in our lives and love our brothers and sisters better. I'd already done that. Anybody who knew me could tell you that.

I took two baths a day trying to keep the sweat down, but it did no good. Sweat poured off me worse than I ever remember. I was even dreaming at night, bad dreams, about what happens to those who don't lead good lives and those who are hypocrites; then I'd wake up sweating and wondering if that was my punishment for being a hypocrite. I was going to sweat myself to death and die of dehydration. Dehydration is bound to happen in hell. That was it! I was going to hell.

While I was pondering the wages of my sin, the men from all the churches came over on Thursday night and talked into the late hours outside in our back yard. Their voices rose and fell as they pondered what to do, but except for the fact that a lot of sinners were showing up at church for the first time ever, they didn't have one wrong thing they could pin on him. They couldn't ask Brother Roland to leave and they sure couldn't ask those folks that were coming to leave.

The leaders were in an awful uproar. I wished I could go talk to Texie about it all, but we weren't that good friends. She couldn't possibly understand about the trials and tribulations of Christianity. And what could I say? "I'm a hypocrite; I'm a sinner; I sweat too much; I may go to hell; how about you?" That's all I could think of. I tossed and turned in my sleep that night and dreamed of the altar where I was on my knees moaning, "Just as I am . . . just as I am."

The last night of the revival came. Earlier in the afternoon, I asked my mother to French-braid my hair.

"Nancy Ann, why would you want to do that again? I thought you liked having your hair more grown-up. You're fourteen years old now. Besides I'm tired of doing it." Mother seemed put out, but she was braiding the whole time she was talking. Her hands were cool and soft against my moist and sticky neck. I couldn't tell her why I wanted my hair braided. I just did. Something ought to be like it used to be. Braiding my hair was the only familiar thing I could remember after the week I'd been through—we'd all been through.

I arrived early but not early enough to beat the crowd. I'll bet there were a hundred and fifty people there, and the whole population couldn't have been more than two hundred. Folks from off the ranches and farms who didn't get to town for sometimes six months were coming in buggies, wagons and a-horseback. The word had sure spread. Folks were gathering, flipping their fans like mad already and hunting good seats. There were plenty of aisle places left in case I wanted one.

You will absolutely not believe what happened then. Just as I was about to find me a spot, I saw Texie coming across the road toward the tent! Seeing her coming at a distance was like an answer to prayer. "Thank you, Lord, for bringing my heathen friend. You will love Texie. She is so good and so pretty. Thank you, precious Lord," I murmured under my breath. If ever I needed someone with me who didn't know me, it was now. Texie could sit with me, and whatever I decided about going down the aisle or not would be OK. Boy, I fairly ran toward her.

The crowd was in the way and not inclined to get out of the way and I got tangled up. When I caught sight of her again, she wasn't alone. Bubba Ray and another boy were with her. They were still a good ways away but I didn't have to be close to know by the looks on their faces that they were talking dirty. And they didn't even know her! How dare they speak to a stranger so! And Texie a visitor to a revival. I fairly flew toward her. Just as I got close, I heard Texie call Bubba Ray by name and tell him to leave her alone. He laughed, said something else I couldn't hear, and ran off, the other boy following close behind. How in the world would she have known Bubba?

"Texie, Texie," I hollered breathlessly. "I'm so sorry. You just wait 'til I get my hands on . . ." I was cut short and never finished my sentence because someone else was calling my name.

"Nancy Ann. You come here. Don't you go near

that woman." It was Sister Andrews, Bubba's step-mother, and there was anger in her voice.

"But, Sister Andrews, she's my friend, Texie. She's come to the revival and she is going to sit with me. It's all right."

I looked at Texie and smiled and waved and tried with the look on my face to make it all right. The look on Texie's face scared me. But even in the midst of it all, I'll never forget how Texie looked. Her black-as-midnight hair was pulled up and a beautiful white hat was on her head. She had on a soft sky-blue dress with little print flowers in it and white gloves and white shoes. Never in all my life had I seen or known such a good and beautiful creature, and never had I seen such hurt on a face that pretty.

It was just like a dream then. Sister Andrews grabbed me by the arm and shouted—yes, shouted—for my mother. Mother was pretty close by for her to have heard, and she must have thought something had happened to me because she came running, scared nearly to death. There were twenty or so people within hearing of what was going on. Every eye was on us.

"Take your girl and tell her about her friend while I deal with this harlot," commanded Mrs. Andrews.

"Nancy, are you all right? What is going on? What did you do?" my mother demanded to know.

"Mother, I didn't do anything wrong. I just asked Texie to sit with me. I told her she could come and be welcome and maybe get saved. And she came because I told her that the preacher was different and the music and all. Brother and Sister Roland even went to see her and they asked her to come, I think. They asked lots of folks to come."

I was hysterical and fought to get back through the crowd that had gathered around us. By the time I pushed my way through, Texie was gone, just disappeared. Mrs. Andrews was marching back to the arbor, and I mean marching.

Even though there were plenty of folks at the back where we were, a bunch of others were beginning to sing from their paperback books, and in an instant those around us turned and went to their seats, their curiosity satisfied. Whatever they were saying, I couldn't hear, and I didn't care anyway.

I just stood there sobbing with Mother's arms around me. "Mother, what did I do? What did I do?"

"Nothing, nothing, Nancy," whispered my mother. She stood right there in the road with her arms around me, rocking me just like a baby. She took her soft, sweet hands and pushed my head down on her shoulder and stroked my cheeks. In words simple and true she explained about Texie. I understood.

But it was her explaining about Sister Andrews that hurt. I can't remember exactly what she said, but when she got through I knew that some people who said they were Christians weren't all the time, but only some of the time, and that I had to honor them for that, but only some of the time and not all the time.

"But can you tell me what I did wrong?" I asked again.

"Nothing wrong. Something good and about the most Christian thing you've ever done in your life. Even better than going down the aisle. Better than going to Africa, even." Mother's voice was shaking, and she cried just like her heart would break. Her tears covered me sweeter than a baptism. "Let's go home, Nancy. We don't have to stay tonight."

"No, I want to stay. There's something I still have to do." Mother and I wiped our tears and found a seat at the very back. No one noticed our coming. I didn't hear one word of what the preacher was saying. If there was special music it was lost on me. No trumpet or piano penetrated my mind. I spent the whole time thinking, thinking, studying it out.

When the call was given, I kept my seat through all the verses and the repeats. For the first time in my life, I sang all the words, read the meaning clear, gave up the call to Africa and parts unknown. God loved me. God loved Texie—just like we were. Sister Andrews was on her own. I didn't need to go down the aisle or anywhere, anymore.

> *Just as I am! Thou wilt receive,*
> *Wilt welcome, pardon, cleanse,*
> *   relieve,*
> *Because Thy promise I believe;*
> *Oh, Lamb of God! I come! I come!*

Charity

Sandra Whiting

This Spur Award–winning short story by Sandy Whiting delights me because it is the polar opposite of the traditional warlike western short story about the tensions between Indians and whites. This one is about a growing friendship between a white girl and an Indian from the nearby reservation who have every reason to be deeply afraid of each other. Whiting writes, "I wrote it to illustrate that not all encounters between new settlers and the Indians were 'bang, bang, shoot-em-ups.' On many occasions, the settlers had been taught that the people indigenous to the new lands were bad. . . . Only when the two sides came close enough to see the whites of the others' eyes could any misunderstandings be straightened out." The result is a unique and tender love story. This first appeared in Louis L'Amour Western Magazine *in 1995. It is Ms. Whiting's first published work.*

I was thirteen when I met him. He was the first Indian I'd ever seen up close. With the reservation being only five miles south of town, I'd seen plenty of Indians, but always from a distance. This one, however, was barely ten feet away.

There were actually three of them. They rode up to our house just like they owned it, Ma said. They would have walked inside, but she met 'em at the door with the Winchester '66. It was an old rifle, but it still worked. Ma told me later that as soon as the Indians had seen it, they'd given it and her a mighty respectful distance.

I was on my way home from school—walking, of course, 'cause Pa needed our one and only horse, an old bay gelding that had seen at least fifteen years, to plow the fields. As I came over the hill, I saw the Indians in the distance and wondered if I should keep the same. Well, it was my house and if they were plannin' on killin' me, they'd have to do it there. I set my jaw and walked on home.

Pa'd seen the commotion from the fields and hurried to my mother's side. He could talk a little Indian sign language, but not much. When I reached the house, he was asking those half-naked redskins what they wanted.

Just as I walked within spittin' distance of those Indians, one of 'em turned and looked at me. He had black, waist-length hair, and even with him on horseback I could tell he was tall. He had an eagle feather and several hawk feathers woven into his hair. He also had two yellow stripes painted on his arm. I didn't know what any of it meant or if any of it meant anything. At thirteen, I was more interested in the beautiful chestnut horse he was sitting on. He saw me admiring his horse and motioned for me to come close, but I wouldn't go up to him because, I must admit,

I was a tad afraid. We kids used to say we weren't afraid and dare each other to sneak onto the Indian reservation that lay just south of town, but in truth, we were terrified of Indians. We should have been more afraid of rattlesnakes.

Pa saw the Indian looking at me and shooed me into the house, where Ma could keep a watchful eye on me. I was the youngest of four children and the only girl. If I wasn't in school or at church, Ma always made sure I was with her or her spinster sister, or at least alone. She said I wouldn't get into trouble that way. The boys could do anything, but not me. It made me so mad.

Finally, Pa figured out the Indians wanted to trade with us. It seemed they wanted an old iron cooking pot that had long since been demoted to flowerpot once Ma'd inherited her mother's brand-spankin'-new one.

Ma cleaned up the pot. I stood beside her at the door as she traded. She could have just given it to them outright, but she didn't want them to think they were getting a handout. The Indian who'd stared at me just minutes before did the swapping. He looked at me and smiled. I blushed and felt silly about it afterward. He also seemed to me to be the youngest of the three, although he did look older than my eldest brother, Matthew. Matthew was sixteen goin' on six, my mother was wont to say when Matthew threw a fit about doin' chores.

A price of five rabbit skins was agreed upon for the old pot and the Indians left. I looked at Ma, holding those rabbit skins in her hand. "Whatcha gonna do with them?" I asked.

She held them up. They were fine quality, not a mark on them. "I guess I'll make a baby blanket out of them. There's not enough there to do much else with." I knew by the tone of her voice that Mother felt like she'd robbed them. She'd always been one to trade fairly with everyone—not like them cutthroats Back East, as she'd say.

School had been out for the summer a week already before I saw him again. He was riding up the road with two other Indians. I supposed they were the same ones as before. As there were three of them again, I assumed they traveled in groups, perhaps for safety's sake, which brought to my attention the fact that I was traveling in a group of one—me—and I was afoot.

Again he looked at me, but this time he winked. This was a revelation to me. I never guessed Indians could wink. I didn't say anything, but quickened my pace to the wild strawberry patch. I heard them laughing behind me.

Spring rains had been plentiful that year and I'd already picked at least thirty quarts from that patch. I expected to get at least ten more before summer took over completely and wilted the little plants into the dust.

From the berry patch, I could see a summer squall brewing to the northwest. I figured I had about an hour left before it came calling. I picked faster and faster, never minding if I didn't get all the green caps off. I could do that later. My mouth watered with the thought of fresh strawberry pie.

My two buckets full, I was fixin' to leave when lightning struck a nearby tree. I was so close to it, I felt the electricity bounce off the tree and into me. Stunned, I stepped backwards, right into a prairie dog hole.

I don't recollect how long I lay there on the ground with my foot in that darned hole. Next thing I knew I was soaked to the skin from the pounding rain and there was someone standing over me—someone with long, black hair. I blinked my eyes to clear them and tried to sit up. That was a mistake. Pain shot through my leg like a bullet and I fainted.

When I came to, I was lying under a crude lean-to that had *Army* written across it. I rather suspected it had been part of a tent at one time or another. I then discovered that except for my underdrawers, I was completely naked. There had been a blanket wrapped around me, but still, someone had to have taken my clothes off in the first place. I was mortified. I never, ever let anyone see me that way.

In the dim evening light, I looked for my clothes. They were hanging on that same tree that lightning had struck, blowing like flags in the wind. By now I figured out that my leg was broken, so there was no way under God's great heaven I was going to be able to fetch them myself. Whoever was my benefactor was going to have to do it for me.

I lay back and contemplated my predicament. If I hadn't been in such a hurry to pick all the berries I'd have been home before the lightning struck and this unladylike and embarrassing situation wouldn't be happening to me.

I was lying there, feeling rather sorry for myself, when my rescuer put in an appearance. Horror of horrors! It was that same Indian who'd winked at me. I then remembered him standing over me in the rain before I had fainted. I pulled the blanket around my body as tight as I could and then some. It was hard to say at the time if I was more embarrassed at knowing he'd removed my clothes or scared of what he was going to do to me.

Frantic, I pointed to my clothes, hoping he'd get the message that I wanted them back. He shook his head, then pointed to a nearby puddle. I assumed he was telling me that they were still wet. I didn't care. Unfortunately, I wasn't in a position to argue.

I looked around my small shelter. The berry buckets were at my head, still full of berries. At least I hadn't lost those, I thought to myself. I peeked around the side of the lean-to and saw his two friends leaving. I thought they would head in the direction of my home to fetch Pa, but instead they headed directly the other way—south, away from town. My hopes dashed, I lay back down. I resigned myself to being an Indian squaw for the rest of my life. *Squaw*—how I detested the word. The men said it with such disgust. Why couldn't they be called wives?

Right at sundown, my benefactor brought my clothes to me. They were still damp in spots, but not drenched, as before. I thought he would leave me to dress in private, but he sat down under the lean-to with me. If he was expecting me to put on a show for him, he had another thing coming. No matter how much it made my leg hurt, I kept that blanket around me and dressed under it.

Again it started to rain. As it did, my Indian started to help himself to a handful of my hard-earned berries. Before I could think, I slapped his hand away, just like I did my brothers' when they got too friendly with my berries.

He was surprised, and his face showed it. I thought his eyes were going to pop clean out of their sockets. I quickly imagined myself without my scalp. I snatched a few berries out of the bucket and held them out in the rain to wash them, pretending I only wanted to stop him from eating dirty ones. I fed them to him one at a time. I think he forgave me for slapping his hand. It also seemed to me he was amused at having me feed them to him.

With the sun gone and the rain still pouring, it was pitch-black and there I was, out on the prairie, with a nearly naked Indian beside me. Having resigned myself to the fact that I was now his squaw, I decided that the first thing I was going to do for him was make him a shirt—a bright red one, so I could see him comin'.

I'd just gotten myself settled down from the initial fright of having him sit so close to me when he lay down beside me and covered us both with his blanket. Fear once again held me in its clutches—so overwhelming that my body was temporarily paralyzed. I'd supposed he would sit beside me all night but there he was, on the outside of the lean-to, and I, on the inside. My fate was sealed. There was absolutely no way I could or would crawl over him to get out. I crossed my arms over my chest and waited to die.

In my sleep, as I waited for angels to take me to their heavenly home, I was suddenly awakened by the most wretched noise I'd ever heard. I opened my eyes, fully expecting to see a large carnivorous animal waiting to feast upon my body, but there was nothing there. The noise came again. It was from my lean-to companion. He was snoring! I wanted to laugh out loud, but instead I pushed on his shoulder so he would roll over, just as Ma did to Pa each night. At last I had found common ground between red man and white man, though I did not think it would be written up in the annals of history.

Morning came without a hint of storm. I sat up. I knew my hair was untidy, so I pulled out the pink ribbon that hung at the end of my solitary braid and ran my fingers through my hair. By now, my Indian was awake and watching me. My hair was light brown and he seemed to like it. Feeling slightly embarrassed at the way he was looking at me, rather like he was interested in me, I turned my back to him. As soon as I did, he ran his fingers through my hair. Startled, and surprised he'd do such a thing, I nearly came clean out of my skin. He saw me start and pulled his hand back, as though he'd touched fire. I reassured him with a smile that I'd only been startled and not frightened, even though I really was the latter—at least a little bit.

Cautiously, so as not to scare me, he caressed my hair. He pulled it around to the front and laid it on my shoulders, then smiled and said something I didn't understand. I've always thought he was telling me I was pretty. Once again, I blushed. He only smiled in return. He then pulled my hair to the back and without braiding it, tied the ribbon around it in a bow. Chalk up another one for Indians. I didn't know they knew how to tie bows.

My companion's friends arrived and, much to my dismay, helped themselves most liberally to my berries. The lean-to was folded and put on a horse. Next, I was loaded up onto the chestnut horse I'd admired when I'd first laid eyes on my Indian weeks before. I was wondering where its owner was going to ride when he quickly got on behind me.

My injured leg, now splinted up with sticks and tied with vines, stuck out awkwardly from the horse. As we traveled, I found pain would run the gamut of my leg with each little jostle. I tried not to cry, as I didn't want him to think I was a baby, but every once in a while, a tear would sneak out anyway. He must have noticed my distress because he shifted me around just a bit so I could put my leg up higher. This, however, required that I lean back on his chest, which I was most reluctant to do, but a quick smile from him assured me he had only my comfort in mind.

Those two miles home from the berry patch seemed like twenty by the time we arrived. There was a small gathering of people at my house, which I assumed was a search party out to hunt for me now that the rain had let up. Several of the men who'd gathered held their rifles up with a look on their faces that made it seem like they'd shoot if the Indians were to make any sudden moves. I thought they should be grateful I wasn't dead. I looked at my Indian. He wasn't smiling anymore. Maybe he expected everyone to thank him for rescuing me. I suppose you could say he was thanked by the fact that no one decided to shoot him.

My Indian wouldn't let Pa carry me into the house, but chose instead to carry me himself, as if proving that his intentions were of the honorable kind. I wanted to thank him for helping me, but I didn't know the words. I then remembered my hair ribbon. I pulled it out and gave it to him. He looked at it, then me, smiled, and left.

When I told the story of my rescue, I only said that the Indians had found me and brought me home. I didn't want anyone to know I had spent the night right beside one of them. I was afraid they'd think something else had happened, so I led everyone to believe I was found that morning.

My new friend came to check on me several times over the next few weeks. Each time he came, he brought a handful of berries, which I washed and fed to him, but only if no one else was around to see. I also let him run his fingers through my hair on several occasions. He was nice. I began to trust him.

I made him that bright-red shirt I had silently promised him, as well. It fit him just right. I also noticed he wore my pink ribbon in his hair. My brothers wouldn't be caught dead with a ribbon in their hair, but my Indian friend didn't mind.

One day, my youngest brother came running into the house, completely out of breath. "They're gonna hang your Indian!" he blurted out.

"Why?" I asked him, disbelieving him.

"Some folks think he and the two Indians who were with him stole horses and killed some folks up north." Horse stealing and killing—those were serious offenses.

"When?" I asked.

"When what?" my brother asked back.

"When did they steal the horses and kill those folks?"

"It was that night you broke your leg, back in the

big rain. Folks say they was on their way back from doin' it when they found you and the only reason they rescued you was to mislead everyone as to what they'd done. That's why all those men were at our house that morning—to hunt down them killers. They supposed you was dead already, They say they now know it was them because your friend was seen snooping around the place the other day and they say a killer always returns to the scene of the crime."

"That's utter nonsense!" I exclaimed. "They were . . ." I didn't finish the sentence.

"Come on, Luke, we've got to get to town and stop this hanging!" By now I was all of fourteen, but I had the lives of three innocent human beings in my hands. As we hadn't any other horse, Luke helped me up onto the old bay and got up behind me. We ran that horse for all it was worth and prayed he wouldn't keel over and die before we got to town.

The gallows was almost finished when we arrived. I was always amazed at how fast timber could be found to build one, where it took weeks to find enough to build a house.

I saw my friend, in the red shirt I'd made him, along with his companions, in shackles. I begged the sheriff to let me talk to them but he said they were dangerous men—killers—and wouldn't let me near. When I asked him what evidence there was to convict the Indians, he showed me a scrap of red cloth and nothing more.

As I couldn't get near my friend, I hobbled around on my nearly mended leg and asked everyone I thought was involved to help me stop this hanging at least until a judge could be found and give them a fair trial. But, because I was young and female, no one would listen to me.

I was in a panic. After having talked to a slew of different folks and eavesdropping on others, I knew the full story, and knew without a doubt my friend was innocent. He was going to die and I was helpless to stop it.

As the three were being taken up to the gallows, like lambs to the slaughter, the words of the circuit preacher echoed in my mind. "No greater love hath a man than he lay down his life for his brother." I assumed it also meant dignity.

Quickly, before I chickened out and before anyone could stop me, Luke helped me up onto the gallows. The gathering crowd grew silent. I took a deep breath. It was now or never.

"Listen to me!" I shouted. "These men are innocent. They were nowhere near the old Drigger place the night them folks were killed."

"How do you know?" came a voice from the crowd.

It was hard to tell them how I knew, but it was either swallow my pride or live with three dead people on my conscience for the rest of my life. "They were with me all night. They found me the same night I broke my leg—not the next morning, as I led everyone to believe." Several of the ladies gasped out loud at this revelation. A young girl and a man simply did not spend the night together without benefit of marriage, and for her to spend the night with an Indian and still have any of her virtue left was unthinkable.

"How do we know you're tellin' the truth?" came another voice.

"Because, because—" I hesitated.

"Kill them redskins!" shouted a voice.

"No. Wait. I know they were with me all night because this one snored and kept me awake!" I pointed to my Indian. It wasn't exactly the truth, as he'd been the only one to stay the night, but I had seen his friends and they'd certainly not been headed north to the Drigger place. I had to give them the benefit of the doubt. I was sure no one else would, not with them being Indians.

"Hang 'em anyway, then we won't have to ever worry about 'em killin' anyone. Besides, we came to see a hangin'!" shouted two different voices.

This made me mad. I had a stubborn streak, still do, and it chose that moment to come out. I hobbled over to my Indian, took the noose from around his neck, and put it around my own. It almost choked the life out of me as it was, my being much shorter than he. "There, now you can have your hangin'! I have given you testimony of their innocence. If you choose to hang someone, I also choose to take his place. I will not let an innocent man die and my lifeless body, hanging here, will haunt each and every one of you the rest of your lives!" I did favor the dramatic side.

"Charity, have you plumb lost your mind?" It was my brother hollering up at me. I refused to look at him. I didn't think anyone would hang me, but I wasn't exactly sure.

The sheriff came up to me. "Are you sure of your facts, miss?"

I looked up at him, but couldn't see his eyes, as his hat shaded them. "Just as sure as I'm standing here with this noose around my neck," I said stubbornly.

At last, the sheriff was having his doubts. A hanging was forever; there was no taking it back. I played on his doubts. "One of your men said he'd found shoed horse tracks and another horse had a nail missing from its shoe. These Indians don't have shoes on their horses. You also said yourself, Sheriff, that the only thing found at the house was a piece of red cloth that matched this man's shirt. I made that man's shirt a week after he found me and took me home. He couldn't have had it the night of the murders and besides, he was right next to me all night, like I done already said." I trembled with worry. Was it enough? I prayed it was.

"Thomas," the sheriff called to one of the townsmen, "did you find any unshod pony tracks out there?"

"No."

"Then all the evidence against these men is very iffy. I warned you about this when you insisted on doin' the investigatin'. Horse tracks and a scrap of cloth aren't enough to condemn 'em and we have a witness who says they were nowhere near the Drigger place that night." The sheriff hollered this to the posse and townsfolk as well. He then whispered to me, "You better be damn sure you're tellin' me the truth, miss, 'cause if you're not, you'll be hung 'longside these three as a conspirator to murder." I nodded my head vigorously, or as vigorously as I could with a rope around it.

The sheriff removed the noose from my neck as well as the others'. No one there spoke much Indian, but with hand gestures, the three formerly condemned men were given back their horses and told to get out of town. My Indian gave me one last mystified look as he departed. I felt sorry for him. He probably didn't even know what he was going to be hanged for.

I stepped down off the gallows, happy my Indian had been spared, but anxious as to what folks would say about me after finding out I'd spent the night with a man. Whatever happened, I knew I'd done the right thing.

By the time school started again, my leg was mended enough to allow me to walk without crutches. I endured the stares of my classmates as they pointed their fingers at me and wagged their tongues. I ignored them to the best of my ability. Soon they left me alone.

It was right after the first snow that I saw my Indian again. This time he was alone and had considerable more clothes on, including the red shirt. He must have been watching the house because he arrived just after my parents left for town in the wagon. My brothers were away doing whatever boys did when it snowed. I suspected it wasn't work of any kind. I was left to tend the house and keep the fires burning.

Having not seen him in a while, I was greatly surprised when I opened the door and found him standing there in the cold. I motioned for him to come in and sit on the floor by the fire. Having no berries at this time of year to feed him, I cut a huge slice of apple pie and fed it to him. I could tell he liked it as he readily opened his mouth for each bite.

As we sat on the floor, he gazed at the fire, then

at me. I somehow knew he wanted to talk, but his mouth simply couldn't form the white man words and I couldn't speak his. I thought how terrible it must be to be a foreigner and not know the language. It struck me then that I was a foreigner and this was his land, but we white folk had changed it to make it appear as though they were the intruders and not us.

Finally he stood and bade me come outside with him. I pulled on my coat and bonnet, for it had started to snow again, and followed him out. He led me over to his horse that I so admired. I patted the horse on her neck. She was the most beautiful creature I'd ever seen.

My friend handed me the rope that was around the animal's neck and said something I did not understand. Mystified, I stared at him. He said it again, only this time he tied the rope to my wrist. I pointed to the horse, then to myself. He smiled and nodded his head. I was stunned. He was giving me his horse. I tried to give it back, but he would have nothing to do with it.

Without further explanation, my red-shirted friend disappeared into the snow. I thought about him for a long time. I'd heard that sometimes when an Indian man wants to marry a woman, he offers horses to her father. I wondered if this young man wished me for his wife. I was no longer repulsed by the thought of being a squaw but I knew, deep down inside, that I would never be able to live in his world and he could never live in mine. Our homes were separated by more than the miles between them.

It was two summers later when I saw him again.

I was nearly sixteen and my interests had gone beyond horses. There were several young men I'd taken a fancy to, but somehow, I always ended up comparing them to my Indian.

Once again I was out picking berries at the patch, only this time there wasn't a cloud in the sky. I stood to move to a richer plant when all of a sudden, there he was. I liked to drop my bucket of berries. He began to laugh. I suppose he thought it funny he'd managed to sneak up on me. I gave him a snooty face. He poked me in the ribs and I threw a strawberry at him. He wasn't the least bit deterred. Right then and there I knew I had a lifelong friend.

He followed me around as I picked, then we sat down under the sole cottonwood. I fed him some berries, thinking that's what he wanted. He ate a few, then stopped. He wanted to talk.

He drew a stick picture on the ground and pointed to himself, then another one, obviously a woman, beside him. He'd married. Part of me was happy for him and part of me was crushed. Somehow, I'd always considered him mine. He then drew a small stick picture and held his arms as if he were cradling a baby. He was telling me he had a baby. I inquired, with a crude drawing of my own, if the baby was a boy or girl. It was a girl.

He pointed to himself and said something, then to several other things and called each one something. He was naming them. He pointed to me and I said *Charity*. He pulled a scrap of tree bark and a small piece of charcoal out of a bag and made as if he was writing. He handed me the tree bark and charcoal. I gathered he wanted me to write my name. I thought

that unusual, for I'd heard the Indians had no written language, but I complied.

I handed him what I'd written. He repeated it out
loud several times, pointed to me and said it, then to
the stick figure of his baby and said it. I was flattered.
He was naming his daughter after me.

He stood to leave. It was then that I noticed the
tear in his shirt. On closer inspection, I discovered
that it was not only torn, but threadbare. He needed
a new one. I would make it for him.

I held up three fingers and pointed to the sun, laid
my hands beside my head as if to sleep, then pointed
to the tree. I wanted him to come back in three days.
He made as if he understood, then left.

Three days later, with a new red shirt, I was back
at the tree and so was he. I had also made a small
blanket for his baby out of those five rabbit skins Ma
had received in payment for the iron pot and had
never used. He thanked me with a nod of the head
and left me once again.

This went on for years, even after I'd married and
raised four fine sons and two daughters. Each spring,
when the strawberries were ripe, I'd meet Red Shirt—
the name he'd been given when the final rolls were
taken—at the berry patch, gifts in hand to give his
family, along with a new red shirt for him. He learned
a smattering of English, but I could barely say his
name in his language.

His first wife died after producing two daughters
and one son. One daughter lived only two days longer
than her mother. I grieved for him. His second wife
produced one son and one daughter.

On occasion he'd show up at my door, but only

when my husband was away, and ask for food. My husband was a good man and had only cautioned me not to give so much away that our own family would starve. My children, after they were older, disapproved of my giving away our food to Indians, but I told them it was our duty, as taught in the Bible, to help those less fortunate. It could be us in their shoes. I'd then give him all he could carry and then some. I prayed it was enough. I'd saved his life and wasn't about to let him die by starvation. At least, that's what I told myself. Actually, he was my friend and I was determined to help him.

The years aged us both. My hair turned a silvery gray and I was no longer the spry young thing I used to be. Red Shirt had adopted the white man way of dress and tucked his hair up under his hat to disguise the fact he was Indian. He wouldn't cut it, and I was glad.

A few more years found me a widow. I also knew his second wife no longer walked this earth. My grown children begged me to come stay with them and I would for a little while, but the itch to be in my own home soon drove me back there. Even though the facilities were outside and I had to pump my own water, it was mine.

It had now been close to fifty years since I had first met Red Shirt. Hitler was coming to power in Europe and my sixth sense told me he'd be a far worse menace than any Indian ever was. Red Shirt came to visit me once a week, despite the disapproval of my children and his. There was very little conversation, but having company was good. I'd feed him a piece of pie and a glass of lemonade. Sometimes we'd play checkers—he let me win every once in a while—and sometimes we'd simply sit in front of the fire. He still liked to run his fingers through my now nearly white hair and tie a bow in it, as if I were still thirteen. I didn't mind.

I'd made him a new red shirt last week. I must have made at least fifty of them by now. He looked handsome in it. But even as he strutted around in it like a young buck, I knew his health was failing. Proper nutrition had been hard to come by on the reservation, and a single piece of apple pie and whatever else he'd eat when he was with me once a week simply wasn't enough to make up for sixty-plus years without it.

I somehow suspected I'd not see him again after that last visit. There weren't many things we could do together, as old Indian men had a habit of being run off from anything and everything in town. Some of the younger folks are changing, but until the young become old, the hatred and distrust will remain. But no one could tell us what we could and could not do in my own home.

"And now you've come to tell me he's gone. I think soon I'll join him. I will miss our visits," I said in a barely audible voice.

"My father made me promise to come see you after he died. I didn't want to, and to tell the truth, I never liked him seeing a woman who was not of our people, even though I was named after you. But I'm glad I did. Would you mind if I came back from time to time?"

"Of course not. You're always welcome. I would

like to find out more about your people before there isn't anyone left who knows."

Charity Red Shirt handed me a small parcel. "He wanted me to give this to you."

I opened it. Inside was my pink ribbon. He still had it after all these years. I held it to my breast. Words could not express what I felt. "Would you tie it in my hair, please? My fingers just can't do it any-more."

"Yes, I'd be happy to," she replied. "You know, my father loved you."

Yes, I knew. And I think he knew I loved him, too.

Continuity

Elmer Kelton

In this beautiful, quiet story about a family ranch and the generations who inherit it, Elmer Kelton turns to one of his favorite themes, the seamless traditions of stockgrowing. "My point in this story," he writes, "is that each generation takes what has been given by previous generations and enlarges upon it. When we are young we tend to embrace new ideas and welcome change. As we become older we tend to become more and more resistant to change and cling to the familiar And perhaps that is as it should be. . . ." This story, like so much of Kelton's work, transcends the material world and plunges us into values and beliefs, and understandings of how the world should be. "Continuity" first appeared in Louis L'Amour Western Magazine *in 1995. It departs from the traditional western action story, focusing on human relationships. Elmer Kelton has won six Spur Awards, more than any other author, and is among the most respected and honored novelists in western literature.*

Ed Whitley would always remember where he was and what he was doing when the old man had his heart attack: in the dusty corrals behind the barn, preg-checking a set of Bar W black baldy heifers.

It was not a dignified job for a cowboy who would much rather be on horseback, doing something else—anything else. It was not the pastoral western scene depicted on calendars or Christmas cards, and certainly not the stuff of song and story. It was messy work and smelled a little, but it had become an economic necessity of life for a rancher in a time of tight or negative profit margins. A dollar saved was better than a dollar earned, for it was not subject to income tax.

To Ed's knowledge, his father had had no previous indications that a coronary was imminent. If there had been, the old man had remained tight-lipped about them. Tom Whitley had always regarded aches and pains as a personal affront, to be borne in silence. To complain was to give them importance.

Ed's probing fingers had just confirmed the presence of a developing calf when he saw Tom fall against the steel squeeze chute, one hand grasping for a rail, the other clutching at his chest. The old man's eyes were wide in surprise and pain and confusion, his mouth open for a cry that choked off before it started. Ed jerked his arm free and ripped off the shoulder-length plastic glove that had covered his hand and sleeve. He caught Tom and eased him to a sitting position on the ground.

Ed's grown son Clay vaulted over the crowding-pen fence and came running, along with ranch hand Miguel Cervantes.

The old man wheezed, "I'm all right. It's just that sausage I had for breakfast."

Ed knew better. He had seen that look before, when his neighbor Alex Hawkins had collapsed and died at the bankruptcy auction that sold out his cattle and rolling stock two years ago.

"Help me get him to the pickup," he shouted.

He had never understood how doctors could have such a dispassionate attitude in the face of suffering and human mortality. With no more emotion than if he was reading the cafeteria menu, the emergency-room doctor confirmed Ed's opinion that his father had suffered a heart attack.

"We will not know the extent of muscle damage or blockage until we have done an angiogram. We must assume, though, that it has been severe. I do not wish to sound alarmist, but you had better prepare yourself and your family for the worst."

"Dad's got a constitution like a horse. He hasn't had a sick day in his life, hardly."

"With an eighty-year-old heart, it may take only one."

Tom was eighty-two, if one wished to be technical about it, but he acted as if he was twenty or thirty years younger. He rode more miles a-horseback than Ed and far more than Clay, who lived in town and held down an eight-hours-a-day job at the feed mill. Clay helped at the ranch on weekends.

Tom persisted in wrestling fifty-pound feed sacks two at a time when Ed was not looking. Somewhere in his sixties he seemed to have made up his mind not to get any older, but not to die, either. He had gotten away with it, except for a little arthritis in his joints that occasionally forced him into minor retreat but never into surrender. He had also come into increasing reliance on reading glasses. But he still ate beef for dinner and supper every day, using his own teeth.

In the back of his mind Ed had known his father could not live forever, but he had never allowed himself to dwell upon that. He could not visualize the ranch without Tom Whitley. From Ed's earliest memories, Tom and the home place had been one and the same, inseparable. Tom's father, Ed's grandfather, had acquired the nucleus of the ranch around the turn of the century, homesteading four sections under Texas law. Tom had been born there and over the years had more than doubled the size of the place. With Ed's help he had cleared the land debt so that the ranch now was free and clear.

"Ready to pass on, without no encumbrance," Tom had said when they paid the final note. But Tom had shown no inclination to pass it on. Now Ed had to face the shattering probability that the time had come. Nothing would ever again be as it had been. He could see no continuity between the past and the future. Losing Tom would be like cutting a tree off from its roots.

They moved Tom into the intensive care unit. The hospital had rules about visitation, but it was lax on enforcement in regard to family members. Ed never asked permission to stay in the room with his father, and nobody contested him. For a long time Tom seemed to be asleep. He was hooked to a monitor, its green screen showing heartbeats as a series of bobbles up and down from a straight line. Ed would watch the screen awhile, then stare at Tom, forcing up old memories as if he had to retrieve them now or lose them as he was losing his father. Most were pleasant, or at least benign.

He could not remember a great deal about his grandfather. The face that came to his mind's eye owed more to old photographs than to life. He knew that Morgan Whitley had come of age in the waning years of the great trail drives and the open range. The ranch's outside fence still retained segments of the original wire and posts that Morgan had installed some ninety years ago, though the toll of time had caused most to be rebuilt in recent years. Even when replacing it, Tom and Ed had coiled and saved some of the rusty old wire and hung it on the barn wall as a keepsake, for Morgan's strong hands had once gripped it. A lively imagination could fantasize that his fingerprints were still fixed upon the steel strands.

Many ranches had unbroken family ownership into the third, fourth, and fifth generations. It conveyed, in a peculiar way, a sort of immortality to those who had gone on. This continuity fostered a reverence for the land as if it were a living member of the family. It engendered in the later generations a strong urge to protect and improve rather than to mine the land for immediate gain at the expense of the future.

But Ed feared for that continuity when Tom was gone. Tom's boots made big tracks, as his father's had before him. Ed felt inadequate to fill them. His life had been relatively easy compared to Tom's and to Morgan's. Most of the building had been completed before he had come of age. He had inherited the fruit without having to dig through the rock and plant the tree.

This was Saturday, so Clay was not on duty at the mill. He had remained at the corrals to finish the day's job. It was an unwritten tenet of ranch life that not even an emergency should interrupt work in progress if any alternative was available. Ed arose from the hard chair as Clay, and Ed's wife, Frances, came into the room. Neither asked aloud, for they could not be certain that Tom would not hear. Ed answered just as silently with a shrug of his shoulders, followed by a solemn shaking of his head. Frances slipped her arm around his waist, offering him emotional support. Clay said his young wife, Susan, was downstairs with their five-year-old son. The hospital did not allow children into ICU.

Clay moved close to his grandfather's bedside and stared down gravely into the lined face that had been a part of his daily life as far back as memory went. Tears welled into his eyes.

When Ed had been a boy, Tom had been demanding of him—often unreasonably demanding, in Ed's view. He remembered a time when Tom had taken a dislike to Ed's way of mounting a horse and had made him practice getting on and off until Ed had thought his legs would collapse. Tom had drilled him mercilessly in the art of roping, making him do it over and over, day after day, until he rarely missed a loop. Not until years later did Tom confide that his own father had done the same thing to him. It was not enough to pass on property. It was necessary to pass on knowledge and skills if the property was to have meaning and continuity.

Tom had mellowed by the time his grandson had come along. He had shown infinitely more patience in teaching Clay the cowboy trade. At those rare times when discipline was called for, Tom had walked away and left that painful duty to Ed.

Odd, Ed thought, how sometimes the further apart people were in age, the closer they seemed in their relationships with one another.

The boy had learned diligently, polishing the horseback skills passed down from his great-grandfather Morgan through Tom, then through Ed and finally to Clay.

Frontier realities had limited Morgan Whitley's formal schooling to a couple of years, though he had acquired a liberal education in the school of practical experience, with graduate honors in hard knocks. Better times had allowed Tom to finish high school before turning to a full-time career as a working cowpuncher and eventual partnership with his father.

Ed, the third generation, had gone on to earn a degree in animal husbandry at Texas A&M. It was an accomplishment Tom had always regarded with a conflicting mixture of pride and distrust. "Most of what I know about a cow," he had often declared, "you ain't goin' to find in no Aggie textbook."

Tom's eyelids fluttered awhile before he opened his eyes, blinking as his vision adjusted itself to the fluorescent lights of the hospital room. He focused first on Ed and Frances, then let his gaze drift to Clay. At first he seemed confused about his surroundings. Ed grasped his father's hand to keep him from tearing loose the tube that fed him glucose.

Anyone else might have asked how he had come to be where he was or what kind of shape he was in, but not Tom. He had always been one to take care of business first. "You-all finish with them heifers?"

Clay said, "We did, Granddad—Miguel and me. They were all settled but three."

"Hell of a note, stoppin' work to rush me in here like this when there wasn't nothin' wrong except that sausage. I could tell the minute I ate it . . ."

Ed said, "It's a lot more than the sausage. Doctor says it's your heart." He stopped there. He thought it best not to tell his father how serious his condition really was unless it became necessary to prevent him from climbing out of bed. It would be like Tom to get in the pickup and head for the ranch in his hospital gown if they wouldn't give him his shirt and Levi's.

Tom grumbled, "Probably just overdone myself workin' that squeeze chute. Never did see that we need to preg-test those heifers. You can tell soon enough which ones come up heavy with calf and which ones don't."

Ed could have told him, as he had before, that checking the heifers early for pregnancy allowed for culling of the slow breeders before they had time to run up an unnecessary feed bill. Moreover, high fertility was a heritable characteristic. The early breeders were the kind a rancher wanted to keep in his herd, for they passed that trait on to their offspring. The slow ones were a drag on the bottom line.

But to Tom, that had always been an Aggie textbook notion. He distrusted selection judgments based on records or mechanical measurements. He preferred to rely upon his eyes.

He had not thought much of artificial insemination either, when Ed had first brought it to the ranch.

Tom had not always been so reluctant to try new ideas. Neither, for that matter, had Ed's grandfather Morgan, up to a point. Though Morgan had been a product of the open range, he had built a barbed-wire fence around the perimeter of his holdings as soon as he had been financially able to buy cedar posts and wire. That had allowed him to keep his own cattle in and his neighbors' out. He had gradually upgraded the quality of his herd through use of better sires without his cows being subject to the amorous attentions of inferior stray bulls.

But as the years went by, Morgan had become increasingly conservative, content with things as they were and quick to reject the innovations of a younger generation. He had looked askance upon the advent of the automobile and truck as tools of the ranching trade. He argued that anything he needed could be carried by a good wagon and team. As for cattle and horses, they could walk anywhere it was needful for them to go; they didn't have to be hauled.

He and his son had almost come to a fistfight over Tom's purchase of a light truck. In time he became accepting enough to ride in a truck or car, but to the end he stubbornly refused to place his hands on the wheel of one.

Tom often told about building his first horse trailer. He had long wished for a way to eliminate the waste of time involved in riding horseback to a far corner of the ranch to do a job, then returning home the same slow way. It took longer to get there and back than to do the work. He acquired the chassis of a wrecked Model-T and stripped it down to the wheels and frame. Atop this he built a three-sided wooden box with a gate in the rear. Crude though it was, it could haul two horses, pulled by the truck.

Morgan had ridiculed the idea. "First thing you know, you'll never see a cowboy ridin' anymore, or a horse walkin'."

Gradually, however, the horse trailer became a regular and accepted fact of survival in the ranching business. It allowed more work to be done in less time and with less labor.

Through thrift and careful borrowing, Tom had managed to add on to the ranch, each addition and each mortgage coming over Morgan's strong objections and predictions of imminent ruin. He had brought a telephone to the ranch, and a gasoline-driven generator to furnish limited 32-volt power so the two houses and the barn could have electric lights. He had even bought Morgan a radio in hopes it would keep his widowed father from feeling so lonely when he sat alone at night in the original old ranch house. At least, he argued, Morgan could keep up with the world news.

"You're wastin' your money," Morgan had declared. "I won't ever listen to the thing. I won't even turn it on."

Tom had often delighted in telling about the time a few weeks later when conversation somehow turned to country music, and old Morgan exclaimed, "Say, that Uncle Dave Macon can sure play the banjo, can't he?"

The aging open-range cowboy had died just before the outbreak of World War II, leaving Tom to run the ranch after his own lights. Tom had sometimes wondered aloud how his father would have reacted to the technological innovations that war and its aftermath had wrought upon the ranching industry.

Tom had cross-fenced the ranch for better control of grazing. He had replaced the generator with REA electricity. But in time he had settled into the same brand of conservatism as his father when it came to modern innovations. He treated with skepticism many of the ideas Ed brought home from A&M.

"Aggie textbook notions," he would snort. Some he accepted after a time. Others he never did.

Despite heavy medication, Tom awoke in the early morning hours, as he was accustomed to doing at home. Ed's back ached from sitting up all night in the straight hard-backed chair. He suspected that hospitals purposely installed uncomfortable furniture to discourage visitors from staying too long. Tom stared at his son with concern in his eyes.

"You ever get anything to eat last night?"

"I slipped away for a bite with Frances while Clay was here."

"You better go and get you some breakfast, else you'll be the one sick in here instead of me."

"Later. I don't want to miss seein' the doctor."

"Ain't no doctor goin' to show up this early unless he's still here this late."

"I'll be all right."

Tom stared at him awhile. "Sure, you'll be all right. Ever since you were old enough to straddle a horse, I've been tryin' to get you ready for this. Now it's come time, ready or not."

Ed realized his father was not just thinking about Ed's immediate need for nourishment. "Don't you be talkin' thataway. You'll be out of here in a few days if you'll do what they tell you."

"I'm goin' out of here in that long black wagon. We both know that. I could feel old St. Peter breathin' on my neck half the night. But you'll be all right. What you goin' to do about Clay?"

"What's there to do about him?"

"You'll have to talk him into leavin' that piddlin' job at the mill. You'll need his help full-time when I'm gone."

Ed's throat tightened painfully. He did not want to talk about this, but Tom was persistent. He seemed to sense that he did not have a lot of time to get the talking done.

Tom said, "He's a good boy, even if he *has* got some newfangled ideas. Some of them'll work, and some won't. You'll have to get a feel for how tight to hold the reins, and how loose, same as I did with you and my daddy did with me."

Ed did not know how to reply. It hurt too much to acknowledge what Tom was saying. "You'll come through this all right," he said, though the words were hollow. He knew differently, and so did Tom.

Tom said, "That's the way of the world. It's up to the young ones to keep movin' forward, and up to the older ones to keep the young from runnin' the train off of the track. And it's why the old have to pass out of the picture, so the train won't come to a stop altogether and maybe even slide back down the hill."

"Things wouldn't ever be the same out there without you."

"They ain't meant to be. If my daddy had had his

way, we'd still be drivin' cattle afoot to the railroad.
If *his* daddy had had his way, there wouldn't even be
no railroad. We don't none of us—old or young—ever
have it just the way we'd want it, and that's probably a good thing."

Though some ranchers saw Sunday as just another
day for work—it seemed there never were enough
days to do it all—Tom Whitley had always accepted
Sunday as a day of rest. It was fitting, Ed thought
later, that on a Sunday he slipped away into his final
rest. Helplessly Ed watched the monitor screen as the
line jumped violently up and down, then flattened.
The most strenuous efforts of doctor and nurses could
not alter the inexorable course of nature.

Frances was with Ed at the end, and so was Clay.
It helped, not having to face this dark moment alone.

Ed said quietly, "I don't know how we'll survive
without him, son."

"What did he do when *his* dad died?"

"He picked himself up and went his own way."

Clay gently laid a hand on his father's shoulder.
"Then that's what we'll do."

The return to the ranch after the funeral was one
of the most trying ordeals of Ed's life. He tried to find
comfort in the fact that nothing physical had changed.
The entrance gate, the headquarters layout, all looked
the same as he drove in. Four horses stood near the
barn, waiting for someone to fork hay into the steel
rack. Either Tom or Ed customarily did so in the late
afternoon. A jersey milk cow stood outside the milk-
pen gate, patiently awaiting the bucket of ground feed
that would be poured for her as she took her place

in the stanchion. All these things were the same as they had been for years and years. In these, at least, there was constancy.

But Tom's red dog, tail wagging, came out to meet the car. It watched Ed and Frances get out, then looked expectantly for its master. It turned away, its tail drooping in disappointment. It retreated toward the house where Tom had lived since Ed's mother had died, and Tom had turned the larger, newer house over to Ed and Frances. Ed watched the dog and felt anew the pain of loss.

"We'll have to get Red used to comin' to our house for his supper," he said.

Frances nodded. "It'll take him a while to quit missin' Tom."

Ed winced. "I doubt I ever will."

The dog never did become accustomed to staying around the bigger house. It did not have to. Clay resigned his job at the feed mill, and he and Susan moved into Tom's house. Though it was old and still bore much of Morgan Whitley's imprint, as well as Tom's, it had most of the modern conveniences that a town girl like Susan was used to.

Clay's being around all the time helped Ed's adjustment to the change. Before, Ed had tried to see to it that he and Miguel did the heavier and more menial work, leaving the lighter chores for Tom. Now Clay and Miguel took on most of the heavier lifting, and Ed found himself doing more of the things that Tom had regarded as his own province. Ed resented it a little at first, though he kept his feelings to himself. It seemed they now considered him an old man

who had to be sheltered. He was not old, not by a
damn sight. But after a time he began to appreciate
their deference. His back did not hurt as much as it
used to, and he found himself able to spend more
time on horseback, riding over the country the way
he liked to do.

It warmed Ed's soul, too, to look toward the older
house and see Clay's boy Billy riding a stick horse in
the front yard. It was high time, Ed thought, to find
a pony so the boy could start learning to ride. Billy's
cowboy education had been neglected in town. Ed
would get him a rope, too, and a plastic steer head
to attach to a bale of hay so he could learn to throw
a loop around the horns.

Ed sensed that something had begun to nag at Clay.
His son became subject to long periods of thoughtful
silence, as if he had something on his mind that he
was reluctant to voice.

Whatever the problem was, Ed decided the time
had come to bring it into the open air. One possibility had occurred to him early. "Is it Susan and that
house? I know it's old, and I guess it's got Dad's brand
all over it. My granddad's, too. But she's welcome to
redo it any way she wants to. It's her house now."

Clay seemed surprised at the thought. "The house
is fine. She loves it. We like the idea that we're the
fourth generation of Whitleys that's lived in it, and
Billy's the fifth. It's like they're all still with us, that
nobody's gone."

Ed wished he could see it that way. Tom *was* gone.
The root had been severed. The feeling of continuum
was lost.

"Well, if it's not the house, what's the trouble?"

Clay frowned, and he took a while in bringing himself to answer. "I've been workin' on an idea. I've been kind of shy about bringin' it up because I don't know how you'll take it."

"Spill it, and we'll find out."

"You've heard them talk about cell grazin' plans, where they take a pasture and fence it up into twelve or fifteen small paddocks. They throw all their cattle onto one at a time and move them every two or three days. That way most of the ranch is restin', and the grass has a chance to grow. It makes for a healthier range."

Ed could only stare at him.

Clay took a sheet of paper from his shirt pocket and unfolded it. Ed recognized a pencil-drawn map of the ranch. Clay placed a finger on the spot that marked the headquarters. "I've figured how we can divide up all our pastures with cheap electric fence and have ourselves four grazin' cells. It's worked on lots of other ranches."

"But this isn't some other ranch." Ed's impatience bubbled to the top. He could imagine Morgan's or Tom's reaction to such a far-fetched idea. "Where did you ever come up with such a radical notion—some Aggie textbook?"

Aggie textbook! Ed wondered for a moment how that expression had popped into his head. Then he remembered. He had heard it from Tom—more times than he wanted to recall.

Looking deflated, Clay studied the paper. "I've had the idea for a long while. I knew better than to try it on Granddad, but I thought you might give it a chance."

"He would've said what I did."

"In the same voice, and the same words, more than likely." Clay managed a wry smile through his disappointment. "You even look like him at a little distance. Funny, you were worried that things could never be the same with Granddad gone. But you've fitted right into his boots."

Ed pondered on what Tom had said about it being the responsibility of the young to originate fresh ideas while the old held the reins, loosening or tightening them as the need came.

Ed compromised, as Tom often had. "Tell you what: We'll try your idea, but we'll go at it slow. We'll take the northeast pasture first and see how it works out. In two or three years, if we like it, we'll talk about doin' the rest of the place. This is a drastic change you're throwin' at me."

"As drastic as Granddad buyin' the first truck, or buildin' the first trailer? Or you startin' artificial insemination and preg-checkin'?"

Ed stared toward the old house. Billy was in the front yard, playing with the red dog. Red had taken right up with the boy, tagging along with him as he had tagged after Tom. Ed thought about Tom, and about Morgan Whitley. The word came to him from somewhere. "Continuity."

Clay puzzled. "What do you mean, continuity?"

"Just thinkin' about somethin' your granddad said. I'll tell you someday, when it's time for you to think about it."

All or Nothing

Gary Svee

Gary Svee is the opinion page editor of the Billings
Gazette, *as well as a Spur Award–winning western
novelist. His Passion for the West and for Montana
history simply doesn't fit into the traditional western story, so he ranges far afield, writing unortho-
dox, tender, and powerful stories about the people
who came west, or the people who were here before
Europeans showed up. There is a profound spiritual
element in each of his novels, as well as a special car-
ing for struggling, oppressed, and desperate people
settling a hard land. Hand and hand with that is a
wry humor that threads his stories, gently poking fun
at human folly. His Norwegian roots show up in this
story of the Great Depression, and to what lengths
people went just to put food on the table. He tells me
that this memorable and haunting story, set in the
early thirties, is essentially true and a part of his own
family history.*

They stood in light spilling from the front window
of the Board of Trade Cafe. Lars had come earlier than most, nodding to some of the regulars as
they arrived. "Cold," one said, the word riding a cloud

of vapor into the light. Nobody replied, words too precious to waste in the brittle air. Every day they came to this corner in the dark—bank clerks, insurance salesmen, farmers and railroad workers, all caught in the winter of their Depression.

A farm truck, black as the men's prospects, edged to the curb, idling as the man inside evaluated the circle of men. The window squeaked down, and the man peered out. Light and shadow the face was, eyes hidden from the men.

"Picking beets," the man growled, his voice colder even than the air that crept under the men's collars. "Two dollars a day and soup. All or nothing."

All or nothing. Bet your body could hold this old man's pace for a day. Win and you got two dollars. Lose and you got nothing.

Lars stepped away from the other men and into the light. He was shorter than most of the men there, but stocky, shoulders broadened in hard work on a farm lost to the Depression. He stared at the man in the truck until the man nodded, and then he climbed into the truck's box. The others followed. The bet was on.

The truck carved its way through the Arctic air, and the men tried to turn themselves inside out. The cold played with them as a small child might play with a kitten, not realizing the cruelty of poking fingers into bright eyes. Icy fingers reached under their collars, stinging their faces and turning their ears numb. They tried not to pay attention to the cold. They had work for the day—all or nothing.

The truck stopped and the men dropped to the ground. Hard as concrete it was and unyielding as poverty and hunger. Other trucks were there, the red dots of glowing cigarettes the only sign of life in their cabs.

"Get at it," growled the boss man, and the men danced in the trucks' headlights, bowing to the beets, pirouetting as they threw the frozen roots into the beds of the trucks. When they slowed, when the cold and the pain of their backs made them hesitate a moment, the son of a bitch leaned out the window of the truck's heated cab, yelling at them as he might exhort horses to pit their muscles against a stubborn cottonwood stump.

First light gave them hope. Maybe the day would warm. Maybe the old man would see that they could break, too, just like the beet picker slumped at the edge of the field, its steel back broken by frozen gumbo.

But the old man drove them as he had driven the beet picker, and they broke, too, slumping into the snow covering the field. Some lay too exhausted to move. Others twitched as the muscle spasms twisted their backs. The son of a bitch left them lying where they fell, leaking out their warmth into the snow.

All or nothing, the son of a bitch had said when he leaned out of the truck window and into the morning's darkness. All or nothing.

The casualties stiffened the resolve of the remaining farmers and clerks and barkeeps and bankers. They would show him that the Depression hadn't brittled their backs. They would show that son of a bitch, and ease the knot in their bellies where breakfast should have been.

But as the morning drew on, more men fell. Walking casualties rose then from the smoking fires at the edges of the field to help. The rescuers had no words to share, just a shoulder to cling to as the fallen made their way to the fires.

At noon the women came. They moved among the men, fueling them with soup steaming feebly in the cold. Mostly water, it was, with an occasional piece of potato or a slice of carrot swimming in the tepid water. Still, Lars felt guilty drinking it, knowing that Inga would likely have nothing, saving what little they had for dinner.

Lars stared at the ground as he ate his soup, not wanting to catch the eyes of the men watching from the edges of the field. He didn't want them to share their shame with him. All or nothing, it was, and they had nothing.

He dropped his chin to his chest, easing the muscles of his neck. He rose, swaying a little on the uneven ground. He carried his bowl of soup to a group huddled around a little campfire at the edge of the field, offering his bowl to the men. A young man took the soup, his hands shaking with the cold or his need for nourishment.

The son of a bitch screamed from the cab of the truck. "I am not feeding those men."

Lars turned to stare at the truck. "I am."

The son of a bitch's eyes roved over the field, measuring the number of men still on the field. He muttered something that Lars couldn't hear, and his head disappeared behind the rising window.

Lars stepped back into the field. "We came here to work," he shouted at the truck. "Let us work."

His hands died sometime that afternoon, his fingers giving up to the cold and going away. So he pressed his dead hands against the beets with the strength of his shoulders, throwing the roots awkwardly into the beds of the trucks.

He thought he might die that afternoon, abandoning the Earth as the sun had. But he would have to stop working to die, and he couldn't do that. Not with that son of a bitch watching him through the truck window, not with Inga waiting in the cabin.

Then in the darkness, the trucks stopped. He lined up with the other men to walk past the black truck, past the thin arm reaching into the darkness. He stared into the eyes of the son of a bitch as he took the silver dollars, and the son of a bitch looked away, muttering that there would be half a day's work tomorrow.

He didn't remember the ride back to the Board of Trade Cafe. He must have fallen asleep, hands shoved under his arms so that the warmth of his body would drive the frost away.

The dollars felt heavy in his pocket as he walked along the lane toward their home. They were hundred-pound sacks of potatoes and flour. They were a little bacon and maybe a doctor for Inga.

The door scuffed as he opened it, and the heat from the Majestic felt like the kiss of the summer sun. Inga was standing beside the table, a pan of soup in her hand.

"You found work," she said, as she might whisper a prayer in church.

Lars nodded. "Two dollars," he said, reaching into his pockets with fingers still sore from frostbite.

She reached behind her for the tin can on the back

of the stove. He dropped the coins into the can one at a time, enjoying the delight on his wife's face.

"You feel better?"

She nodded.

"You don't look so yellow."

"Yellow jaundice. Mrs. Smith said I had yellow jaundice. She said it would go away."

"Now that we have the money, I think you should see the doctor."

She shook her head.

Lars stood at the stove, washing his hands and face and neck, trying to get the stain of the day off him.

The two settled into the table, taking each other's hands, and he said, *"Takk for maten,"* thanking God for the food He had placed on their table.

"I have half a day of work tomorrow, too," Lars said, smiling at his wife. She beamed, and he thrust his spoon into the bowl. Bean soup. Good soup. His eyebrows crawled up his forehead with each bite, as though each bean were an explosion of flavor. When his spoon could glean no more nourishment from the bowl, he took a piece of bread and wiped the bottom clean.

Inga toyed with her soup. Her portion had been smaller than Lars', and she struggled to eat even that.

"I think you should go to the doctor."

"No, I'll be fine. Mrs. Smith said I would be fine."

She sat at the table, her head downcast. "Lars, I think I know why I am sick."

He stared across the table at her.

"I think it was that sugar beet."

It had seemed like a gift that morning, lying at the corner of the lane as she walked down to check the mailbox. How could it have been placed precisely beside their mailbox if God had not meant for them to have it? So she had carried it back to the house, washing it and peeling it and cutting it into thin slices. She simmered the slices on the stove all day, tasting the sweetness draining from the beet into the broth.

Syrup it would be, with a little of the brown sugar they still had. When they next had eggs, she would make French bread and surprise Lars with the syrup. But as the day went on, she found herself eating the slices of the beet, the boiling water rendering its woodiness edible. The next day, she was sick. It had to be the beet.

Inga looked down in her lap, then her back stiffened and she looked Lars full in the eyes. "I think God was testing me," she said. "I think he wanted to know if I would steal something that didn't belong to me."

Lars reached across the table, taking both of his wife's hands in his own. "That beet fell beside the mailbox. It didn't belong to anyone."

"It didn't belong to me."

"Who would you have returned it to? Would you have stopped every truck, asking them if they had lost one of their beets? Don't be silly."

Inga's smile didn't quite reach across the table, falling wanly amid the dinner dishes.

"Why did I get sick, then?"

"I don't know. That's the reason I want you to see a doctor."

Inga pulled her hands away from Lars, clenching them to her lips, her elbows digging into her breasts. "I think maybe God wants to take my child from me. Maybe he doesn't want my child to have a thief for a mother."

Tears spilled from her eyes, falling on her clenched fists.

Lars stepped around the table, kneeling beside his wife, taking her into his arms. She cried then, her face falling to her husband's shoulder.

"It will be fine, Inga. Everything will be fine. I got work today."

Inga smiled at him, but the tears still hid her eyes from him.

"Yes, you got work. What did you do?"

"I picked beets."

"Oh, Lars. . . ."

He rushed to explain. "The machine broke, the picker. So we picked beets. It was a blessing, Inga."

"He was a good man, the man who hired you?"

The muscles clenched in Lars' jaws. "No, he has no heart."

Inga nodded. She was silent for some time, and when she spoke her voice was little more than a whisper. "Maybe he has more heart than you think, Lars. Maybe he's afraid he will lose his farm. You know how you felt when they came to take our farm."

Lars looked at her for a long moment, remembering as the sheriff's deputies had taken each of his milch cows, each named and coddled. They had loaded them mooing into a truck, and Lars had wondered if they would live to see the calves they carried.

Lars remembered the deputies going through his home, taking those things they thought had value and piling the rest in the yard to burn. The spinning wheel

from Norway, decorated with his grandmother's rose-
maling, had been burned. Nearly everything had gone
into the burning pile.

All those years of hard work, the early mornings
and the late nights, raising sheep and tilling the silty
river-bottom soil, encouraging it to yield a living,
burned in that fire, too. Inga and he had left the farm
with only their clothing and the family Bible with en-
tries going back to the old country.

"Yes," Lars said. "I remember."

He rose, then, stepping to the door. He leaned over,
picking up a gunnysack. "I found coal today along
the railroad track, maybe enough to last all night."

Inga beamed. "That's good. We will be warm and
cozy, tonight." She stepped to the bedroom door,
opening it. Cold air rushed into the kitchen, ruffling
the hem of her skirt.

"You know it is cold when even the air rushes to
the stove to warm itself." Her attempt at humor
brought a smile to Lars's face. "We put this coal in
the stove, and it will warm up soon enough."

Lars stepped into the bedroom—a lean-to, really—
pitched against the north side of the house. It was
cold there, cold enough for him to see his breath
against the kitchen's light. He stepped out of his
clothes, leaving them in a heap on the floor. He shivered, wondering if he would ever really be warm
again.

A moment later, he heard the last of the dinner
dishes clatter from the washbasin to the sideboard.
The lights went out as Lars climbed into bed, dread-
ing the touch of cold sheets. Inga joined him, and he

wrapped himself around her back, each warming the other.

"Lars?" The word drew him back from the edge of sleep.

"Yes."

"Mrs. Smith said they would be hiring people this spring to work on trails in the Beartooth Mountains. I know how you feel about the government, but the pay would be steady and . . ."

"No." The word came gruffly, final.

"But . . ."

"Inga, do you want me to work for the people who took our farm?"

Inga could feel her husband tossing on the bed, all thought of sleep driven from his mind.

"They had a job last week," Lars said. "You know what it was?" No.

"Killing sheep. They would have paid me to kill sheep and burn them. They do that so the price of mutton and wool won't fall any further. Do you think I could kill and burn sheep when I know how many people are hungry? Do you think I could do that when I know the wool could be carded and spun and knit into clothing to keep children warm? I'm sorry, Inga, I can't work for people who do things like that."

Lars felt his wife shudder, and he pulled himself tighter to her, willing the warmth of his body to warm hers.

"I have work, Inga. I had work today, and I have half a day of work tomorrow. God will take care of us. He always does."

"Yes," Inga said. "He always does." But a tear dropped to Lars's arm where Inga lay her head.

Lars stood in line, waiting his turn at the window of the black truck. Not so many men had come this morning, and not so many men had fallen. So the old man was paying nearly everyone. One dollar for seven hours of work.

Lars' eyes roved over the field, remembering a particularly stubborn beet there, the frost of the field unwilling to yield its prize. There the young man had fallen, the young man he had shared his soup with. The boy didn't come today, and Lars sighed, a cloud of vapor marking the gesture.

They had done this thing, picked the field clean. Lars felt good about that, a general sense of satisfaction almost erasing the ache of his bones and muscles. But then his revery was broken. On the other side, near the windbreak of Russian olive, one beet lay still under its cover of snow.

He looked away and then looked back. The beet was still there, no figment of his imagination. The beet irritated him, representing a job undone. People had worked hard on this field. They had suffered cold and pain to pick this field clean, and the work was not done, not with that one beet lying on the other side of the field.

Lars sighed and willed his feet to move, to leave his place in the line. He stumbled as he walked across the frozen clods, catching himself before he fell. The beet was frozen into the ground as solidly as though it had been welded there. He kicked at it until it broke free. Lars carried the root back to the truck, throwing it on the top of the load.

Maybe that would return the beet Inga had found. Maybe God would make her well now.

The work was done. Lars took his place at the end and waited his turn at the window of the truck with the skinny arm and the face he had seen only in the darkness. Two dollars yesterday and one today. Three dollars. They would have enough to buy food. Maybe he would buy something special for Inga, some of those mints she liked so well. The two of them would walk into the grocery story with real money in their pockets, and the hard looks of the clerks would soften.

Lars stepped up to the window and the arm came out. Two dollars! The old man had given him two dollars. It was a mistake and it would be dishonest to keep the second coin, so he handed it back. The old man shook his head. His mouth opened but no words came, and he gave the dollar back to Lars. Lars stared at him and nodded. Inga was right. The old man had a heart. He just kept it hidden under the worry for his farm.

Lars stepped to the back of the truck and an arm reached out. He took the hand and pulled himself into the back of the truck.

Five miles isn't so far, Lars told himself, not even with fifty pounds of flour and fifty pounds of potatoes on his shoulders. The gunnysack of potatoes and the cloth sack of flour bracketed his head, giving him pillows for his stiff neck.

He walked on, the snow squeaking its protest. Cold, he thought, when the snow cries out. The sun was bright but without warmth, like an icicle held up to a lamp. But the cold didn't seem to sting so much on a sunny day.

Lars would have liked Inga to come with him, to

visit the Andersons, but she was still feeling a little
light-headed. Her color was back, but she said she
didn't feel up to a five-mile walk. Lars was beginning
to wonder if he were up to the walk when he spotted the Anderson place.

Smoke was streaming from the kitchen. That was
good. That meant they were home, and they had wood
to burn. Soon they would have potatoes and flour. If
Bertha Anderson had some cream, maybe she would
make some lefse. That would be good.

The Anderson place might have been built from
the same plan as Lars and Inga's, had there been any
plan. One room for kitchen, living room, and parlor.
Another room for Axel and Bertha's bedroom. George
Holmstad slept in the kitchen.

Lars smiled. They would be pleased to have the
potatoes and flour. He turned into the lane and crossed
the dry irrigation ditch, separating the home from the
county road out front. He frowned as he stepped into
the yard. A drag trail of crushed snow, spotted with
pink and red, marked the way to a willow thicket farther down the ditch.

They had shot a deer, Axel probably, George's feet
being what they were. Shooting deer out of season
and without licenses was not thought of as an evil.
Surely the animals were a gift from God for his hungry people. But the state thought otherwise. Killing
the king's deer was a serious matter, made more so
by that game warden, Alvin Oswald.

Lars's concern grew as he followed the spoor toward the house. Deer hair was scattered here and
there, and a pile of pink snow marked where Axel
had scoured the creature's gut cavity with snow.

This was bad. The neighbors would have heard the shot. They might have seen Axel dragging the deer. Someone might have reported Axel to that game warden.

Lars's teeth ground together. That man had no heart. He liked to hurt people. He strutted around in his uniform like a little king. That damn government paid him more than he was worth. He didn't have to choose between starvation and killing a deer out of season.

Bertha stepped from the house, carrying a bag of steaming laundry to hang on the line. How clothing froze and then dried was beyond Lars's understanding, but it did and that was all that mattered.

She looked up and saw Lars, throwing her head back in a nod that would have to take the place of a wave, her arms being weighed down with laundry.

"Go on in," she called. "They're both in there. I'll be there in a minute."

Lars nodded. He stepped to the door, shifting the flour and potatoes to one arm before knocking. Axel answered the door, smiling with delight at seeing his friend.

"*Velkommen*," Axel said, and Lars smiled at his friend's language lapse. They lived in America now, and they would speak English. They reminded themselves of that constantly.

George was sitting in a chair by the stove, his feet wrapped in shreds of an old sheet. He smiled, too, but the smile didn't have energy enough to color his face.

"Axel, George," Lars said. "I brought you some potatoes and some flour."

"You have work?"

"A day and a half, picking beets."

"I should have come."

"How many days have we stood there in the dark? How could you have known the day that a truck would come?"

"I didn't, but . . ."

"It looks as though you've been busy, anyway."

Axel blanched. "What do you mean?"

"The deer you killed. You left too much sign. I told you, you should carry the deer back. Not leave a drag trail. Your neighbors. Would they . . . ?"

"I don't know. They might report me if they thought Oswald would give them a break."

"That son of a bitch doesn't give anyone a break."

"Maybe they don't know him as well as we do."

"He sure as hell doesn't know us as well as he would like to," Lars said, grinning.

"No, he would like to have us in jail for about six months so he could talk to us every day."

The two laughed, and Lars turned to George. "How are your feet?"

"They're fine. I think they're getting better."

But Lars saw Axel shake his head.

Lars stepped toward George, and he pulled his feet under the chair, wincing with the effort.

Lars kneeled in front of his friend, but he didn't have to remove the bandages to know what was happening. George's feet had the smell of rotting flesh.

"Inga and me have got some money now. Maybe you should come with me to see the doctor."

George shook his head. "I couldn't walk that far. Just walking to the outhouse . . ."

"Maybe I could carry you. Axel, do you still have that wheelbarrow?"

"No, I had to sell it. We didn't have anything to . . . I didn't need it. Not 'til now, anyway."

"Axel and me could take turns carrying you. We could get you to town in no time."

"No, I'm not going to town like that."

Lars whispered, "George, if you don't get those feet looked at, you're going to lose them. How are you going to work if you have no feet?"

"I haven't been working, anyway. Axel and Bertha have been taking care of me as though I were a baby." George shook his head. "I can't keep doing that. I just can't."

Lars stared into his friend's eye. He stood abruptly, separating himself from the truth he had seen written there.

Bertha returned from hanging her wash on the line, gasping in delight when she saw the flour and potatoes, "You play cards," she told the men. "I'll fix something to eat. Then we'll all play some whist."

Lars pushed himself back from the table. "I better be going home. Inga will be wondering what happened to me. Besides, I think that George, he's been dealing from the bottom of the deck."

George squinted one eye, looking as dastardly as he could manage. "You have to cheat your friends," he said. "Your enemies won't let you."

They all laughed.

"Lars, you take some of that venison home with you. We have it outside in the rain barrel."

"Yes, I will. Thank you. Inga will love to have some meat for a stew."

Lars stepped out the door, and the three settled again at the table, finishing their coffee. Outside, they heard the squeak of Lars's steps as he walked down the lane.

Axel stretched. "I think I go outside now," he said, making an unspoken first claim to the outhouse. When no one said anything, he stepped out into a night black and clear. The stars seemed especially close, little points of light too far away to provide warmth on the Montana prairie.

Lars was a quarter mile or more on his way home, a dark shape against the snow. Axel was pleased that he was home and not making so long a walk on this night. He stepped back toward the outhouse, not pleased with the promise it offered. Cold it would be with wind blowing through the cracks in the wall. Still, it was better than summer and the stink and the flies. Winter was replete with blessings, too, if you just gave yourself time to think about them.

He stepped into the outhouse, gasping as his bare bottom hit the layer of frost and snow on the throne, as he called it. An inside bathroom would be nice, very nice, but that was not to be. It was better to think about the blessings visited upon the Andersons this night than those things which would be "nice." They had deer meat and potatoes and flour from Lars. There would be no hunger in this place, and that was more than many Montana families could say in this Depression.

Axel stopped on the way back to the house to look at his treasure of fresh meat. He stepped back from the rain barrel in surprise and walked into the house with his forehead wrinkled into a frown.

Bertha could read her husband's expressions as well as she could understand his words. "What's wrong?" she asked.

"Lars took both high quarters and most of the loin. We have only the front shoulders and ribs."

"That isn't like Lars."

"He's the one who did it. No one else could have, and him having work, too."

"He brought us the flour and the potatoes."

"But he stole our venison."

"No, you told him to take some home."

"I didn't tell him to take it all."

"We'll go to sleep now. We'll go look in the morning. Maybe it just looked like it was missing in the dark."

"Ya, maybe."

But Axel lay awake that night, watching his breath dissipate into tiny clouds. Lars had stolen from him. His best friend had stolen the food from his table. This Depression was hard on people and friendships.

Lars walked up to his house, stopping at the wooden box he had nailed to the cabin wall. It was better than an icebox this winter. No dogs could reach it from the ground, and no birds could break through its sturdy door. Lars was pleased with his work.

He placed the venison inside the box, taking care to make no noise. He had one more stop to make this night in town, and he didn't want Inga to know where he had gone. Lars stepped down the road, looking over his shoulder at the cabin, wishing that the snow didn't so protest his passing.

The sun cracked the eastern horizon just as Warden Oswald and Lars reached the Andersons' lane. Lars would have preferred that this work be done in the dark, but it was Oswald's way to humiliate people. He wanted neighbors to see the shame that came with killing the king's deer. Oswald turned on the truck's siren and roared up to the house. Nobody would miss this show.

The two climbed from the truck, but Bertha was standing on the porch before their feet touched the earth.

Lars couldn't hear Oswald's words. He seemed apart from what was happening to his friends, the warden's words only a babble in his ears. But he could see the tears streaming down Bertha's face. He understood those words as clearly as though they had been shouted in his face. The Andersons had broken the law, Bertha's tears said. They would be shamed forever, unable to hold up their faces in their neighbors' eyes. Bertha saw her future bleak as this winter day.

Axel stepped through the door. He saw Lars, and his back stiffened. So now his friend was running with Oswald?

Oswald prowled the yard, looking at the deer hair strewn there, checking each sign of blood in the snow.

"Where'd you hide it, Anderson?"

Axel stared sullenly at the warden, and Lars edged closer. Axel might try to get his rifle. That would be bad. That would be very bad.

"Mrs. Anderson?"

She was sobbing now, pointing at the rain barrel.

The warden stepped over to the barrel and looked inside. He turned then to Lars.

"You get any of this meat, Lars?"

Lars stepped over to the barrel and looked inside.

"No, I didn't get any of *that* meat," he said.

Axel's face was burning a dull red, and he looked with hatred at his friend. Sold out. His best friend had sold him out. Flour and potatoes one day, and selling his friends out the next. That Lars was a piece of work.

"What was the price, Lars, your thirty pieces of silver?" Axel hissed.

"My rifle, Axel. I shouldn't have left my rifle here. You shouldn't have let George use my rifle to kill that deer."

"George? Your rifle?"

"George made a mess of this poaching. If one of the neighbors had reported it, Oswald would have taken my rifle. I had to turn George in, Axel, so I wouldn't lose my rifle."

Axel's face wrinkled into a map of confusion.

Lars stared into his friend's eyes, willing him to understand. "George might as well plead guilty and go to jail. If he tries to fight this he won't have a leg to stand on."

A light came on in Axel's eyes. He shook his head. "A leg to stand on. You're some piece of work, Lars. Some piece of work."

Lars's chin dropped to his chest, and the game warden sneered. "Everyone has a price. Just that the price for you square heads is so damn low."

Axel glared at Lars. "I will get George now. I will deal with you later."

Oswald edged closer to the two. "No. Lars, you go get him. I don't want any funny stuff inside the house. Bring out the rifle, too."

Lars stepped into the house, leaning over George, whispering to him as he helped his friend to his feet. George limped through the door.

"What the hell's wrong with you?" Oswald growled.

"Froze my feet," George said.

"Getting the deer. He froze his feet," Lars said.

"I don't give a damn if he froze his"—Oswald looked at Mrs. Anderson—"feet off. You load that venison in the truck. That's the only exercise you're going to get for a month or two."

Lars said, "I will load the truck. George, you get in."

George nodded, limping toward the truck, grimacing with each step.

Oswald grinned, a mean, evil grin. "Dumb sons a bitches. Dumb as posts."

Lars nodded. "But now I got my rifle."

Oswald nodded. "Yeah, you've got your rifle. Considering you traded the rifle for this bunch, you made a good deal."

Oswald stepped toward the truck, stopping to stare back at Lars. "You'd best be damn careful, stool pigeon. You watch over your shoulder or Axel will walk up behind you some dark night. Don't come whining to me if he does. Only one thing lower than a poacher and that's a stool pigeon."

Oswald climbed into his truck, spinning the vehicle in a circle and roaring toward the road.

Lars turned to look at Axel. Axel glared back. "You should have told me, Lars."

"I couldn't tell you."

"Coming on like you did with Oswald. I might have shot you. I sure as hell wanted to."

"But you didn't."

"No, I didn't."

"Well, that was good, then."

Lars handed Axel his rifle and scuffed the snow with his boot.

"I was thinking that maybe you and Bertha would like to walk back with me. We'll cut up the venison, and then play some whist. Inga's feeling better, and I know she'd like to see you two."

"Ya, that'll be good," Axel said, cocking his head to one side. "You think maybe that jail doctor will save George's feet?"

"Better chance than if he just sat out here."

"Ya, that's a blessing. God takes care of us, doesn't he, Lars?"

"Ya, but sometimes I think he likes it when we help out."

The School at the Bucket of Blood

Jeanne Williams

One of Jeanne Williams's special gifts—perhaps we should call it a mission—has been to focus on the women and children and domestic life of the frontier. In novel after novel, she has shown us that the settlement of the West was not a male enterprise by any means. In this vivid, warm, and comic story she describes what happens when some progressive people want to borrow a rough and grubby saloon during daytime hours for a schoolhouse. The result is an education—but not entirely for the lucky children who receive their first schooling. The story is based on a true episode that occurred near San Luis Pass in New Mexico, where a certain rancher began operating a school by day and a saloon at night in his own house. Williams has won four Spur Awards for her novels, is a past President of Western Writers of America, and the winner of the Levi Strauss Saddleman Award for lifetime achievement in the literature of the West. She lives in the Chiricahua Mountains of Arizona, which became the setting for this delightful story.

Jim Halloran wiped off the bar, shook his head, then winced at the memory of the night before, and squinted at the painting of Pinkie flanked by rows of bottles. That was his idea of a lady. Pretty and sweet, wind tugging her skirts and hair and bonnet. Not that you ever saw a woman like that out here. Why would you, down in the very heel of New Mexico Territory, where even in late September, rattlesnakes and lizards hid from the sun before it got much above the San Luis Mountains?

You had to be tough to take this country, tough like the Chiricahua Apaches who cantered through here down into the Sierra Madres in Mexico till just a few years ago. Geronimo and his holdouts had given up in 1886 and been shipped to Florida, which made Jim sorry for them—penned up after roaming the mountains and deserts, hard to catch as the shadows of clouds—but he slept better than he had back then.

He jumped at a sound from the door, wondered if he should grab his shotgun from beneath the bar, and thought he was having delayed delirium tremens when he heard a woman's voice.

"What are you doing in my schoolhouse, sir?"

What she said took a moment to penetrate. Jaw hanging, Jim thought, *There she stands. Pinkie!* Except that her hair was almost black and instead of a white gown with pink sash, she wore a longsleeved bottle-green dress buttoned right up to her chin. She tapped her small stylish foot, raised her eyebrows, and the meaning of her words struck him.

"Your *what*, ma'am?"

"Schoolhouse. S-c-h-o-o—"

"I can spell, ma'am. Some, that is." He scratched his head and wished he had washed his hair lately and shaved that morning. Man got slack about that kind of thing when all he saw day in, day out was cowboys or shady characters who looked worse than he did. "But this—well, it's the Bucket of Blood Saloon."

She sniffed in delicate fashion and looked around. As if a pleasant, cozy veil was ripped away, Jim saw sardine tins running over with the remains of cigarettes, hand-rolled in both paper and corn shucks. He saw the cobwebs festooning the corners, hunks of dried caliche mud adding texture to the regular dirt, windows filigreed with dust and—

"Watch out!" his visitor shrieked.

She gasped as Old Bill sprang to Jim's shoulder from his summer perch in the length of a small hollow log Jim had placed on the mantel for him, thinking it would serve instead of an earth burrow. Fast as a striking diamondback, the woman swung her satchel at Old Bill.

Jim ducked. The bag missed Bill but caught Jim alongside his head. The *thunk!* reverberated through his skull. He staggered, blinking at lightning flashes, and reeled against the bar. His vision cleared as she started to swing again.

"Wait! Hold on, ma'am. This is only Old Bill." She stared at him as if she reckoned the blow had addled whatever brains he had. He managed to stand more or less straight. "Bill won't hurt me, but you'd likely better keep clear of him even if his sting's no worse than a bee's. He's not used to ladies and—"

"What is that hideous thing?"

"Why, he's a tarantula, ma'am." Jim held up his arm so Bill could stroll up it, his favorite promenade. "Must be a pretty smart little guy, too. Hasn't got eaten up by any of his lady loves though he sure goes huntin' one after a nice rain."

"You mean—"

Jim nodded. "Black widows have a bad name, but they're not the only critters that make a free lunch off their fellas."

He nodded again, remembering a few human females who'd lassoed him in their webs. If he hadn't been pretty fast once he recognized danger—well, he could be running Clara Dalrymple's ornery old daddy's store, bossed around by both Clara and her mama, or he'd have lost his life as well as his money when Lorena Schatz never told him she was engaged to the blacksmith. There was Minette, the gambling woman who declared he'd won both her hands, and across in Mexico, Angelita Torres's cousins, uncles, father, grandfathers, and godfather would forevermore be on the watch for him.

Absentmindedly, he rubbed a weal at the side of his neck. Close. Must have been the godfather. All Angelita's kin were lousy shots.

"Your knowledge of arachnids is fascinating, Mr.—" She lifted those eyebrows again, curved like the wing of a raven and as dark. He'd never seen eyes that color of gray with no hint of blue or hazel.

"Name's Jim Halloran, ma'am."

She extended a hand that surprised Jim, a good, useful strong hand with short fingernails. Her handshake was firm, too. A chill and a jolt more potent than that of mescal with a snake pickled in it ran through Jim at her touch, and at her smile, though he sensed it was a careful one, not the sunburst kind hinted at by some depth in her eyes.

"I'm Sally Wright, Mr. Halloran. Now, about my school—"

Fetching as she was, she wasn't going to flummox him. "My saloon, Miss Wright. I made a year's deal with Jethro Honeywell. For letting me use this old 'dobe, he gets a tenth of my profits." At the protest in her face, he added quickly, "That's all the good Lord asks for, a tithe of ten percent. Anyhow, Jethro was just lettin' it melt back into the ground."

She frowned. "There seems to be a misunderstanding."

"There sure does."

"I mean, you don't understand." She started for the door. "You'd better have a word with Mr. Honeywell." She called that gentleman's name.

Having hitched his team of matched bays, Jethro puffed inside. A chunky solid man with a ruddy face and bushy gray hair, he was considerably more duded up than Jim had ever seen him in black coat with a starched white shirt and string tie. His boots were a tad dusty but they had started out polished. His bristly eyebrows puckered above his light-blue eyes.

"Didn't you get my letter, Jim?"

"Letter?" Jim rubbed his ear. It still tingled from the wallop aimed at Old Bill, who had retired to the mantel to catch flies. "I haven't been to Perdition for a week or so." Perdition, thirty miles away, was Jasper Higgs's saloon squatted across the road from the general store where folks for miles around picked up their mail.

"Reckoned one of the boys would drop it off." Jethro sounded accusing, but Jim figured he was just embarrassed.

"Now you're here," Jim suggested, "you can tell me what the letter said."

Jethro's color deepened under the combined stares of Jim and Miss Sally Wright. Gazing at some distant point between them, he cleared his throat. "Well, Jim, the fact is that while I was buying that new"—he glanced at Miss Wright—"that purebred male brute in Kansas City, I met the sweetest, prettiest widder with eight kids."

Jim gulped at the very idea but managed to say, "Good for you, Jeth."

He snuck what was meant to be a piercing, critical look at Sally Wright but, shucks, he couldn't be critical. Her nose might be a trifle snub and her mouth too generous for some tastes, but she suited Jim right down to the caliche. There was no way she could have eight kids, though he reckoned from the laugh lines at her eyes that the dew had dried off her four or five years ago. Fine with Jim. He never took advantage of an innocent.

Jethro toed the baked bare ground with an elegant toe. "What it comes down to, Jim, is Lilia wouldn't budge from the city till I promised her a school and teacher for her young 'uns."

"Fine. Looks like you got the teacher. All you need to do is build a school."

"I'm going to, one of milled lumber with a wood floor and nice windows, just like Lilia wants, but I can't get to that till after branding next spring. Right now I got a lot of fixing to do to make my place fit for my family." He squinted at the Bucket of Blood. "Needs some shoveling out but it'll do till I can get at the real school."

"Hey, it's rented to me!"

"Can't exactly call it rented, Jim." Honeywell's voice was mild but his shoulders had a stubborn set. "If you don't sell any booze, I don't get a cent."

"How about that shingled roof?" Jim demanded.

Honeywell eyed it and beamed. "You sure did a first-rate job of it. Be nice and dry for Miss Wright and the kiddies."

"Now, look here—" Jim exploded.

"Jim, I thought you'd be glad to sacrifice a little for the education of our little ones—"

"I don't have any!"

"Speaking in the broad sense." At Jim's snort, Honeywell sighed. "Since you feel that way, I'll pay you for the roof. Now, the shingles didn't cost you anything—"

"Except a couple of trips to the Chiricahuas and back, and the work of cutting the trees and splitting the shingles, *and* swapping a couple days of building fence to Dan MacDonald for the use of his team and wagon." Jim stared off at the marching mountains, each range a softer blue with distance, rested his eyes on the green of oak and sycamore banding the river. "I don't want money for the roof, just to be under it. I like it here."

He was surprised to hear the words. Then it hit him that they were true. He'd been thinking of adding a ramada out back, planting some wild grapevines and honeysuckle to twine around nice and shady, maybe even scrub the windows. He folded his arms and looked down his broken nose at his fickle landlord. "I like it here," he repeated.

Miss Sally Wright had been poking around inside,

but she must have had an ear trained toward the men. "Since the school won't be here after the new one's ready," she said, "maybe we could work something out."

"What?" Jim was as doubtful as Honeywell looked.

"Don't most of your customers come in the evening?"

"Generally. Start driftin' in as the sun sinks."

"And they're all gone by morning?"

"They are, if I have to tie 'em on their horses. Don't want drunks sleeping it off around the place."

"Fastidious of you, Mr. Halloran." Was that a chuckle or a sniff?. "In other words, you don't need the building during school hours, say nine to three?"

"Reckon I wouldn't, ma'am." Jim rubbed his assaulted ear again, not because it hurt now, but because her hand had been at the other end of the satchel. "And you wouldn't need it in the evenings."

She dipped her chin and smiled at Honeywell. "If Mr. Halloran will cover his bar and bottles, I'll see the school things are out of his way when I leave." She slanted Jim a mischievous twinkle. "'*Pinkie*' can stay where she is. She'll help the children appreciate art."

Honeywell brightened before he dimmed. "Uh— Lilia's real strong on temperance. Her hubby owned a bar and drank up all the profits. She's determined her boy Cal isn't going to get stuck in his daddy's footsteps."

"I don't sell to anyone who's not shavin'," said Jim.

Sally Wright chuckled. "Then you wouldn't sell to yourself, would you?"

He blushed and touched his cheek. When did he

shave last? "Well, you bet I sell to men with whiskers. What I meant was—"

"Let me talk to Mrs. Honeywell," the teacher suggested. "After all, church services are held in saloons all over the West. Why not have a school in one? It's only for a year, and her boys must still be small."

"Cal's only sixteen but he's husky," said Honeywell. "He plain wouldn't go to school anymore after fourth grade. The kids teased him on account of he was so much bigger than them. His mama's sure it'll be different out here in a little school."

"Looks like he could've put a stop to that." In the few winter terms he'd had of school back in Texas, Jim had licked many a boy for making fun of his jug ears.

Honeywell shook his head. "Cal's scared of hurting someone if he gets started so he just takes it. Got such a gentle nature it's probably lucky he is big, else he'd get run right into the ground."

"I'll keep the peace." Sally Wright gave the saloon a last appraisal, including Jim, as if deciding what had to be done to bring things up to her standards. "Shall we go, Mr. Honeywell? I'm sure your wife will be reasonable."

"You haven't met her yet," muttered the rancher. He looked at Jim. "When I said Lilia was purty and sweet, she is, but she's also—well, determined." He followed Miss Sally to the buckboard, gave her a hand up, and unhitched the team.

Jim stared after them, thoughts spinning like a dust devil. Kids trooping into the Bucket of Blood instead of the toughest men along a tough border? Shrill voices piping the alphabet instead of telling raunchy jokes and cussing? But it'd only be till summer. Then he'd have his saloon back to himself.

"Bill, you lazy galoot, get after the flies!" he adjured. He found a shovel out back and began applying it to the debris in the corners. When his first customers rode in, as usual, Red Tolliver and Jack Monteith, they stared as Jim swept a last flurry of dirt through the door with a kind of broom fashioned from willow limbs he'd cut down by the river and bound together with a piece of wire.

"What's the matter with you?" Red inquired. He was a lanky freckled cowboy who worked for Dan MacDonald, as did Jack, a good-looking fellow with curly black hair.

"We're going to have school here till afternoons." Jim handed them a bucket of water, sudsy from pounded yucca roots, and an old shirt he'd torn in half. "If you boys'll get the windows clean enough to see through, I'll stand you to drinks and tell you all about the school."

Mizzou Bates was the next one along. He was wanted in his home state and not wanted most other places. His reek of tobacco and sweat, new over rancid, horse and human, reached the door before he did. At Jim's proposal, he tilted his sombrero back from greasy black hair and chortled.

"Good joke, Halloran! Now get behind that bar and pour my mescal."

Jim kept rubbing tallow into the bar's chips and scratches. "If you can't help me, guess I can't help you." Mizzou's whiskery jaw gaped.

"Huh?"

"Anyone as drinks tonight works first."

Mizzou's hand streaked for his gun. Jim kicked the wrist up, splashed what was left of Red's whiskey in Mizzou's face, poked the shotgun into Mizzou's gut, and heisted his gun. "Go drink at Perdition, Mizzou. I'll send your gun there the first time someone goes that way."

Holding his wrist, Mizzou turned the air blue. A prod from the shotgun sent him stomping off. Red whistled. "Didn't know you could move that fast, Jim."

"Or knew the moves." Jack grinned. "You might should have fanned his brisket while you had the chance, though."

Jim shrugged. "If I'd meant to do that, I'd have let him get his gun out." Both cowboys looked questions. Jim said no more. They all went back to work.

By the time Jim hit his bunk in the lean-to that night, he had swapped drinks for elbow grease from twenty customers and was tireder than he'd been since he worked his last roundup, but he was filled with a warm glow of accomplishment, or maybe that was the result of washing his hair and scrubbing off in a tub he filled with water from the creek.

"Bill," he said, as his buddy made a good-night creep along his arm before going out to hunt, "Just wait till Miss Sally Wright sees this place! Cans and bottles hauled off and covered with rocks at the end of the arroyo, weeds chopped away so snakes can't hide in 'em to bite the kids, furniture polished, serape draped over the bar—yeah, she's going to be surprised!"

Bill gave his cheek a feathery pat and set forth to prowl. Nestling into his pillow, Jim thought of Mizzou. Not since he was a U.S. deputy marshal in Indian Territory chasing bad guys for Hanging Judge Isaac Parker's court had he used that kick and whiskey-in-the-face play, but he'd had to do it so often then that it must have become sort of automatic. He'd never had to kill anyone and didn't mean to start now he'd met Sally.

Comparing his three pairs of Levi's next morning, he donned the cleanest ones and tucked a practically clean plaid shirt into them. While the coffee brewed, he shaved, whetting the razor twice and stanching his wounds with juice from a broken off point of the agave by the door. Frowning at the speckled mirror, he wished his nose didn't have that hump in the middle where the last horse thief he'd arrested had slugged him. Seemed to be a lot more crinkles at the edges of his eyes and mouth than when he'd last looked, but Clara, Lorena, Minette, and Angelita had all said they liked the way his eyes changed with the light, from gray to green. There wasn't much gray in his straw-colored hair—gold, Lorena called it, but she was kind of poetical.

Bill sauntered in while Jim was washing down cold biscuits with coffee, ran up his arm and rested companionably on his shoulder. A coyote trotted past, melting into the dried grass. A red-tailed hawk hunkered on the corral gate, which was open so that Dusty, Jim's buckskin gelding, and Pardner, the white mule, could go in and out at will. Pard was company for Dusty. Jim thought it plumb cruel to keep a horse alone, they were such sociable critters.

The two-day-old biscuits were too hard to save for another meal. Jim took them down to Dusty and Pard.

"Wait till you see Pinkie," he told them. "That is, Miss Sally Wright." The rattle of a wagon reached him.

Who were the early birds? Most folks in wagons were peaceable, but just in case these weren't Jim went in to wait by the bar. Hmm. The shotgun was hidden by the serape, but it wasn't a good idea to have it where a curious young 'un might find it. As the wagon stopped, he looked vainly for a safe place to stow the weapon.

"Don't you know it's dangerous to wave firearms around, sir?" The voice sliced him like a whip. He turned to look at Miss Sally Wright and the short, plump blond woman beside her who advanced on him with wrath in her delft-blue eyes. "You certainly can't keep it in the school."

"In the *saloon*, ma'am, it's a part of the equipment."

They glared at each other. Putting her lovely form half between them, Miss Sally introduced them. "I can't say it's pleasure," snipped Jethro's pertest, sweetest no longer widder woman.

Jim bowed. "Likewise, ma'am, I'm sure."

As she glanced around the room, Miss Sally Wright's eyes widened. She cast Jim a questioning look. But as Lilia Honeywell surveyed what Jim considered a pretty respectable room, her eyes widened, too, then narrowed.

"We've got our work cut out for us, Miss Sally." She pushed the toe of her buttoned shoe against the earth. "Is there a wood floor down there somewhere?"

Jim enjoyed his chuckle. "Caliche and rock all the way to China."

"Then Mr. Honeywell will just have to get some more lumber after he brings the wood we bought in town for desks and benches and privies. I suppose there *is* a sawmill in the region?"

"Kind of. Over in Morse Canyon in the Chiricahuas about eighty miles the way a wagon would have to travel to get through the Peloncillos."

Lilia groaned. "I never in all my life saw such a hodgepodge of tacky little mountain ranges, all with outlandish names!"

Experience had taught Jim there was no profit in wasting breath and opinions on some folks and she was one of them. Pitying Honeywell right down to the ground, Jim remembered something he'd thought of doing every now and then when he got tired of spending his spare time poking around the mountains. His excuse was prospecting, but he simply enjoyed knowing where to find a spring or whether a canyon ran all the way through a range, like Skeleton did through the Peloncillos, or ended at impassable rock walls.

"There's lots of nice smooth rocks in the creek. Probably be less trouble to haul 'em up and lay 'em in sand." He considered. "I'd help. A good stone floor would be dandy for my saloon."

Lilia surveyed him warily. "I'll look at the rocks, Mr. Halloran. Coming, Miss Sally?"

"If you don't mind, I'll try to decide how to arrange the school so the children don't face the bar."

"If I had my way, there wouldn't be one!" Lilia proclaimed. "'*Wine is a mocker, strong drink is raging . . .*'"

Jim strode off with the shotgun, trying to think where to put it. Kids might get in the shed where he kept his saddle, horse feed, and such. Even more hopeless was the ramada in the corral that he'd closed in on three sides with cottonwood poles to shelter Pard and Dusty. But that old dead cottonwood tree by the ramada had a big hollow in it. Was it long enough?

He tied his bandana around the barrel to keep it from getting full of whatever had accumulated in the hole and lowered the shotgun till it touched bottom, relieved that the butt was four or five inches from the top, which was too high for a young 'un to peek into. He put a box of shells in a little cavity and thought he'd solved *that* problem.

Lilia puffed up from the river as Jim stepped in the Bucket to find Miss Sally attacking the windows. A frilled gingham apron covered her brown dress, and he doubted she'd have rolled up her sleeves if she could have guessed the effect a glimpse of her rounded arm had on him. Look at the dirt she was scrubbing off, specks and blobs he'd thought were permanent! Sure, the panes had been grimy when he moved in three years ago, but he felt guilty for Miss Sally having to work so hard.

He was about to offer to try his hand again when Lilia said, "I suppose the rocks will do. They could be pretty with all the different colors." She sprinkled water over the floor, getting some on him either by accident or by design. "You could start picking them out, or begin whitewashing the walls. There's brushes and whitewash in the wagon."

"I'm your husband's tenant, ma'am, not his hired man."

"The floor will improve your saloon, Mr. Halloran." That was true, but it was Miss Sally's look of appeal that made him shrug.

"I don't have a wagon so I'll have to use yours to haul the rocks."

She stared in disbelief. "How do you bring in your whiskey?"

"Pard has a packsaddle. I stow the rest in my saddlebags and bedroll."

"I doubt if Mr. Honeywell would want you using his team."

"I'll water them at the river," Jim said pointedly. "And when I'm through, I'll unharness them, rub them down, and turn them into the corral."

She flushed. "You can't expect me to take care of horses!"

"I reckon Jethro will if you're going to take a team without a man along."

Her mouth tightened. She began to sweep the dampened floor with a real broom. "Use the team, then, but mind you're careful."

Honeywell's bays were dandy horses. Jim stroked their necks and got acquainted before unloading the whitewash, brushes, a big kettle that smelled aromatically of beans, and a woven covered basket of what he hoped were Lupe's marvel-thin tortillas. The wife of Chuey Sanchez, a top cowhand as well as the JH's carpenter and fix-it man, Lupe cooked and kept house for Honeywell while the three Sanchez kids played in and around the spraddled-out adobe, bringing some life to it. Jim hoped Lilia would be a darn sight nicer to Lupe than she'd been to him.

Driving down to the ford, he let the bays drink all that was good for them at one time, hitched them where they could browse, and began to choose rocks with one flat surface. The pointy end would be buried in sand.

Gray rocks, white rocks, yellow, rose, black, some streaked with orange. Jim searched up and down, admiring the way a plain rock looked jewel-like under the sparkle of water. He started to the Bucket with his first load when Honeywell drove up with the lumber, Chuey Sanchez beside him. Dan MacDonald was a little ways behind on his strawberry roan.

Short, sinewy, and bowlegged, Chuey took a saw to the boards as soon as they were unloaded while Honeywell, with a harried greeting to Jim, unhitched his team and led them to water before turning them into the corral to roll happily in the dirt.

"Our *chicos*, they are excited about coming to school," Chuey told Jim with a white smile. "I must smooth the wood so no little hands or bottoms get splinters. What, Jim, are you doing with all those stones?"

Jim rubbed his back but surveyed his collection with pride. "They're going to make the handsomest floor in all New Mexico Territory, Chuey."

"Your back will ache much more than now, I think, by the time that pretty floor is made."

"Reckon you'll ache right along with me," Jim kidded. He stuck his head in the door. Somehow, Lilia had rustled a heap of debris out of nooks and corners. "Not much use going to all that trouble, ma'am," he said cautiously. "We'll just be shoveling sand in here."

With a martyred glare, she poked her broom at bottle shards, tobacco cans, worn-down horseshoes, and all manner of trash that had hid out from Jim's willow brush yesterday. "It'd serve you right to get a hunk of glass in your knee, Mr. Halloran, while you're setting stones, but I don't want some innocent man suffering."

"Don't think there are any innocent men around here," Jim said under his breath. He could tell her some things about her husband that would sure straighten out the waves in her hair. He seized inspiration from Miss Sally's pretty arm, uplifted as she finished the top pane, and went out to unload.

Dan, a big yellow-headed man with merry blue eyes, gave Jim a hand after he put his roan in the corral. "It's sure good of you to share the Bucket, Jim. Mary's tickled to death about the school. She's been worried that our kids won't know more than she can teach them, and she only had a few years of school. Which is more than I did."

Wagon empty, Jim started for another load while Dan helped Chuey and Honeywell stir whitewash. His moustache drooped today. Jim felt a stir of compassion. He hoped Lilia wasn't going to make Jethro sorry he'd taken on a ready-made family. Likely she'd be sweet again once she got what she wanted.

It was hot now the sun was high. Jim was considering a drink from the creek when Miss Sally appeared with a jar of what proved to be lemonade. "Talk about angels!" He took a few swallows and grinned, pleased to pieces that she'd thought of him. "Best drink I ever had."

"What do you do outside of bar hours?" she demanded suddenly.

None of her business, but he was kind of flattered that she wondered. He wasn't going to tell her he enjoyed *The Meditations of Marcus Aurelius* and reading a fellow named Thoreau who'd found plenty to see and think about up in the New England woods. If she could ask such a question, he could make a small test of her character.

"Oh, there's lots of things to see and to admire." He was quoting someone whose name he couldn't remember. "I might go watch young coatimundis. They're interestin' critters that look like a short-eared raccoon got mixed up with a monkey. The little ones play on the ledge under a big madrone tree while their mamas visit and comb each other's hair—"

"I'm not that green, Mr. Halloran."

"Well, of course they comb with their claws. And there's always a chance to see a mountain lion."

"I'd rather not." She looked around. "Are they numerous?"

"Bless you, no. I've only ever seen one. Looked like he was growing right out of some oak leaves that were just his shade of kind of faded yellow-brown. Long tail, and that head, pale around the muzzle, and those gold-green eyes! Prettiest critter I've ever seen."

Her eyelashes flickered, but he didn't apologize. "Sometimes in the fall I put up the GONE sign and go to a canyon I know in the Chiricahuas where the maples turn red and the aspens yellow by a waterfall where drops fall on the mossy cliff and sparkle every color there is. In the spring that cliff just shines with red-and-yellow columbines blooming on the ledges."

She wasn't sneering. He ventured further. "About that time of year, I like to know who's nesting where. Sometimes I get to see the little fellers learning to fly.

I keep wondering when a pair of curve-billed thrash-ers will stop nesting in that big cholla yonder and find a place where snakes can't wipe 'em out. They raise two, three broods a summer, a regular picnic for the snakes."

"You could kill the snakes."

"Could but I won't."

"Why?"

"If the thrashers can't figure out they'd better find a better place to nest, then their babies are probably just as dumb. Anyhow, snakes don't bite unless you bother them, and they keep down mice and rats."

Now she did give him a scornful look. "Next you're going to say they're part of nature. Well, Mr. Hallo-ran, I'm part of nature, too, and if I see a mean old snake shinnying up a cactus to eat baby birds, I'll use a hoe to toss him so far away his fangs'll rattle!"

"He'll come back." They weren't talking about snakes.

"Then he's as dumb as the thrashers."

"There's one snake you better not run off unless you wants rats and mice dancin' on your toes," Jim warned. "Old Spot—he's a bull snake and harmless to humans—has a den under the southwest wall."

"The children—"

"If they don't know he's useful, Miss Wright, teach-ing them that would be a sight better than parsing paragraphs." He didn't know how you did that but it sounded good. "You've heard what they say about building a better mousetrap. Well, Old Spot's the best mousetrap there'll ever be."

She took the jar and marched off. That's what he got for telling the truth, Jim thought dourly. But he thought of how she'd looked when he talked about his gold, and, scarlet canyon. If she didn't squash Old Bill or try to drown out Old Spot, he could go on hoping she was the one woman who'd understand the things he enjoyed.

He was dumping his last load when Lilia hollered for him to wash up and come eat. Amongst them, they put away the spicy beef and beans and buttermilk biscuits that melted in your mouth even if they were as cold as anything looking up at the hot New Mexican sky could be. To finish, there were big chunks of toothsome gingerbread. Lilia went up several notches in Jim's esteem, to plummet again when she screeched at poor Jethro.

"There certainly does need to be some kind of wall around the side and front of the privies, at least the girls'. I won't have my daughters stand outside getting teased while they wait to go in."

Honeywell sighed. "I reckon we can cut a mort of young cottonwoods and make poles out of them."

Jim hated to think of that many trees being killed for such a damfool reason. "Be a sight quicker and easier to use a few poles to anchor a sotol, yucca, and agave fence." He waved his hand at the myriad dead stalks of all three plants that, according to age and wind, spiked straight or leaned or had fallen. "We could twist a couple of lengths of wire to hold the stalks in place." Lilia still looked skeptical. "I can bring up some wild grapevines to plant along the fence."

"That sounds sensible to me, Mrs. Honeywell," put in Miss Sally. "The—whatever they are—are already dead and might as well be put to use instead of cutting live trees."

Jim could have hugged her. "We'll try it," Lilia grudged.

Jim's bar had been moved outside because of the whitewashing and stone-laying. He readied it for the evening's customers, if any, and reported for duty. Not much sense hauling up sand till the whitewashers were through so, after Lilia and Miss Sally agreed on where to have the privies, he got his pickax and shovel and attacked the caliche accompanied by Dan's and Chuey's hammering.

Kind of fun to be working with other folks for something good for the young 'uns. When Jim quit marshaling, he was so sick and tired of the sorrier brands of humanity that he'd reckoned the Bucket would provide all the society he could stand, but as he sweated and dug and caught a glimpse now and then of Miss Sally plying her brush inside, he knew he had been lonesome.

"Bill," he said to his friend, who was doubtless snoozing in his burrow, "you're a good buddy, but it's time I was sayin' good night to somebody quite a bit different!"

Red and Jack dropped by late that afternoon and took turns with the pick for free drinks. "Hear the teacher's real pretty," Red blurted after unsuccessful efforts to get Jim to describe her. "Couldn't you—uh—kind of introduce us since we're helpin' out and all?"

Red was too young to be a rival, but Jack was old enough and mighty good-looking to boot. "I'll give you another drink," said Jim.

Two days later, many colors of stones paved the floor and white walls lightened the Bucket past recognition. The bar was back in place, polished to gleaming. So that the kids would have their backs turned on even serape-draped iniquity, the teacher's desk was across the room from it in front of the window. A big colored map of the United States hung on one side of the window and a blackboard the Honeywells brought from Kansas City was attached to the other. The two fourteen-year-olds, Lilia's Cal and Mary Thompson from across the valley, would work at the burnished and purified old saloon table back of three long desks and benches of varying heights. In front was the lowest desk and bench with room for the six six-year-olds. Next was the medium desk for five eight- and nine-year-olds. The highest desk would hold the four ten- and twelve-year-olds. After school, the desks stored neatly on top of each other with the benches tucked just as neatly beneath.

Pegs were fixed in a side wall to hang coats. Next to these was a bench to hold lunch pails and a stand for the shiny new water bucket. Lilia had decreed that her children weren't drinking water from the river, so Honeywell would haul water along with the kids till a well was dug.

Out back, a sotol, yucca, and agave fence interwoven with long bear grass shielded each whitewashed privy from view. Looking around with a glow of accomplishment, Jim grinned at the Honeywells, Chuey, Dan, Miss Sally, and Bax Thompson and Harry Bridewell, who had kids and pitched in when they heard about the school.

"I think we're entitled to drink a toast to the new school." The men gathered at the bar as Jim flipped off the serape. "Ladies, there's sarsaparilla, ginger beer, or some wild raspberry shrub I made out of just fruit, water, and sugar."

Lilia eyed him skeptically. "It's not alcoholic?"

"Not unless you'd like me to stir in a little brandy."

She ignored that and dimpled at Jethro, who was looking thirstily at his favorite bourbon. Unless he had a bottle stashed someplace, he probably hadn't had a sniff since he got married. "Mr. Honeywell and I will have the raspberry shrub, please."

Jim nodded and glanced at Miss Sally as he reached for glasses. "The shrub sounds nice." She stepped around the bar to stand beside him, dark hair so close to his chin that he got a clean sweet whiff of lilac. "Let me pour it while you get the other gentleman's drinks."

Dan and Chuey picked rye whiskey. Bax and Harry asked for bourbon. Lilia was jaunting around the room, taking pride in what she had wrought. Jim didn't exactly see it happen, but when he set down the bourbon, it was a third full. When he looked again, it was more like a quarter.

Miss Sally finished filling three glasses with raspberry shrub. Where had she learned that handy way with a bottle? She carried a pair of drinks to the Honeywells. When Lilia reached for the glass in the teacher's right hand, Miss Sally deftly gave her the one in her left and offered the other to Jethro.

Honeywell took a dispirited sip. The ends of his moustache seemed to curl and his eyes got a shine in them. Hoisting his glass, he bellowed, "Here's to the Bucket of Blood School!"

"We can't call our school Bucket of Blood!" protested Lilia. "It sounds dreadful!"

Dan drew bleached eyebrows together. "Reckon it does, at that."

"My wife wouldn't like it," said dark, skinny Bax Thompson.

"Why not just Bucket School?" Jim suggested. He nodded toward the water pail. "We've got one."

"I suppose it'll do till we get our real school built," decided Lilia.

Honeywell drew inspiration from another swig and swept his glass around in a salute. "Here's to you gents who helped fix up Bucket School! And here's to the little woman who's behind it!"

Amid cheers, he flourished a bow to his wife and took a long, happy swallow. "Sure is good raspberry shrub, Jim. If you make any more, I'd admire to buy all you can spare."

"I'll remember that," said Jim.

The refurbishing wound up on a Friday. Monday morning, sunbrowned Mary Thompson, one plump honey-brown plait hanging down her back, drove up in a wagon with prim little blond Jane Bridewell beside her, while the six-year-olds, Tammy Bridewell and Tad Thompson, gleefully predicted horrors for each other.

"You'll bawl like a branded calf when the teacher calls you to the front," was Tad's final shot as, ignoring his sister's chiding, he jumped down and ran off to join the race yellow-headed Larry and Pete Mac-Donald were running with Miguel Sanchez.

"I—I hope he wets his pants!" sobbed Tammy.

"Mind *you* don't," warned her hard-hearted older sister.

"He'll behave on the way home," Mary said, "or I'll tell Pa and Tad'll get a hiding."

Jim was going to help the tall, awkward girl unhitch but a youngster with hair as fluffy and yellow as a chick's stepped up to the team and took charge. "Let me take care of your horses, sis."

"I'm not your sister!"

"Oh." The boy was almost as tall as Jim, and broader through the shoulders. His sky-blue eyes puzzled at the flustered girl. "What shall I call you, then? I'm Cal Barclay." He added doubtfully, "Mama says I'm a Honeywell now, but I don't feel like I know Mr. Honeywell good enough to use his name."

Mary softened. "I'm pleased to know you, Cal, whatever your last name is. I'm Mary Thompson." She sighed. "I'm fourteen but I've never been to school before. Coming from Kansas City, you must have lots of schooling."

Cal dug his toe in the dirt. "No. You see—"

Jim moved off to turn Pard and Dusty out of the corral where Honeywell's bays were munching hay Honeywell had previously brought for them. Cal had driven the wagon that morning, hauling his brothers, sisters, and the three Sanchez kids. Florrie, the gray mule ridden by the two youngest MacDonald boys, was hobbled down by the river along with the blue roan twelve-year-old Ben rode.

Miss Sally appeared in the door. How could anyone look that pretty in a snuff-colored dress even if it did have white cuffs and collar? She rang a cowbell. The race broke off, Cal left the horses with gentle pats, and a jumble of skirts and trousers vanished into the Bucket. In a few minutes Jim heard a clear voice that must be Miss Sally's soar into "The Star-Spangled Banner."

Jim peeked through the back door. The teacher had written the first verse and chorus on the blackboard. She stood beside it, smiling, encouraging the children with those capable hands that rose and fell with the tune.

Quite a sight, three rows of black, brown, yellow, and red heads, straight and curly, slicked down or untamed, with Mary and Cal standing by their table in back and little Daisy Honeywell beside her stool by the teacher's desk. Only four, she'd begged so hard to come and promised to be so good that Miss Sally interceded for her. Lilia's other kids, all girls except for Cal, had various shades of yellow and light-brown hair and were named for flowers or trees like eight-year-old Myrtle, nine-year-old Hazel, and ten-year-old Olive. The twins, six-year-old Pansy and Violet, bloomed on either side of cute little Anita Sanchez and longingly eyed the small gold hoops in her ears.

On the last row, twelve-year-old Rose Honeywell loftily ignored the ten-year-olds, her sister Olive and Carlos Sanchez, but stole interested glances at freckled Ben MacDonald, whose voice was just beginning to squeak in its abrupt changes from deep to shrill.

From what Jim could see, the kids had brought whatever books the families had, readers, spellers, arithmetics, a few geographies, a U.S. history, even a few Bibles and hymnbooks. Miss Sally gave out pencils and tablets and told those who could write to start stories about themselves, their families, and this valley between the mountains. Then she asked those who could read to look through the readers and find the one they should start with. While most of the pupils were absorbed in one task or the other, she called the primer class and began to teach them how to sound out and spell their own and each other's names.

Tippy-toeing away, Jim bent to howdy Old Spot, who was sunning himself by the lean-to, a big handsome cream-colored critter with red-brown splotches that were near enough a rough diamond shape to get his kind killed for rattlers. Not that most folks worried much. A snake was a snake.

"Mind you keep the mice and pack rats out of there so Miss Sally'll take a liking to you," Jim exhorted. "You know what, you rusty old serpent? After seeing that bouquet of all kinds and sizes and shapes of kids, I don't grudge the kinks in my back or the blisters on my hands."

All the same, he put on his goatskin gloves before he got the pick and started on the well.

By the end of the week, the windlass over the well was drawing up sweet, cold water, none of the alkali-tainted stuff that gave man and beast the trots. Bax Thompson, who'd been a miner at Tombstone, used dynamite to blow out a layer of otherwise impenetrable rock. After that, with some men resting while the others dug, it had gone pretty fast. When Jim knocked off after school let out, he found everything ready for the Bucket's transformation from education to recreation: desks and benches stowed away, blackboard erased, and the floor swept.

The water bucket was also full. He grinned at the wishful thinking. "Bill," he murmured to his friend, who leaped from the mantel to his shoulder as if grateful that they had the place to themselves, "the onliest way any of the boys are goin' to taste that good, pure water is if they're skunked enough to think it's gin."

"Really?" The voice at his elbow was soft but had an edge to it that made his neck tighten up. "I should think a truly thirsty man would prefer water to alcohol."

"Probably do back in the States, ma'am, but the fellas who hang out around here have mostly pickled their gizzards."

"Indeed?" Miss Sally lifted an eyebrow and plunked Walden down in front of him. "Is this yours, Mr. Halloran?"

His name was written in the front so he couldn't deny it. He started to demand why she'd been in his lean-to but remembered just in time that he'd likely left the book on the bench by Old Spot's hole where he'd been reading it last night while Bill feathered up and down his arm. He felt his face go as red as if he'd been caught watering the booze he sold.

"I guess it is," he admitted.

Her gray eyes darkened to the color of deep twilight. "Why do you pretend to be ignorant?" Her tone was more grieved than angry, but Bill must not have liked it. He reared up and waved several of his front legs at her.

"Nasty thing!" Miss Sally retreated.

The moment gave Jim a chance to recover and pose the question that had been eating at him. "Why do you happen to be teaching?"

"I have to earn a living."

"Yeah, but . . ." His voice trailed off. She might be sensitive about being an old maid.

Dangerous glints flickered in her eyes. "You mean why am I not married to some man who'd feed and clothe his body servant?"

Servant? The word raised Jim's hackles. "It takes a sorry varmint to make a slave of his wife."

She curled her lip. "Have you noticed any lack of sorry varmints?"

Jim curled his lip back at her. "Have you noticed the plumb shameful way Jethro Honeywell's makin' a servant out of Miss Lilia?"

"Exceptions prove the rule."

"That sounds smart but it's silly. If there are exceptions, Miss Sally Wright, then there isn't any rule."

She looked as shocked as if Bill had made the retort. Jim softened, but before he could smooth things over, she grabbed her books and hurried out to where Cal waited with the kids and wagon.

Jim gave them a cheery wave and watched them until they were out of sight.

Miss Sally was good with Cal, but the kid had to be mortified to be in Second Reader with his younger sisters, Hazel and Olive. The week after the well was finished, he started tagging Jim at recess and lunch, instead of trying to play with the smaller boys. He helped gather branches from trees along the river and chop them for fuel, enlarge and improve the horse ramada in the corral, and transplant wild grapevines to twine along the fences shielding the privies.

At first he was a little nervous of Bill and Old Spot, but he was soon letting Bill prance up his arm and he kept the MacDonald boys from bashing Old Spot, holding the three of them off. "Spot's our friend," he explained laboriously. "He keeps down the mice and rats. No, Ben, he isn't a rattlesnake. See, he doesn't have those pits between his eyes and nose like all rattlers do."

"Looks like a sidewinder to me," muttered Ben.

"Then you must not of ever seen a sidewinder!" retorted Cal. "Mr. Halloran showed me one. He had little horn-like ridges above his eyes. So all of you just leave Spot alone!"

The thing was, Cal's shy nature didn't fit with school any more than his size. Jim decided to give him a responsibility that should make him feel important. While they were scattering hay for the horses one morning, Jim asked, "Know how to use a shotgun, Cal?"

"Chuey's been teaching me."

Glad the vaquero, too, had noticed the boy's lonesomeness, Jim nodded at the hollow tree. "There's a shotgun stashed in that hole, barrel down, and a box of shells in a cavity on the right. I keep the shotgun under the bar during business hours but put it in the tree every morning." Jim paused, and put his hand on Cal's shoulder. "Some pretty tough fellas ride through here sometimes. It would ease my mind to know you'd handle any trouble that might come up while I'm away."

Cal straightened till his eyes were level with Jim's. His shoulders settled back instead of drooping and his smile was a burst of sunshine. "You can count on me, Mr. Halloran. Don't you worry a bit."

"That's a load off me." Jim put out his hand and

got a good firm squeeze. "I reckon, Cal, that you should call me Jim, at least when we're by ourselves."

Cal nearly wrung his hand off but the light in his eyes was worth it. "Jim—thanks! Thanks a heap."

As the third week of school began, Lilia visited all one morning, and that noon, Jim heard her proposing to Miss Sally that they have a spelling bee and pie supper that Friday night to raise money for the school.

"It would be nice to have new texts instead of the jumble we use now," Miss Sally agreed. "But your older girls are the only pupils who'd do very well at a spelling bee."

Lilia's expression showed she didn't see any problem with that, but she lifted and let fall one plump shoulder. "I'm sure you can figure out some kind of little program just to show parents their children are learning."

Miss Sally turned to Jim. "That would be during saloon hours. What do you think, Mr. Halloran?"

Three weeks ago he'd have said a bargain was a bargain and after four o'clock the Bucket was his. Now he looked at Miss Sally, saw she wanted to have the affair, and said, "You can send notes home with all the kids and ask their folks to spread the word the bar'll be closed that night. I'll put up a sign at Perdition when I pick up my mail tomorrow."

"That's more than kind of you, Mr. Halloran." Miss Sally's words were formal, but his real thanks was the brightening of her color.

"He knows how much he's benefiting from the

school," snipped Lilia. "Hasn't he got the dump cleaned up and a good well and privies and—"

"I seem to recall that he worked harder than anyone on all of that. Now, Mrs. Honeywell, if you'll just help me write these notes . . ."

By sundown Friday, extra lanterns hung from the rafters of the Bucket. Examples of students' work were tacked to the walls, from the littlest ones' drawings to handsomely penned compositions by Rose Honeywell and Mary Thompson. The girls had filled jars with asters and sunflowers. WELCOME TO BUCKET SCHOOL was written on the blackboard, and Carlos had added: BIENVENIDOS. The two shortest desks would serve as seating, as would the lunch pail bench. Kegs and boxes were tucked wherever there was room.

Shaved, scrubbed, duded up in coat, tie, and a white shirt he'd had laundered last time he was in Silver City, Jim went kind of misty-eyed as he looked around. Doggoned if he didn't feel almost as proud of the kids as if they'd been his own!

"What do you think of it, honey girl?" he asked Pinkie, who smiled inscrutably.

Horses. Well, it was time folks started to arrive. He was lighting lanterns when Red Tolliver and Jack Monteith strode in, halting so abruptly that they were bumped into by the three men behind them.

"Holy smoke!" gasped Red. "What's goin' on?"

"Didn't you see the sign in Perdition about the program and pie supper and how the bar would be closed?"

"Closed?" the five moaned.

"We didn't see any sign," grunted Red. "Been delivering cows to a ranch in Mexico and came from there just today."

"Nobody's here yet," Jack said hopefully. "If you could just give us a quick snort—"

"I'll sell you a bottle but you can't drink it here," Jim decreed. "The kids and their families will be coming any minute."

Red perked up. "And that pretty teacher we been hearin' about?"

"Well, of course she'll be here!"

Jack and Red exchanged glances. "She'll have a pie!" they chorused.

"Now, boys," said Jim, "you're tired and dusty and headed home. Let me get your bottle and—"

"We're staying! " declared Jack and Red, who were beginning to sound like a vaudeville act. "We'll go out to the well and get cleaned up."

Labe Pierce, a sandy-haired paunchy man with a tobacco-stained handlebar moustache, looked sourly after the younger cowboys. "Guess my thirst'll wait till we hit Perdition, Halloran. When I stop at a saloon, I want a drink in a glass and I want to drink it there."

"This isn't a saloon tonight,"

Pierce blew through his moustache. "You might get away with not openin' up till in the evening, but what the hell kind of a bar is closed at night? That's not doin' your customers right, Halloran, and you damn well know it!"

"Go drink in Perdition," Jim said.

For a second, Pierce's hand strayed toward his six-shooter. Then he shrugged, spat brown juice close to Jim's boot, and headed for the hitching rack. His companions slogged after him. Jim didn't care if they never came back. He scowled as Red and Jack came from the well. They'd sloshed water over their faces and hair, and in spite of trail-weary clothes, they looked more respectable than they had any right to.

Without really planning, Jim had from the start of this whole idea figured he'd be sitting with Miss Sally that night, sharing her pie. If he wanted that to happen, he was going to have to take steps. The Honeywells and Sanchezes drove up just then, Cal and Chuey in the wagon with the kids, Jethro driving a fancy new carriage containing his wife, Miss Sally, and Lupe Sanchez.

Jim hurried to help the ladies down. He hoped to see how Miss Sally's box was decorated, but each woman had a towel wrapped around her offering. Maybe Cal would know.

Cal looked at him with stricken eyes. "I—I'm real sorry, but I promised not to tell, Jim—I mean, Mr. Halloran."

Jim managed a weak smile and pushed a light fist against Cal's shoulder. "I'm still Jim, son."

Would the Honeywell girls be as honor-bound? Maybe they hadn't promised. To his horror at such a lack of scruples, he saw Jack Monteith over by the door slipping the twins, Violet and Pansy, a silver dollar apiece. They giggled, the flaxen-haired traitors, and whispered something in Jack's ear.

At least, thought Jim, *I'll know which pie is Miss Sally's when Jack starts bidding. And I've got eighty-two dollars and fifty cents in my old sock.*

Every seat in the Bucket was taken by women and kids from up and down the valley and the canyons of three mountain ranges. Men and bigger boys stood against the walls and spilled out the back. Most folks, evidently, had gotten the word, even if a few roaming cowboys hadn't. The highest desk, and the teacher's, ranged against the wall, were crammed with all manner of fancy boxes and baskets, decorated with frills, bows, and paper flowers.

Didn't Miss Sally have anything but brown dresses? At least the one she wore tonight was sprigged with tiny yellow and purple flowers. Nothing could disguise her figure. When she went to the front and smiled at all four corners and the middle, Jim scowled at the sighs and intaken breaths that filled the air around him.

"Thank you all for coming and welcome to our school," she said in a clear, carrying voice. "Shall we stand to sing 'The Star-Spangled Banner'? First and last verses," she mercifully added.

By now, the kids knew the words and tune pretty well. There was something about singing that brought people closer together who were many of them almost strangers. You could tell a difference, as the crowd settled, in how they smiled or nodded at their neighbors.

Bucket pupils were seated on the front row. The primer class trooped up to stand in front of Miss Sally, took one look at their audience, and fixed six pairs of eyes on the floor. Violet Honeywell nudged her twin, Pansy, who quavered: *"The coyote trotted out one starry night—"*

"And begged of the moon to give him light," carried on Violet.

"He'd many a mile to go that night," from Anita.

"Before he reached his den-o," mumbled Tad Thompson to his new shoes.

The little ones got through Miss Sally's version of "The Fox and the Goose" with the goose replaced by a quail, and, amidst wild applause, fled to their seats in glory and relief. The five eight- and nine-year-olds marched up as if to battle, turned and stared determinedly at the rafters.

Each gave a description of a favorite animal. Myrtle Honeywell praised her tabby cat. Her sister, Hazel, preferred their spaniel. Miguel Sanchez and Pete MacDonald bragged on their ponies. To Jim's surprised pleasure, though he figured she wanted to horrify her elders, demure Jane Bridewell declared that she liked Old Bill best of all. She'd go to see him first thing after getting to school and he'd come out of his burrow and hop onto her hand.

Her mama choked, "Gracious sakes alive!"

To Jim's glee, Miss Sally pointed out that tarantulas ate flies, cockroaches, lice, mosquitoes, and other unwelcome visitors. She'd been listening to him even when she hadn't seemed to be. Next, the big kids took their places, except for Cal, who was hiding out someplace.

"We're well-known Arizonans. We'll tell you a little about ourselves and see if you can guess our names." Blushing, Mary Thompson fiddled with her wheat-colored single plait. She glanced at Miss Sally, got some kind of silent encouragement, and drew herself erect. "I ran a boardinghouse in a tough mining town, but my reputation has always been good. When four men were sentenced to hang for murder and someone built a grandstand so he could sell tickets to people who wanted to watch, I got friends to tear the seats down. Sometimes I've prayed with condemned men so they trusted in God's grace when they went to their deaths."

"Nellie Cashman!" several men called. "The Angel of Tombstone!"

Mary smiled, nodded, and stepped back. Ben MacDonald's General George Crook was guessed, as was Carlos's Geronimo, but no one could figure out Olive's and Rose Honeywell's characters.

Olive said she had helped Rose's person make arrangements for the Apaches to hold peace talks with the soldiers. "I was a warrior and good at breaking horses," Rose declared. "I raided with Nana and Victorio and Geronimo. My power told me when the enemy was near. I was sent to Florida with Geronimo and the Chiricahuas three years ago. I miss the mountains and deserts and riding through this valley and across the San Luis Mountains into Mexico and our Sierra Madre."

When the crowd had guessed the name of every Apache leader they'd heard of, Rose said, "I'm Lozen, the warrior woman. My brother Victorio called me his right hand and a shield to my people."

"And I'm her friend, Dahteste," put in Olive.

Lilia's mouth tucked down. Apparently, she didn't much like her daughters putting themselves in the moccasins of Apache women, even for a program. There were a few frowns and a lot more puzzlement, but when Jim led the clapping, everyone joined in.

Dan MacDonald dodged through the men to stand beside the pies. "Boy howdy, folks, do you smell these dee-licious pies? None of 'em's going for less than a dollar. The kids need new books. Every dime raised tonight helps educate these young 'uns, so loosen up your money bags, gents! Let's show Miss Sally Wright we appreciate her!"

The older girls took turns handing him pies. He showed the first one with its big gingham bow and sniffed ecstatically. "Smells like lemon meringue to me, boys! Who'll bid a dollar and a dime?"

"Here!" called three or four men.

It sold for $2.75. Mary wrote the buyer's name on the box and put it at the far end of the bench. A half dozen pies fetched between two and four dollars. Red and Jack threw in a bid now and then but dropped out early so Jim knew Miss Sally's box was still to come.

Dan joked and heckled and prodded, getting eight dollars from one newly wed husband, and twelve and fourteen dollars from the male half of two courting couples whose friends had a fine old time running them up. Over half the boxes were sold when Dan flourished one with paper sunflowers adorning the top and sides.

Red and Jack traded meaningful grins so Jim wasn't deceived when they didn't bid till Dan was about ready to let the pie go at four dollars. "Five!" sang out Red. "Six!" hollered Jack.

Others leaped into the bidding. When it hit thirty dollars, Jack and Red looked at each other, whispered a second, and Jack bid thirty-five. From then on, one or the other bid, but not both. Pooled their money, but Jim didn't think they could top his stash. To put an end to the nonsense, he called, "Fifty dollars!"

Red and Jack looked at him and horse-laughed. "Sixty bucks!" yelled Red.

"Seventy!" came back Jim, but he was sweating. He had more money, but it was at the bank in Silver City. What was the matter with these crazy cowboys? A month's wages apiece to have a piece of pie with the teacher?

"Seventy-five," said Jack.

"You guys have been in the loco weed!" hissed Jim.

"How about you?" Red chuckled.

"Seventy-five!" intoned Dan. "Do I hear eighty?"

Jim closed his eyes. "Eighty-two dollars and fifty cents," he croaked through a throat gone dry.

"Eight-five!" triumphed Jack and Red together.

"Will you take a check?" Jim asked.

Dan shook his head. "Sorry, I know your check's good, Jim, but if I take it, I might have to take some I'm not so sure about. Cash on the barrelhead." He frowned at the jubilant cowboys. "You fellas do have cash?"

"You just bet we do!" They dug in all their pockets and forked the contents over to the hovering giggling girls.

Jim felt like slinking off but it wouldn't do to let folks see how crushed he was, like a kid who'd thought he could afford ice cream and instead could only buy a penny candy. He bought the next pie for ten bucks, and damned if he didn't wind up chomping vinegar pie—which suited his mood—with Lilia, who didn't.

"I must say I didn't guess you were so public-spirited, Mr. Halloran," she said with what he decided was a cackle. "You must get a lot of satisfaction from knowing how much money you raised for the school."

"Sure." Jim glumly watched Red and Jack sit indecently close on either side of Miss Sally. Whatever balderdash they might think up couldn't be as funny as she seemed to find it, laughing up at each of them in turn.

Jim craned his neck. Bitterness ate into his soul like the vinegar pie into his stomach. Yep, the final insult and injury was that sure looked like cherry pie, his absolute, always and forever favorite. *Pinkie,* he thought in anguish, *Pinkie, how could you?*

He was not greatly cheered when Lilia patted back a yawn and promised that she, Honeywell, Cal, and the teacher would come over next morning to help clean up since it was getting too late tonight.

Somehow, he managed to shake hands with Red and Jack instead of slugging them, and tell people till his jaw was sore about yes, how fine it was the school had plenty of money now for books and supplies, but his spirit was bruised and it was small comfort that his sock still held $72.50.

He had a bad, short night. By the time the Honeywells and Miss Sally drove up next morning, he'd carried the kegs and boxes out back and was picking up bits of paper, ribbon, trampled tissue flowers, and discarded crusts.

"People are hogs, Bill," he grouched to his buddy. "Specially those two wastrels who ganged up to do me in! I hope they got bellyaches from that cherry pie. And you just wait till they come in here wantin' drinks on credit!"

Lilia was still over the moon about all the books and maps and things the school could have now without Jethro, having to foot the bill. "We can even get a flagpole and flag," she planned as she helped the teacher stow away the desks and benches. "There might even be enough to start saving for a piano. Wouldn't that be grand, Sally?"

"Oh, certainly." Miss Sally didn't look as bright and shiny as Jim expected. She hadn't met his eyes when she said good morning but had put a bag over behind the bar and gone to work without any chitchat. Not that anyone else had much chance when Lilia was around.

She was shrilling questions at her husband about various people who'd been at the supper when the sound of hoofs drowned out her voice. Jim peered out the door.

Drat the luck! His shotgun was in the hollow tree and here came Labe Pierce, Mizzou Bates, and half a dozen no-goods who hung around the Perdition saloon, including its owner, Jasper Higgs.

"Howdy, boys." The only handy weapon Jim could think of was his flipping iron or loggerhead he heated to make hot buttered rum or grog. Not much against eight revolvers. Honeywell wasn't armed. Might have a rifle or shotgun under the wagon seat but that was on the far side of the advancing crew.

Still, even this bunch wasn't likely to cause real trouble in front of two ladies. "Mizzou," said Jim, standing in the door, "you don't come in the Bucket anymore."

Mizzou showed yellow teeth at his following.

"How's that for a saloon keeper? Running off anyone he doesn't like."

Labe squinched his beer-colored eyes at Jim. "How's about the rest of us, Halloran? Do we get a drink on this fine no-school Saturday mornin'?"

"Nope. We're cleaning up. If you want to wait a couple of hours—"

Jasper's tobacco juice splattered the side of the Bucket door. "Have I ever said a thing like that to you boys?"

"No, and never would!" growled Labe.

Mizzou kept his hand near his gun and gave Jim a mean smile. "Since you can't seem to decide to stay in business, Halloran, we're goin' to do you a favor and close you down."

"If you go bustin' up the school," said Jim, fading back to the bar and digging out the flipping iron, "I'll hang all your mangy hides out to dry."

Mizzou winked at Labe. "Listen at him. You'd think he was still ridin' for Hanging Judge Parker. Yeah, I ran into a fella you roughed up in Indian Territory just the way you done me, Halloran, but the story up there is you lost your guts. I'm bettin' you ain't found 'em. Anyhow, we ain't botherin' the school. We're just going to toss your on-again, off-again bar into the river."

He and Labe started for Jim with their guns out. He figured he was in for a pistol-whipping, not a killing, and got a good grip on the iron. A couple of men flanked the spluttering Honeywell, and the rest ranged in front of the women.

"Hold it," came a voice from the door that started deep and ended high. "Drop your guns, all of you."

It was Cal, aiming the shotgun from the hollow tree. That many men could have rushed the kid or shot him but who, even amongst this gang, would do that with the kid's mama looking on? The guns were all placed gently on the floor.

"You better go now." Cal's voice quivered but he held the shotgun steady.

"Wait a minute." Miss Sally stepped through the men and swept all of them with those clear gray eyes. "You men need to get settled in your minds about what you value in a saloon." She smiled at a gangly kid, who blinked and nearly strangled on his convulsing Adam's apple. "Please, won't you tell me what you think's important?"

He looked around desperately. "A—a clean place, ma'am?"

She beamed. "That helps."

Another cowboy said, "I like a place that don't water its whiskey."

"Or color it with tobacco," added another.

They all, even Mizzou and Labe, looked at Jasper, who cleared his throat and began to fidget. "Or flavor it with horse liniment and chilis," mused a grizzled hand from Lordsburg.

Miss Sally nodded as if they should go to the head of the class. "Very true, gentlemen. But wouldn't you say it's desirable to be able to order something out of the ordinary and know it's going to be good?"

Most had probably never thought beyond whiskey or gin but now they considered. Jasper sneered uneasily, "I don't go in for that fancy stuff like Tom and Jerries and hot buttered rum. just plain good booze—"

"Not always so good," said Labe. He studied Miss Sally. "What are you gettin' at, ma'am?"

She uncovered the bar and turned up her sleeves. "I'm saying I can mix any drink you ask for, providing we have the ingredients."

There was a general gasp with the loudest breath coming from Lilia. "I'm saying," Miss Sally went on, "that if Mr. Halloran doesn't know how to make your favorite tipple, I'll teach him." Her eyes traveled from face to face. "I'm saying Mr. Halloran's helping the children of this valley get their educations and you shouldn't mind a little inconvenience."

Mizzou chuckled. "Ma'am, I hailed from Kentucky before I roamed over into Missouri. You ever hear tell of syllabub?"

"Coming up—that is if Mr. Halloran has some evaporated milk and sugar."

"I've got lemons, too," he assured her. "Kind of shriveled since I got them in Lordsburg a couple of weeks ago."

Once in Fort Smith he'd had the rich dessert drink at the home of a family from Virginia. He'd asked how it was made but had never tried it. Miss Sally gave him a funny look, but it was probably no more puzzled than the one he gave her. Where had she learned enough about tending bar to challenge Jasper?

"I need a bowl, too," she called after him.

Into the bowl went sherry, brandy, a can of Borden's, sugar, and what juice she could squeeze from puckered lemons. She whisked the ingredients till they bubbled, took a taste, and added a tinch more brandy, a procedure that brought a nod of approval from Mizzou.

"You know"—she smiled at him—"that syllabub began by milking a cow into a bucket of wine." Lilia winced at the indelicate remark, but the teacher didn't notice. She poured the frothy mixture into glasses, filling Mizzou's and divvying up the rest so his companions could at least have a taste.

All eyes were on Mizzou. He sniffed, savored, took a sip, fixed his gaze on the rafters, and looked nearer to bliss with each swallow. "You know, ma'am," he said at last, "I like that Borden's even better than cream." He turned to the others. "Roll it over your tongues, boys, and see what you've been missing."

"Tastes like puddin' to me," said Labe, making a face.

"Why, you uncivilized mossyhorn!" scorned Mizzou. "Give me that glass if you can't appreciate a gentleman's drink!" He finished Labe's share in a gulp and looked around for more. There wasn't any, though the men's expressions ranged from happy surprise to disgust.

Turning to Jim, Mizzou bristled his eyebrows. "You goin' to learn to make syllabub, Halloran?"

"Why, I reckon," said Jim, "that I'm going to learn every single blessed thing Miss Wright's willing to teach me."

Mizzou nodded. "Could we start over, Jim?"

"Why not? Just so you understand that when the Bucket's a school, it's not a bar." Mizzou put out his hand and Jim took it.

When the defanged raiders departed, Lilia gave

Miss Sally a grim stare. "I think, Miss Wright, you've got some explaining to do."

"Not if she doesn't want to," said Jim. "You hired a teacher, Mrs. Honeywell, and got a damned good one. That's all that's any of your business."

Lilia spluttered, but Honeywell spoke with amazing firmness. "Jim's right, angel. Your—our kids are learnin'. You say yourself it's the first time Cal's liked school."

"Thank you, Mr. Honeywell, but I'd like to explain." Miss Sally looked at Jim, not her employers. "I was an orphan, sent out west on an orphan train when I was twelve. I was placed with a farmer who—well, never mind! I ran away to a mining camp and got room and board for slaving in a boardinghouse. A woman called Big Marie felt sorry for me and paid me wages to work at her hotel and restaurant. It had a bar and a bartender who taught me to fill in when he drank a little too much of his own whiskey."

"Good heavens!" Lilia shuddered.

"When I turned sixteen, Big Marie fired me."

"Why?" asked Jim.

Miss Sally smiled. "She didn't want me to live the way she had. She lent me money so that with what I'd saved, I could go to normal school. I paid her back as soon as I could. We still write to each other."

Lilia's jaw looked unhinged. She didn't say anything, but her husband took the teacher's hands in his. "Young woman, you're a better teacher—and a person—for what you've been through. We're lucky to have you." He blinked a time or two and turned to Cal. "Son, we are mightily proud of you!"

They finished setting the Bucket to rights. As the

Honeywells and Miss Sally were leaving, she said to Jim, "That's a cherry pie in the bag I left behind the bar. I—I was sorry you didn't get one after bidding so high."

"Wasn't the pie I wanted most," said Jim. He felt his face burn right up to the roots of his hair.

She blushed, too. "Really?"

Her confusion gave Jim courage. "Won't you stay and eat with me?" he blurted. "I'll take you home later."

"Lilia," said Honeywell, hustling her toward the door, "We've done all we need to here. Come on, Cal. You can drive."

Jim watched Miss Sally, the shine in her eyes, the lovely color in her cheeks. He couldn't believe his luck. Here they were alone, with cherry pie to boot! "Miss Sally—*Sally*—"

He moved toward her, but she put up her hands. "I guess I deceived you—Jim—but you deceived me, too."

He stopped in his tracks. "How?" Lordy, she hadn't someway found out about Minette, Lorena, Clara, and Angelita?

"Pretending to be an ignoramus—never letting on that you were a marshal in Indian Territory—"

Jim laughed and caught her hands. "Sally, we'll have a lot of fun finding out about each other. That's why I won't ask you to marry me till, oh—about Christmas."

"You want to marry me?" Her voice shattered. "Knowing I've tended bar?"

"All the more, honey. You can teach me about syllabub, cordials, and other fancy things. But right this minute," he murmured, taking her in his arms while Pinkie smiled benignly upon them and Old Bill waved his front legs, "won't you teach me how you like to be kissed?"

She laughed and put her arms around his neck. "We'll learn together."

SIGNET BOOKS

JUDSON GRAY

Introducing a brand-new post-Civil War western
saga from the author of the Hunter Trilogy...

DOWN TO MARROWBONE

Jim McCutcheon had squandered his Southern family's fortune
and had to find a way to rebuild it among that boomstowns
of the West...
Jake Penn had escaped the bonds of slavery and had to find
his long-lost sister...
Together, they're an unlikely team—but with danger down
every trail, nothing's worth more than a friend you can count
on...

❏ 0-451-20158-2/$5.99

Also Available:
HUNTER'S JOURNEY   ❏ 0-451-19819-0/$5.99
HUNTER'S WAR   ❏ 0-451-19564-7/$5.99

Prices slightly higher in Canada

Payable by Visa, MC or AMEX only ($10.00 min.), No cash, checks or COD. Shipping & handling:
US/Can. $2.75 for one book, $1.00 for each add'l book; Int'l $5.00 for one book, $1.00 for each
add'l. Call (800) 788-6262 or (201) 933-9292, fax (201) 896-8569 or mail your orders to:

Penguin Putnam Inc.   Bill my: ❏ Visa ❏ MasterCard ❏ Amex _____(expires)
P.O. Box 12289, Dept. B
Newark, NJ 07101-5289   Card# _____
Please allow 4-6 weeks for delivery.   Signature _____
Foreign and Canadian delivery 6-8 weeks.

Bill to:
Name _____
Address _____City _____
State/ZIP _____Daytime Phone # _____
Ship to:
Name _____Book Total $ _____
Address _____Applicable Sales Tax $ _____
City _____Postage & Handling $ _____
State/ZIP _____Total Amount Due $ _____
This offer subject to change without notice.   Ad # SHFIC2 (3/01)

∅ SIGNET

Jason Manning

❏ Mountain Passage
0-451-19569-8/$5.99

Leaving Ireland for the shores of America, a young man loses his parents
en route—one to death, one to insanity—and falls victim to the sadistic
captain of the ship. Luckily, he is befriended by a legendary Scottish
adventurer, whom he accompanies to the wild American frontier. But
along the way, new troubles await....

❏ Mountain Massacre
0-451-19689-9/$5.99

Receiving word that his mother has passed away, mountain man Gordon
Hawkes reluctantly returns home to Missouri to pick up the package she
left for him. Upon arrival, he is attacked by a posse looking to collect the
bounty on his head. In order to escape, Hawkes decides to hide out among
the Mormons and guide them to their own promised land. But the trek
turns deadly when the religious order splits into two factions...with
Hawkes caught in the middle!

❏ Mountain Courage
0-451-19870-0/$5.99

Gordon Hawkes's hard-won peace and prosperity are about to be threatened by the bloody clouds of war. While Hawkes is escorting the Crow
tribe's yearly annuity from the U.S. government, the Sioux ambush the
shipment. Captured, Hawkes must decide whether to live as a slave, die as
a prisoner, or renounce his life and join the Sioux tribe. His only hope is
his son Cameron, who must fight his father's captors and bring Hawkes
back alive.

Prices slightly higher in Canada

Payable by Visa, MC or AMEX only ($10.00 min.), No cash, checks or COD. Shipping & handling:
US/Can. $2.75 for one book, $1.00 for each add'l book; Int'l $5.00 for one book, $1.00 for each
add'l. Call (800) 788-6262 or (201) 933-9292, fax (201) 896-8569 or mail your orders to:

Penguin Putnam Inc. P.O. Box 12289, Dept. B Newark, NJ 07101-5289 Please allow 4-6 weeks for delivery. Foreign and Canadian delivery 6-8 weeks.	Bill my: ❏ Visa ❏ MasterCard ❏ Amex _____ (expires) Card# _____ Signature _____

Bill to:

Name _____

Address _____ City _____

State/ZIP _____ Daytime Phone # _____

Ship to:

Name _____	Book Total	$ _____
Address _____	Applicable Sales Tax	$ _____
City _____	Postage & Handling	$ _____
State/ZIP _____	Total Amount Due	$ _____

This offer subject to change without notice.   Ad # N107B (6/00)

🅞 SIGNET HISTORICAL FICTION   (0451)

RALPH COTTON

"Gun-smoked, blood-stained, gritty believability...
Ralph Cotton writes the sort of story we all hope
to find within us."—Terry Johnston

"Authentic Old West detail."—*Wild West Magazine*

❑ **HANGMAN'S CHOICE**   20143-4 / $5.99

They gunned down his father in cold blood. They are his most elusive
enemies, the outlaws known as *Los Pistoleros*, and they're still at large.
But Federal Deputy Hart will not give up....

❑ **MISERY EXPRESS**   19999-5 / $5.99

Ranger Sam Burrack is once again driving the jailwagon filled with a
motley cargo of deadly outlaws, whose buddies are plotting to set them
free. But with the Ranger driving, they're in for quite a ride.

Also available:

❑ **BADLANDS**   19495-0 / $5.99
❑ **BORDER DOGS**   19815-8 / $5.99

Prices slightly higher in Canada

Payable by Visa, MC or AMEX only ($10.00 min.), No cash, checks or COD.
Shipping & handling: US/Can. $2.75 for one book, $1.00 for each add'l book;
Int'l $5.00 for one book, $1.00 for each add'l. Call (800) 788-6262 or (201)
933-9292, fax (201) 896-8569 or mail your orders to:

Penguin Putnam Inc. P.O. Box 12289, Dept. B Newark, NJ 07101-5289 <small>Please allow 4-6 weeks for delivery.</small> <small>Foreign and Canadian delivery 6-8 weeks.</small>	Bill my: ❑ Visa ❑ MasterCard ❑ Amex _____(expires) Card# _____ Signature _____

Bill to:

Name _____

Address_____   City _____

State/ZIP _____   Daytime Phone # _____

Ship to:

Name_____   Book Total $ _____

Address _____   Applicable Sales Tax $_____

City _____   Postage & Handling $_____

State/ZIP _____   Total Amount Due $_____

This offer subject to change without notice.   Ad #CTTN (8/00)

SIGNET BOOKS

"A writer in the tradition of Louis L'Amour and Zane Grey!"—*Huntsville Times*

National Bestselling Author

RALPH COMPTON

❑ **THE AUTUMN OF THE GUN**	0-451-19045-9/$5.99
❑ **THE BORDER EMPIRE**	0-451-19209-5/$5.99
❑ **THE DAWN OF FURY**	0-451-18631-1/$5.99
❑ **DEVIL'S CANYON: The Sundown Riders**	
	0-451-19519-1/$5.99
❑ **THE KILLING SEASON**	0-451-18787-3/$5.99
❑ **SHADOW OF A NOOSE**	0-451-19333-4/$5.99
❑ **SIXGUNS AND DOUBLE EAGLES**	0-451-19331-8/$5.99
❑ **THE SKELETON LODE**	0-451-19762-3/$5.99
❑ **TRAIN TO DURANGO**	0-451-19237-0/$5.99
❑ **WHISKEY RIVER**	0-451-19332-6/$5.99

Prices slightly higher in Canada

Payable by Visa, MC or AMEX only ($10.00 min.), No cash, checks or COD. Shipping & handling: US/Can. $2.75 for one book, $1.00 for each add'l book; Int'l $5.00 for one book, $1.00 for each add'l. Call (800) 788-6262 or (201) 933-9292, fax (201) 896-8569 or mail your orders to:

Penguin Putnam Inc.	Bill my: ❑ Visa ❑ MasterCard ❑ Amex _____ (expires)
P.O. Box 12289, Dept. B	Card# _____
Newark, NJ 07101-5289	Signature _____
Please allow 4-6 weeks for delivery.	
Foreign and Canadian delivery 6-8 weeks.	

Bill to:

Name _____

Address _____ City _____

State/ZIP _____ Daytime Phone # _____

Ship to:

Name _____	Book Total	$ _____
Address _____	Applicable Sales Tax	$ _____
City _____	Postage & Handling	$ _____
State/ZIP _____	Total Amount Due	$ _____

This offer subject to change without notice.   Ad # N108 (5/00)